"Your heart's in good shape," she murmured, half to herself. "And we don't have a whole lot of time locally. Alan, I'm going to prove to you that we can travel in time. I'm going to bring in someone you'll remember."

Norlund felt a new clutch of unreasoning fear as Ginny turned toward the door. "Come in!" she called in a clear voice, and phantoms of the dead chased through his imagination. . . .

The door opened. The figure that entered was not one of the phantoms, but a young man of about nineteen. His right arm, Norlund saw with a shock like that of fear, ended in what was either an odd glove or a very advanced type of artificial hand. The arm lay in a supporting sling at elbow level.

"Al?" the young man asked. It was a familiar voice.

"Andy." Norlund nodded. It wasn't that Andy had been hard to recognize. The problem was that he couldn't help recognizing him. And that was a very great problem indeed, requiring some adjustment. Andy Burns stood before him, solid and three-dimensional, as real as he had been that day over Regensburg in nineteen forty-three when Alan Norlund had tried to tighten the tourniquet on the stump of Andy Burns' right arm, then had tightened up his chute harness for him, clamped his left hand on the D-ring and then had put him out through the right waist gun opening of the burning Fortress.

And Andy was not only still alive but not a day older than he was that day forty years ago. . . .

FRED SABERHAGEN

A CENTURY of PROGRESS

A Tom Doherty Associates Book

A TOR Book

Published by:

Tom Doherty Associates, Inc.
8–10 West 36th Street
New York, New York 10018

First TOR printing, September 1983

ISBN: 48-568-9

Printed in the United States of America

Distributed by:
Pinnacle Books
1430 Broadway
New York, New York 10018

1984

Norlund hadn't killed anyone for decades, but he was getting in the mood for it today.

He came out of the hospital's main entrance, a compact, crag-faced, gray-haired man wearing the rumpled trousers of a gray suit, and a mismatched old corduroy jacket over a white shirt. After standing for a moment he crossed the street to the little park and sat down there in the mild spring sunshine of Chicago. He moved with a slight limp because the old leg wound was bothering him a touch today. But it wasn't his leg that made him feel like killing.

Before he had been sitting on the park bench thirty seconds he had an impulse to jump up and move on to somewhere else. The trouble was the kids playing in the park. They were healthy kids, all up on their feet and running around, and all Norlund could think of, looking at them, was that he was never going to see Sandy doing that again.

But he didn't jump up from the bench and move on, because it wouldn't have helped. Instead he continued to sit there, trying not to think about choking the children who shrieked with their good health and not from pain. He watched the hospital entrance, and he wished, darkly and selfishly, that today Sandy's mother might leave her slowly dying child a little earlier than usual, and come across to the park to comfort her aging father who couldn't take it any more . . .

Norlund, held in isolation by the ugly gray fog of his own feelings, wasn't really aware of the brisk footsteps as they came close to him along the paved walk, then stopped.

"Mr. Norlund?"

"Huh?" The voice of the young woman did get through to him, and he looked up, relieved at any interruption of his thoughts. She was standing almost directly in front of him, almost within reach, wearing a light spring coat. Dark hair and blue eyes; a pretty but completely unfamiliar face. Without really thinking about it, Norlund assumed immediately that she must have some connection with the hospital.

Her smile was businesslike, pleasant but impersonal —it might certainly have been that of a hospital administrator. She spoke to Norlund in a low, attractive voice. "I'm Ginny Butler. I'm so sorry to hear about your granddaughter's illness, and I very much hope to be able to do something to help." After that many words were out, Norlund thought he could detect just a hint of something British in her tones.

Whatever she wanted, he continued to feel grateful for the distraction. "There's not much anyone can do, I'm afraid . . . will you sit down?" And in a symbolic gesture of welcome he slid over a little on the bench, though there would have been room enough anyway.

Meanwhile he squinted up into the sunshine at his visitor. Now that he had had time to think about it, he decided that the hospital probably wouldn't have sent anyone across the street to talk to him. Therefore this young woman must be some friend of Marge. Or possibly one of Sandy's teachers. The number of cards and phone calls Sandy received in the hospital had convinced Norlund that his granddaughter was a popular girl at school.

But his visitor, whoever she was, remained standing. In a voice touched with elegance she replied: "No thanks, I really can't stay now. But I want to assure you that I do expect to be able to do something for Sandy. Something that will make her, and your daughter, and you, all very happy." The young woman's tones were forceful, her trim figure erect and full of purpose. Whatever she really meant, it was something more than polite well-wishing.

Already Norlund's original relief was starting to shade into wariness. The last thing he wanted or needed right now was a confrontation with some kind of crackpot, faith-healer or whatever. Not now on top of what he was already going through.

He could hear his changing attitude reflected in his voice. "I don't think I understand. Are you a doctor, Miss? Connected with the hospital in some way?"

She started to confirm Norlund's suspicions by ignoring the question. She had one of her own, which she now put to him very solemnly: "Mr. Norlund, do you know how to drive a truck? I don't mean a very large one necessarily, but an older type. Say one that might have been in use around nineteen-thirty, with that kind of a stick shift?"

Norlund could feel his newly aroused wariness already flagging. The sheer irrelevance of the question was disarming. It seemed unlikely to form part of any sales pitch or swindle worth bothering about. But it did touch his curiosity, and he answered patiently: "Yes, I know how to do that. I did it often enough when I was young. Why?"

"I expect to be able to offer you a job." This too sounded supremely irrelevant to Norlund, who hadn't known that he was looking for one. But the young lady was still utterly serious, and went on: "We can talk about that later. Right now I have some good news to give you about your granddaughter. During the next few days Sandy's going to experience a dramatic improvement." The announcement was delivered with the calm certainty of a judge awarding a prize in a contest. "And one week from today, after you have witnessed this improvement for yourself, I want you to meet me again."

The attractive blue eyes lifted away from Norlund's face, to gaze around at the park and its surroundings. "I think right here would be a good place. If it should be raining, you can wait for me in one of those doorways across the street—the apartment building, or the drugstore."

Automatically Norlund followed her gaze, then frowningly returned his eyes to his visitor. "What are you saying about my granddaughter?"

The question was received with perfect patience, as if the young woman had fully expected that her announcement would have to be repeated. She said, quietly and distinctly: "I am saying that not only will Sandy be alive one week from today, she will be much improved. Very much improved indeed. There is only one condition: that you say nothing to anyone about my speaking to you, nor repeat what I've said. Not to your daughter or Sandy or anyone else. Is that agreeable?"

"Wait a minute. Wait. What did you say your name was?"

"My name's Ginny Butler. But I can't wait now. Remember, meet me one week from this hour, right here at this bench. Across the street if it's raining. And meanwhile say nothing to anyone." With a last momentary brightening of her smile the young woman turned away. Her retreating heels made light, brisk sounds on the paved walk. Her dark hair—Norlund noticed now that it was somewhat curly—bounced a little as she walked. She moved steadily away from Norlund, not looking back, heading for one of the side streets bordering the park.

"But you . . . " Norlund had risen to his feet at last, and was standing there with one hand raised. For a moment he even thought of chasing after her.

That was on Friday afternoon. By Saturday evening, Norlund had all but forgotten his strange encounter in the park. Because all through Saturday Sandy had been obviously sinking. The little girl was now more often unconscious than awake.

No one, no doctor or nurse, had yet come right out and told Norlund that his only grandchild was on the brink of death. Not that there was any need for them to do so.

All through Sunday, Sandy's mother and grandfather —there were no other relatives in visiting distance— spent most of their time in her room. Norlund and his daughter took turns dozing in chairs, spelling each other for occasional leg-stretching walks down the corridor or visits to the coffee shop.

It didn't help Norlund's weekend at all to be treated to a preview of how his daughter was going to look as an old woman. Marge's hair hung in odd neglected waves; her eyes looked more dead than alive. Her face seemed to have collapsed, as if it were compelled to mimic Sandy's sunken features.

Then, almost imperceptibly at first, starting Sunday evening or Sunday night, the tide somehow turned. Probably the first change that Norlund noticed was that Sandy's breathing had grown easier. A little later, when he looked at her closely, he got the impression of someone sleeping—resting—rather than sinking into death. She was clearly in less pain, even when her prescribed drug dosage was accidentally delayed.

On Monday morning Sandy opened her eyes at something like a normal wake-up time. She looked about her and talked; she said she didn't hurt. In general, she was fully conscious for the first time in several days. She was still painfully weak, and appeared somehow diminished, younger than her twelve years. But Norlund, no matter how fiercely he cautioned himself against starting to hope, could not help seeing what he saw: that life was returning to Sandy's face instead of passing from it.

By breakfast on Tuesday, Sandy was eating again, with almost her normal appetite. She was talking freely, making jokes, telling everyone that she felt better. And on Tuesday afternoon the oncologist, after taking a close look at the patient, pronounced the first official notice of the change. "There's been a certain improvement, I think. Looks like the chemotherapy may be taking hold at last. I don't want to get your hopes up unjustifiably, but—"

Things had already gone too close to the brink, reality had been engaged far too deeply, for mere words from anyone to have much effect now on Norlund's hopes.

But when he looked at Sandy, he could not help seeing what he saw.

And by Wednesday the change for the better was so obvious that hope could no longer be denied. Sandy was sitting up in bed, taking every chance to get up and walk, eating ravenously, and wondering aloud how much school work she was going to have to make up. Sandy's mother, her hair newly styled, was walking about in a lightfooted daze, as if uncertain whether she was going to collapse or dance.

And it was only on Wednesday that Norlund remembered, with a small private shock of fascination, the odd event that he had so completely forgotten: that peculiar interview with the young woman in the park across the street. He happened to be shaving when he first remembered it, alone in his small apartment condo in a moderately expensive area of the North Side. With razor in hand he paused, looking at his angular face in the mirror and wondering if that odd event might have sprung completely from his imagination, a kind of hallucinatory memory provoked by stress.

At Thursday morning's chemotherapy session, Sandy complained more than usual about the discomforts of the process. But it was less an invalid's protest than a well person's energetic crabbing. On Thursday afternoon, sitting in Sandy's overfamiliar hospital room while his daughter and granddaughter walked the corridors arm-in-arm, Norlund found himself staring out the window. But instead of the apartment rooftops opposite he was seeing himself and the young woman talking in the park across the street.

He tried several times to recall exactly what she had looked like, and all the words of their brief dialogue. Most of it was pretty hazy. The name had definitely stayed with him, though: Ginny Butler. He couldn't remember ever knowing anyone by that name. Which didn't prove, he realized, that she wasn't someone he ought to be able to remember. Norlund had never been good at keeping track of marginal relationships, nor did this faculty, at least for him, tend to improve with age.

That young woman had talked so strangely. Unless he had somehow misinterpreted her words. . . . But no. He probably wasn't remembering all the details correctly, but the strange prophecy had been there.

On Thursday morning, immediately after the chemo session, and again on Thursday afternoon, Norlund found himself on the point of mentioning the park incident to Marge. Both times he refrained. Maybe it was just that he didn't want to burden his daughter right now with anything remotely disturbing. Or maybe . . . maybe he was afraid of sounding like he'd had some kind of hallucination, as if he might be cracking up under the strain.

Which last explanation, Norlund had to admit to himself, was for all he knew quite possible. There was no way to be sure. No, there was probably one way.

The patient was doing so well by Friday morning that Marge went back to work. There was talk of Sandy going home in another day or so, barring complications. Norlund had no such clear-cut decision as Marge's to make about work; he was three-fourths retired now anyway. He had been manager and part owner of a small firm wholesaling electronic and electrical parts, and though he still kept his hand in as consultant and stockholder the business could go on quite well without him, and left him a lot of flexibility in his schedule. After looking in on Sandy at the hospital Friday, he came out and stood gazing across the street. He was coatless today, it was warmer now than it had been a week ago. Norlund stood there with hands in his pockets, gazing toward the park.

One week from this hour. That was what she had said. And exactly what hour had that been? A week ago, Norlund had made no effort to fix the time, but now he considered that two o'clock had to be approximately right.

He looked at his watch: one thirty. He strolled left toward the corner, where a traffic light periodically jammed the continual creep of hospital traffic looking for a place to park. Norlund strolled across the street, across grass, then along the paved path to the same bench he had been sitting on a week ago. A shower seemed imminent. *If it's raining, you can stand in one of those doorways.* Norlund looked toward those doorways, again involuntarily, but she wasn't waiting for him there.

A few drops were coming down now, but it wasn't raining all that much. Belatedly, as so often, Chicago's spring was arriving. The park flowerbeds, largely dormant a week ago, today were blooming gorgeously. Sitting on his bench again, Norlund would have been quite willing to accept an hallucination or two as a trivial price to pay for the glory of Sandy's resurrection . . .

The young woman, wearing the light spring coat he remembered, was walking toward him, coming from the direction in which she'd disappeared last Friday. As she drew closer Norlund could see that the dark hair and the blue eyes were as he'd remembered them.

She approached Norlund directly, smiling as she drew near. It was a more relaxed and friendly smile, he thought, than it had been a week ago—almost as if they had somehow spent the week in contact, getting better acquainted. The young woman's shoes clicked on the walk as they had last Friday. And now she was stopping directly in front of him, just as she had before.

Norlund got slowly to his feet, and said: "I wasn't sure just exactly what I remembered from a week ago." He had a momentary impulse to reach out for a handshake—but he didn't.

The young woman nodded, unsurprised. Her smile faded now, but not grimly; only with the sheer urgency of the question she now asked. "You didn't mention me to anyone? I must be sure of that before we can discuss anything else."

Norlund looked around; it would be hard to imagine a more public place. He gestured expansively. "Our meeting is supposed to be a secret? Anyone could see us talking together now."

"Of course. But that's one thing, and your telling someone is something else. For now just take my word for it. Have you mentioned me? If so, I'll find out later anyway; but it will save us both time and effort if you admit it now." She halted, obviously in great suspense as she waited for his answer.

Norlund drew in a breath, to let it out again in a kind of sigh. "No, actually I haven't mentioned you to anyone. Or your prediction about Sandy. I'm not sure *why* I haven't. For a while there I simply forgot—"

"Good." The clear relief in the young woman's face showed how strong had been the tension before it. "Then today I will sit down and talk with you for a while."

"Sure." Norlund sat, then, as before, moved over minimally. Looking at his companion carefully as she sat down, he estimated that she was six or seven years younger than Marge's thirty-two. "Ginny Butler, is that right?"

"Quite right." She nodded, waiting, willing to be questioned.

Now he was sure of the faint British flavor in her voice. "I'm sorry," Norlund said, "but do I know you? Should I?"

"No, not apart from our meeting last week. I do have the advantage of you, as they say. But I think that you are going to get to know me fairly well."

"You're not asking me how Sandy's doing."

"I didn't ask you about that last week either, did I?" Ginny Butler continued to be pleasantly business-like. Definitely a salesperson, thought Norlund. Big-ticket items. She went on: "We both know that Sandy's doing very well right now. So today we can start talking about a certain job that you can do for me, in return."

Norlund cleared his throat. "Wait, now, just a moment." He was interrupted by kids shouting and speeding past them on roller skates—just as, thank God, Sandy ought to be doing again soon. If . . . "Let me get this straight. It sounds to me like you're claiming to be responsible for Sandy's improvement. And you're saying you want me to do something for you in return."

The woman nodded. It was only a slight movement of the head, but it was very firm. "Yes, absolutely, Mr. Norlund. I—or the people I represent—have helped Sandy. And I think you do owe us a return favor now."

Norlund thought that hallucinations would have been relatively easy to understand. He crossed one leg over the other. "I don't even know who you are."

"I've given you my name," the young woman answered patiently. "Telling you my life story wouldn't help right now. I think that by helping your granddaughter we have established a perfectly legitimate claim on your friendship."

"Who's 'we'? Who's this group you say you represent?"

"We ask only for a day or two of your time, time that I know you can well afford to spare. You will not be asked to do anything illegal during that day or two, I promise you that. But at the same time I must continue to insist on secrecy."

"Lady . . ." Norlund paused, sighed, shook his head, and tried again. "Look here, I don't know what you're talking about. I don't admit that you've established any kind of claim on me."

Ginny Butler remained patient. "Mr. Norlund—may I call you Alan?"

"Why not?"

"Alan, then—I certainly wouldn't expect you, at this stage, to completely understand what I'm talking about, as you put it. But I really think we have established a claim. Just think back seven days. You sat here on this bench, and you knew that your granddaughter was dying. And she was. The funeral would have been over by now."

"Just a minute."

"Please, let me finish?"

"A week ago, as I recall, you made no claim that you were going to be responsible for curing her."

"Would you have believed me for a moment if I had? You would have been angry instead of only puzzled. We preferred to make a demonstration instead. I'm sure you remember what I *did* tell you a week ago."

"Not word for word."

The young woman waited silently.

Norlund muttered something like a curse. "All right, you told me she was going to get better."

"And what happened?"

"I don't care for catechisms, lady." Norlund was starting to get angry. He supposed it was largely something bottled up from when Sandy had seemed to be dying. "You come here and talk to the next of kin of all the cancer patients, is that it? And when one of them does get well, you try to cash in."

Ginny Butler did not appear surprised or angered. "No, that isn't it. Have you seen me talking to relatives of any other patients? And I haven't asked you for money; I'll turn down money if you offer it. I say again, I'm asking only for a small amount of your time. Perhaps two days."

"My time, doing what, driving an old truck? You could hire a lot better drivers than I am."

The young lady leaned forward a little on the bench, eagerly, as if she felt that she was starting to get somewhere. "Driving a truck is only part of it. But nothing about it will be very hard for you. You have all the qualifications that we want."

"Such as what?"

"We'll discuss the details when you've told me that in principle you agree. Two days of your time?"

Norlund thought that he would eventually say that he agreed, just to see what came next. But not yet. "No, lady, I just don't buy it. You really claim that this mysterious group of yours is responsible for Sandy's getting well?"

"Yes, I do."

"And how did they work this miracle cure?"

"When you've agreed to give us two days, a lot of things will be explained to you."

"And so I should go and drive your antique truck. And stand on streetcorners and hand out pamphlets for your cult."

It was Ginny Butler's turn to sigh; it was a sound

that spoke of disappointment, but not surprise. And now she surprised Norlund. "All right, Alan, I see we can't get anywhere just yet. You'll be able to meet me here." And she stood up quickly from the bench. Again her dark curls bounced as she walked away, not looking back. This time she left the park in a different direction.

If she was expecting Norlund to come chasing after her, she was disappointed.

That afternoon Norlund went to see Sandy again. They discussed her hopeful plans of being able to go home soon, and tried to figure out how many doctors might have to give their approval. Norlund also had to come up with an opinion as to which of Sandy's girlfriends she ought to telephone first upon her release; this subject took up more time than the question of the doctors, as there were social intricacies involved. Then, with her grandfather's prodding, the patient even summoned up strength enough to write two brief notes in reply to get-well cards.

On Saturday morning Norlund, for some reason feeling newly edgy, was back in Sandy's room. He was early, but the oncologist had been in already, and had ordered another scan. Sandy was once again experiencing some pain and swelling.

Norlund, looking closely into his granddaughter's face, made sure to keep an encouraging smile on his own. Even when he saw signs that the bad days had come again. There was a change around the eyes, the reappearance and waxing of the evil shadow.

He phoned Marge from the hospital, and talked to his daughter gently, trying to prepare her for the setback when she came in later. He repeated the latest hopeful words of one of the doctors about chemotherapy.

And once again, at one thirty in the afternoon, having just seen Sandy ask for and receive her first pain-reliever in almost a week, Norlund was back on the park bench. He waited there through a mild shower, hardly aware that he was getting wet.

This time he didn't notice from which direction Ginny Butler came, but here she was again. Today she had on a translucent plastic raincoat, over jeans and a dark sweater. It was colder again today, but Norlund hadn't noticed it till now.

He found himself standing. "What have you done to her?"

A momentary flash of triumph showed in the woman's eyes. She flinched a little from Norlund's anger, but continued to confront him. She said: "We've done nothing to harm her. Nothing at all."

"She's had a turn for the—"

"Refusal to help someone is not necessarily a crime."

"Oh no?" His throat felt tight.

"Mr. Norlund. If you were to walk off in that direction, in maybe half a mile you'd come to a neighborhood where you wouldn't have to look very hard to find someone who needs help. Some alcoholic passed out in a gutter or a doorway. A life that might very well be saved with some effort on your part, if you were to see that such a man got food and a decent place to sleep and some routine medical care. But you're not going over there to find that man, are you?"

"I'm talking about my own—"

"Yes. Exactly. You concentrate on fighting for your own causes. You can't do everything, save everyone in the world. Besides, maybe that particular man will make it anyway. Well, maybe Sandy will make it anyway, now that she's had some real help for a few days. I wish her well, I really do, and maybe now the hospital's chemotherapy will work." Ginny Butler paused. "If she were my kid, I wouldn't want to bet on it."

Norlund stood there, staring at the young woman in front of him. The two of them were just about of a height. He could imagine himself clubbing her to the ground, or reaching out to choke her. He could imagine himself forcing a laugh, and turning and walking away. No, he couldn't really. Not with Sandy . . .

The young woman, as if perceiving that he had passed some interior turning point, softened her voice. "Now, what do you want to do? You could make a fuss, perhaps try to report me to the police. But I haven't asked you for any money; I repeat that I wouldn't take it if you offered it. I have nothing to fear from your going to the police. But it would end our relationship."

Ginny Butler paused at that point, as if to give Norlund time to consider the implications. Then she went on, in a more optimistic tone: "Or are you ready to do me the favor I requested, and grant me a couple of days of your time? I promise that if you do, Sandy will recover."

Norlund only stood looking at her.

She put a hand on his arm, tentatively, almost timidly, and said: "I swear it solemnly. We want to help her. I want to. If you help us, she will not die of this bone cancer. No tricks, no catches. She'll go home in a short time, happy and healthy."

Norlund heard himself asking: "She won't die?"

"Not in the immediate future. No one can promise immortality."

"She'll be healthy?"

"Just like them." Ginny gave a confident nod toward

the noisy skaters, who were now off on a far loop of the walk.

Norlund had the sensation that he and Ginny Butler were utterly alone, the rest of the surrounding city far away. "Something legal, you say? Driving a truck?"

"As I told you, there's a little more to it than just driving a truck. But it's better than just legal, Alan. In fact it's for a very good cause."

"Ah. I'm not so sure that's a good selling point with me. You ought to use that 'good cause' bit only on your younger clients."

"I didn't want to emphasize it with you. But it is the truth." Ginny Butler had a very winning smile when she turned it on.

"You sure you got the right man, lady? I mean, I'm just an ordinary guy. Getting up in years. There's nothing in my background . . . "

"I know all about your background." Her smile had turned impish. "More than you can imagine." And Norlund could suddenly imagine the possibility of trusting her.

"And when," he asked, "do you want me to start on this job?"

"I want you to come with me right now. The sooner you start, the sooner you'll be finished. If you like we can stop at a phone somewhere, and you can call your daughter and tell her that you're off on a short business trip. Which will be the truth. Marge won't be particularly surprised. You still do go off on business trips once in a while."

Someone had certainly gone to a lot of trouble to set this up. What did he have that could be worth it? "And what about Sandy?"

"You can call the hospital tomorrow morning, and find out how she's doing. Tell you what, Alan. If she's not doing well tomorrow morning the whole thing is off, and you don't owe us anything."

"Tell me how you work the miracle cure."

"We'll go into that at the proper time. Along with other explanations."

"If I do go with you now—" But the young woman had already turned and was walking away. Limping slightly, mumbling swearwords under his breath, Alan Norlund hurried after her.

Ginny Butler's car, one of a solidly parked line on a street a couple of blocks away, was a commonplace, year-old Datsun. Norlund made a mental note of the Illinois license number as he got in on the right side.

She maneuvered the Datsun neatly out of the parking space. "I assume you do want to stop and call Marge?" Ginny was gazing at traffic as she spoke, and her blue eyes were far away, as if she might be thinking two or three moves ahead. "I know where there's a handy booth."

Norlund asked: "You know Margie?"

"Only as I know you."

"You've talked to her?"

"No, I didn't mean that."

Ginny drove in silence for a few blocks. Then she pulled into a small shopping center where there was a large drug store. "There's a public phone in there. I'll wait in the car." She smiled at Norlund's puzzled expression. "I'm assuming that you're with me willingly now, Alan. I'm not kidnapping you, I'm not going to listen to your call. You're keeping what we're doing secret because that's the only way you can help Sandy. Right?"

Norlund got out, then hesitated again before closing the car door. "Two days, you said. Should I buy a toothbrush?"

"No need. We'll provide everything."

Almost to himself, he asked: "Do you think I ought to tell her that Sandy will get well?"

"She will get well. My promise stands. Tell Marge whatever you like, as long as you don't mention me or what we're doing."

Norlund gave her a long look. The blue eyes looked back at him, and he read both sympathy and amusement in them. Then he turned away and went into the drugstore, found the booth and made his call.

He was faintly surprised at how readily Marge accepted his story about a business trip—he supposed that his daughter's attention and energies were focused elsewhere. For a little while he talked with her about Sandy. Norlund was optimistic, but made no direct predictions. Tomorrow morning, he told himself, he would call the hospital from wherever he was. Then he would know . . .

Walking back through the drugstore to the parking lot he felt light-headed, a little crazy. But there was the Datsun waiting for him, as real as any other car. Somehow Norlund could not generate a great deal of worry about himself personally in this situation. He wasn't wealthy enough for anyone to concoct an elaborate plot to kidnap him. And now he was at least doing *something*, which was a hell of a lot better than simply sitting in the hospital waiting for a little girl to die.

He got back into the Datsun, and with an energetic movement closed the door. "Ginny, you say. Short for Virginia."

"Yep." His guide, employer, whatever she was, drove out of the parking lot and slid expertly back into the street's traffic. Now they were heading west.

"Where we going, Ginny?"

He had expected more mystery, but her answer was frank, or at least sounded that way. "Out near Wheaton. There's an old house out there, a former farmhouse actually, that we use as a kind of base. We'll put you up there for tonight, and tomorrow you'll be on your way. Meanwhile, the rest of this afternoon and this evening will be spent largely in explanations."

"Hooray. I'll be on my way where?"

"That's one of the things the explanations are going to cover."

"Do you suppose we could start them now?"

She glanced sideways at him. "It'll be much easier if we do it at the house, believe me. It'll be a sort of show and tell."

"Okay. As long as you guys understand I'm not worth kidnapping, I give the plan a tentative okay." Norlund sat back, watching the passage of ordinary houses and humdrum people. Then he turned to Ginny. "You know, right now I feel like thanking you. I don't know what this is going to turn out to be, but at least it's something. Know what I mean? At this moment, for me, life is not terminally dull and grim."

Ginny showed him her best smile yet. "Now that's the kind of man I like."

With his first look at the place in Wheaton, Norlund silently agreed that it must have been a farmhouse once. It was a large old structure built on a hill, as a lot of farmhouses had been when there was endless land around to choose from. Now it was heavily surrounded by suburbia. Its shingled sides were painted a dull gray-green, as if in some attempt at camouflage, and it was set back a good distance from both of the streets bordering its large corner lot. One of these streets was lined with aging middle-class houses. The other was commercial, with some empty lots, and a scattering of shops and gas stations. The former farm-house looked as if it could not make up its mind which street to belong to. To Norlund, approaching now along the residential way, it displayed an oversized set of sliding garage doors. The garage was obviously a comparatively recent addition, and made the whole structure look something like an auto repair shop. If it was, there were no signs to advertise it.

One of the garage doors rolled up automatically as Ginny pulled in off the street and up the long, shaded drive. Then the car was inside, the only vehicle in a garage easily big enough for three or four. As the door rolled down automatically behind them, she sighed with what sounded like relief.

"So far," she pronounced, looking at Norlund. The look she gave him was for a moment happy, almost twinkly; but in a moment her business-like attitude was back.

"You live here?" Norlund asked, as they got out of the car.

"I stay here from time to time." And she smiled again, this time as if at some private joke.

Norlund stretched his arms and shoulders, damn-ing tiny modern cars as he usually did whenever he had to ride in one of them — how did the big guys manage? Then he looked around the garage. It appeared quite ordinary, maybe somewhat cleaner than most, with less casual junk and debris. Here and there the concrete floor was oil-spotted. Along the rear wall a bench held a few tools and boxes, suggesting that work of some kind was done here at least from time to time.

"Lead on," said Norlund resolutely. And Ginny obligingly led him out of the garage and through an interior door that Norlund expected was going to bring them into a laundry room or kitchen. He was surprised by a narrow passage that traversed the width of the house to deliver them to another garage as big as the first one. The vehicle doors here were on a different wall of the house, and Norlund thought that the driveway approaching them must lead to the commercial street.

The single vehicle now occupying a space in this second garage was facing away from the large doors, straddling an old-fashioned grease pit sunken in the concrete floor. There were a lot more tools in here, including an overhead engine hoist.

But it was the vehicle that drew most of Norlund's attention. It looked at least as old as the grease pit—probably older. It was a small truck, of the kind that in a modern version would have been called a van—a tall, dull black, slab-sided squarish machine that indeed looked as if it had been built sometime around nineteen-thirty. RADIO SURVEY CORPORATION, read the legend painted in hard-to-see dark red on the flat black side, along with an uninspired zigzag of yellow lightning.

Ginny would have led him across the garage to exit by another interior door, but Norlund delayed, looking at the truck. It appeared to have been quite well cared for, but it was no museum piece. There were small dents in the large rounded fenders, and a film of gray road dust on the dark paint. A small old-fashioned nameplate informed Norlund that the vehicle was a Dodge.

Ginny had paused, waiting for him patiently. "Think you can drive it without any trouble?"

Stepping closer to the vehicle, Norlund looked in through the open side window. From the design of the gearshift, and the other old controls, he judged the truck to be even a few years older than his first estimate. Behind the two front seats for driver and passenger, the large windowless interior held two floor-to-ceiling equipment racks with a short aisle between them. Almost in the very rear, at the end of the aisle, was another seat, facing toward the rear with its high back concealing whatever it faced. The two side racks, of three or four shelves each, were mostly filled with what looked like appropriately antique radio equipment. Not for decades had Norlund seen gear remotely like this: wooden cabinets, alternating with black crackle-finished metal boxes, bulky transformers nested in cloth-insulated wiring, exposed vacuum tubes the size of sixty-watt light bulbs. From all this stuff archaic power cables led down into lower wooden cabinets, in which Norlund could picture primitive lead-acid batteries arrayed in series and parallel.

"Don't see why I couldn't drive it," he answered. "But what's all this junk here in back?"

"Come along, Alan. We're going to start explaining that right away. Among other things."

"Good." He followed.

The old building was even larger than it had appeared from the outside. They ascended a narrow stair, old enough to show deep wear on wooden treads. At one place the head clearance closed to a minimum, but Norlund was short enough to negotiate it handily. Once they were upstairs, modernity reasserted itself in the form of a vinyl-floored hallway with fluorescent lighting. The doors on either side of the hall were closed. Norlund hadn't seen anyone else since entering the building, but now he could hear brief footsteps, and a door closing a couple of rooms away.

He looked round sharply when Ginny led him into a

large room, sunlit from a row of windows fronting on trees and lawn, but unoccupied. This room, thought Norlund, looked like the place where the sales force might meet to plan monthly strategy. In the center was a large conference table, the wooden top shiny and unmarred though the edges and legs were definitely experienced. The room still had plenty of space for assorted other furniture; one table against a wall held a small modern coffee-maker, contents looking ready to pour. A light breeze came in through the well-screened windows, to stir casual scatterings of papers on various desks and tabletops.

The most eye-catching thing in the room was a huge photomural that all but completely covered the wall opposite the windows. Blown up black-and-white photographs had been put together on a special board to form a montage of a single scene. It was some kind of a street, or a pedestrian promenade, with a waterfront in the foreground and a row of unusual buildings in the rear. No people or vehicles were to be seen. There was a scattering of trees in full summer leaf, and what appeared to be flowerbeds among the walks. Central among the buildings was a skeletal tower, its top too high to be visible in the picture. In the background beyond the buildings there was more water, some kind of lagoon perhaps, and beyond that land again, with at least one more rank of exotic architecture. The buildings that were clearly visible were a varied lot, and certainly not ordinary houses. The whole thing reminded Norlund somewhat of a zoo—but there were no cages. A design for a museum? The world of tomorrow? Wait a minute . . .

"Have a seat, Alan. Coffee?"

"Sure. Thanks." He pulled out one of the ordinary chairs that surrounded the conference table, and seated himself so he could keep looking at the giant picture. "Sugar and milk if you've got 'em." He couldn't puzzle the picture out.

Norlund glanced around at the empty room at the couple of silent typewriters. "Is your organization somewhat undermanned? Or aren't they back from lunch yet?" Suddenly he was a skeptic again, feeling an urge to needle, to demonstrate independence. Any moment now, he thought, the fanatics are going to burst out of concealment and start teaching me the true path to salvation.

Ginny had removed her raincoat and hung it in a small closet. Now she was busying herself around the coffee-maker. "We come and go. You'll meet some of your co-workers later." She turned her head to Norlund briefly. "I expect you'll be able to recognize one of them."

"Oh?" But it appeared that no details were going to be provided just now. "All right, lady, you know how to keep me interested." Norlund found his eyes kept coming back to the huge picture. Something about it nagged him, as if the scene it showed ought to have been familiar.

He gave up on it for the time being and looked around at the room again, at the papers on a small nearby table. The top one looked like some kind of printout, with columns of incomprehensible numbers. In through the windows came the genteel murmur of traffic from the suburban residential street, invisible behind the summer screen of trees.

"Inconspicuous," Norlund pronounced. "Though not really secret. Is that the note you guys are striving for?"

"All organizations have certain secrets." Ginny came to set down a steaming styrofoam cup on the

big table near his hand. "We do have some we consider vitally important, but we try not to work at it
unnecessarily."

Then, with her other hand, she placed another object on the table for his inspection. Somewhat smaller
than a banana, it was vaguely the same shape, dark,
smooth, hard-looking, a near-cylinder with tapering
ends and a light curve. On each end there were a
couple of small flanges with holes in them, evidently
for mounting. "These will be a part of the job you
do for us—a large part. Go ahead, pick it up and look
it over."

Norlund first took a sip of his coffee, which was hot
and good. Then he picked up the so-far unnamed
object. It was indeed hard and smooth, and moderately heavy. Metal? No, he decided, some unusual
ceramic.

He asked: "What is it?"

Ginny had perched sideways on the big table now,
swinging one foot lightly and sipping from her own
styrofoam cup. The jeans and sweater showed her
figure to good advantage. "It's a kind of recording
device. Think of what we're doing as taking a kind of
survey; your part of the job will be to distribute a
number of objects, twenty or so, similar to this one,
according to a plan that you'll be given."

"A survey of what? What do they record?"

"You don't have to worry about that."

"Huh. So I'll be driving around in that truck downstairs, distributing these?"

"Yes."

He shook his head. "Forget what I just said about
you guys trying to be inconspicuous."

"To distribute the devices properly, you're going to
need help. Either you or your partner will have to take

certain readings on the truck's electronic equipment, while the other person puts the devices in place."

Norlund drank coffee again. "First I've heard about a partner."

"You're going to need one. It could be someone from here—it could, as a remote possibility, even be me. More likely it'll be some local man that you hire when you get where you're going."

"Or woman, I suppose?"

Ginny's smile returned faintly. "Anyone you hire locally for this particular job will almost certainly be a man."

"Let me guess. Saudi Arabia?"

"Oh no." She turned, directing his attention to the huge photo on the wall. "You're going there, in among those buildings—you've been there before, actually. You used to live in that city."

"Mystery, mystery. Is it all right if I have another cup of this? You make good coffee."

"Sure, help yourself. I don't want to be mysterious, really, Alan. I want to get on with the job. It's just that there's a right way and a wrong way to explain things."

"Sounds like I'm being prepared for a shocker." He poured himself coffee, then judiciously measured in a little sugar. He'd go without cream this time. "Sounds foreign. Not that I'd necessarily mind. I've lived in a fair number of countries at one time and another."

"To me it would be foreign. But I think you'll fit right in, Alan, with just a little preparation before you go." A light tap sounded on one of the closed doors at the far end of the room, and Ginny hopped briskly off the table. "Excuse me, be right back." Opening the door, she put her head out and murmured something to whoever was out there. Norlund couldn't make out any of the words.

Gazing at Ginny Butler's back, he thought momentarily of shifting his position to where he might be able to see past her, discover who she was talking with. He decided not. Let them play their games. Instead he went back to drinking coffee, and studying the naggingly half-familiar photomural, while in the background he was aware of the tones of a male voice that spoke to Ginny from just outside the door. Again Norlund was haunted by a sense of cognition; deep in his memory a search was going on, some connection fell just short of being made. . . .

He heard the door close. In a moment Ginny was back at his side, gazing at him as if she expected something of him.

He said: "You were going to tell me what country this is in."

She said decisively: "A far country indeed. But the city is Chicago."

He looked at her; he couldn't believe that she had suddenly started talking total nonsense. But if it was logic that she was talking, it had to be the logic of a dream. Norlund cleared his throat. "I still don't get it. I live in Chicago now. Whereabouts are these buildings in Chicago?"

Ginny moved to stand beside the picture. "They were put up on Northerly Island, for the World's Fair in the early Thirties. Maybe you can remember going to it as a boy. They called it A Century of Progress."

"Where they're talking about having the new fair in Ninety-two."

"That's right."

"Oh." He shook his head. "But those buildings aren't there *now*. On Northerly Island there's the

Planetarium, and a beach, and a small airfield. You said I was going in *among* them — ?"

"You are."

It was quiet in the room, except for the faint murmur of traffic from outside. "I repeat, I still don't get it. You mean they've been — reconstructed somewhere? Or what?"

"No, I don't mean that." Ginny was standing now at the huge photo's right-hand edge. Her hand reached down, pointing. "I said 'a far country', remember, Alan? The name of it is printed down here."

Her voice was encouraging, but still Norlund knew fear, or something very like it. It was not an overpowering feeling, but it was deep. The woman who faced him was not playing games; she was as deeply serious as anyone Norlund had ever seen. This was no cultist's pitch — or, if it was, there was a frightening intensity behind it.

He leaned forward in his chair, trying to see what she was pointing to. There were symbols on the photo at her fingertip. The lettering must have been very small to start with, because even enlarged as it was now, Norlund had trouble reading the dark shapes against the poorly contrasting background of foliage in the picture.

Norlund got up from his chair and moved closer. " 'A Century of Progress' ", he read aloud, and once more knew the feeling of recognition. " 'Chicago, Summer — ' "

Ginny's fingernail, a youthful, red-polished instrument of fate, tapped inexorably at the photo-board. "Here, Alan. Here. You're going here."

And just at her fingertip were four more symbols. Norlund was never sure, afterward, if he had read them aloud or not.

1933

There was traffic again on the road outside, a motor-cycle blatting. Norlund had raised his eyes to the face of Ginny Butler.

"Alan, I promised you an explanation of how we were able to help Sandy. She was treated by medical techniques of the year two thousand and thirty. Exactly how treatment was administered, I'm not free to say, but that's what she's getting. She's a very fortunate little girl. Lucky for her that we wanted to recruit her grandpa."

Norlund shook his head, feeling stupid. He didn't know what he thought, and he certainly couldn't find anything to say. He was slumping slightly now, leaning back on the conference table for support. With a feeling of relief he gave up and let himself sit down.

Ginny came closer, peering into his face. She nodded slightly, like a doctor satisfied with the progress that a patient was making.

"Your heart's in good shape," she murmured, half to herself. "And we don't have a whole lot of time locally. Alan, I'm going to prove to you that we can travel in time. I'm going to bring in someone you'll remember."

Norlund felt a new clutch of unreasoning fear as Ginny turned toward the door where the whispered conference had been conducted. "Come in!" she called in a clear voice, and phantoms of the dead chased through his imagination. . . .

The door opened. The figure that entered was not one of the phantoms, but a young man of about nineteen. He moved tentatively, hesitantly closer. He was wearing ordinary modern jeans and a long-sleeved sport shirt, and he kept staring at Norlund with a strange expression.

Norlund found himself getting to his feet, the connections of dream or madness finally being made deep in his memory. That voice, when he'd heard it outside the door . . . but . . .

The youth who had entered was no taller than Norlund, and thin with the springiness of youth. His light brown hair was just starting to grow out of a crewcut. His right arm, Norlund saw with a shock like that of fear, ended in what was either an odd glove or a very advanced type of artificial hand. The arm lay in a supporting sling at elbow level.

Norlund managed to take in all these things while hardly taking his eyes from the young man's face. He kept on staring at that face, and it was as if the last forty years had gone by in some strange, distorted dream, gone by overnight. . . .

The world had turned gray in front of Norlund, and then briefly disappeared. He was aware of Ginny Butler guiding him, supporting him, helping him back to a chair.

Presently the world was steady again and he looked up. The young man was still there. He was standing even closer now and peering down at Norlund anxiously.

"Al?" the young man asked. It was a familiar voice. Just a minute ago, from outside the door, it had nagged at Norlund's subconscious with its familiarity. The youth leaned a little closer. Norlund felt like an accident victim, with this face looming over him with a look of pity and muffled terror. "Al? It's me. Andy."

"Andy." Norlund nodded. It wasn't that Andy had been hard to recognize. The problem was that he couldn't help recognizing him. And that was a very great problem indeed, requiring some adjustment. Andy Burns stood before him, solid and three-dimensional, as real as he had been that day over Regensburg in nineteen forty-three when Alan Norlund had tried to tighten the tourniquet on the stump of Andy Burns' right arm, then had tightened up his chute harness for him, clamped his left hand on the D-ring and then had put him out through the right waist gun opening of the burning Fortress. And Andy was not only still alive but not a day older than he was that day forty years ago. Or not many days older; his hair had grown longer. . . .

Norlund didn't know that he had finally completely fainted. He knew only that he was coming out of a faint, and that he was once more alone in the room with Ginny Butler. He was lying slumped back in his chair, and his belt had been loosened, and there was dampness on his face and in his hair as if someone had just sprinkled him with water. The old man can't take it any longer, he thought with momentary shame.

Then that feeling was swallowed up in wonder. He stirred under Ginny's touch on his hair, and sat upright. "That was . . ."

She waited for him to complete the statement. When he didn't, she said: "You know who it was. You recognized him instantly."

"Where'd he go?"

"He was called away. You can talk to him again later." Ginny paused. "Like your granddaughter, Andy's very lucky that we need you for a job. You're the main reason that we went back and saved him, out of the air over Germany. It cost to do that."

"Andy Burns." Norlund was sitting a little forward now, leaning his face in his hands.

"I hope that, having seen him, you'll be ready to believe we can send you to the Century of Progress."

"I guess I have to." Norlund looked up. Andy Burns. Two proofs, Sandy and Andy. It sounded like the title of a Thirties comic strip. "I put him out of the aircraft myself, but I never saw his chute open. . . ." His voice trailed off. "My war story," he concluded.

"You flew twenty missions as a waist gunner," Ginny said. "I'm sure there's more than one war story you could tell." For a moment she looked at Norlund almost tenderly. The moment ended in a return to briskness. "However, there's another job to be done now."

She led Norlund out of what he thought of as the planning room, down a rather long hallway to a small bedroom. There was an attached bath, making the quarters look rather like a room in a modern motel.

"Your medical checkup is next, Alan, so get undressed if you will. The doctor will be along in a minute." The room's door closed behind her.

He followed orders in a daze, still too much in shock for examining-room embarrassment. Andy Burns. . . .

The door opened again, without a knock. The white-coated man who entered was in his seventies, if appearance could be relied upon after today, but erect and trim. He wasted no time in introductions or other chitchat, but issued terse instructions and began to administer a physical.

In addition to making tests, he took some of Norlund's body measurements, as if he might be fitting him for a suit of clothes. He checked Norlund's teeth, which were still original issue. Some of the instruments that were used in the exam looked strange and unfamiliar to the patient, but that was nothing out of the ordinary these days. When the examiner had finished, he brusquely told Norlund to get dressed, advised him to get a haircut within the next few days, and departed as uninformatively as he had entered.

Ginny returned not long after the silent man's departure, knocking before she entered.

"How'd I do?" Norlund asked.

"Fine. You're in good health."

"I thought I was. What was that about a haircut? He told me I ought to get one."

"Oh. Well, men's hairstyles are somewhat different in the Thirties, as I'm sure you'll remember. Not that yours is *very* long, but—"

"Oh." And somehow the whole prospect suddenly became real.

Ginny was holding open the door to the hall. "Let's get moving," she murmured abstractedly. "We've got to speed things up."

She led him down again to the garage where the old truck waited. "Let's see how you start the truck, Alan. Then put it in gear and ease it backward and forward a foot or so. We can't open the garage doors just now, but don't worry about the carbon monoxide. We're well ventilated."

"If you say so." He climbed aboard the truck, while Ginny watched from the center of the floor. "Shouldn't be much different from driving a modern stickshift," he told her out the window. "Except here you have a hand choke to fool with too. And a hand brake, I see."

But he had no trouble getting things to work. All the machinery seemed to be in excellent condition, and memory came back as if the skills had been used only yesterday. Every now and then Norlund paused for about two seconds, thinking to himself: What in the *hell* have I got myself into?

Ginny, watching him handle the truck, seemed reassured. "Good, I think we can assume that the driving *per se* is not going to present a real problem." And she looked at her watch.

"Ginny?" It was the first time he had called her by name.

"Yes?"

"How did you manage that? With Andy?"

"We haven't time to go into that now. You'll talk to Andy again before you go. We went and got him, that's all."

"And now there's no time."

Her manner softened briefly. "I realize it may sound crazy. But there are ways in which we can manipulate time, and ways in which we can't, and right now we're in something of a bloody hurry. I've got to start teaching you how to operate the equipment in the rear of the truck."

A door in the inner wall of the garage opened, to admit the septuagenarian medic, still in his white coat. Ginny went to him and they spoke together in low voices. Norlund shut off the truck engine and heard her call him Dr. Harbin. Norlund got out of the truck, not knowing what else he was supposed to be doing.

The doctor approached. He looked into Norlund's eyes for a moment, nodded as if satisfied, and said: "I want you to listen to these numbers. They'll come in three groups. Ready?"

"Whatever."

Harbin then indeed pronounced three groups of numbers, sixteen digits in each group. Norlund to his own amazement found himself effortlessly counting and keeping track. When Norlund had heard all three groups recited, Ginny approached him with a small notebook and pencil in hand. He was expecting to be asked to play the numbers back, but instead she interviewed him on his personal preferences in clothing.

"You know what I was doing in nineteen forty-three and you don't know what color shirts I like to wear?"

"That's not so crazy, if you think about it."

"It isn't?"

"Just answer, please." And Ginny wrote down his answers, as if they mattered, and hurried off.

Harbin confronted him again. "Repeat the second group of numbers for me, please."

To Norlund's considerable surprise, he could still do so, without even hesitating. When he looked for the numbers they were there, sitting in his mind as if projected on a screen.

"Good. Fine. And now the first group, backwards?"

Norlund could rattle those off just as readily. Ginny came hustling back from somewhere while he was at it. "He's ready to learn," the doctor told her.

"Great," she rejoiced quietly. Efficient as usual, she already had the truck door open, gesturing Norlund in. "Step into the back of the vehicle, please, Alan, and sit in the seat there. You've got to learn that equipment."

He went in. The high body of the old vehicle gave Ginny room to stand behind his swivel seat, lean over his shoulder and point things out. The proximity of her young body was pleasant, yet somehow not distracting.

The first thing that became obvious to Norlund about the equipment was that the ancient wires and tubes, even though the filaments were glowing, were no more than window-dressing; modern gear must somehow lie concealed beneath. The modern gear was evidently complex, but he learned how to operate it very quickly—too quickly.

Feeling actually frightened, he interrupted the lesson once. "What've you done to my brain? I can't forget anything if I try."

"Then don't try. It's nothing harmful, Alan, when it's used sparingly. We've just given you something to speed up the learning process temporarily, make it more efficient. Now, these dials here have a code setting, like a safe. They must be set properly for any of the other gears to work."

As soon as the dials were at their proper settings, what had looked like a primitive oscilloscope built into the console in front of Norlund cleared its round gray screen and showed him a color-graphics display as sophisticated as anything he'd seen on equipment of the Eighties.

Ginny started to explain to him how he was going to use it. After she'd made the scope turn gray again, displaying one primitive green-line trace like an ancient A-scan radar, Norlund interrupted the lesson to point at it. "They had scopes like this in nineteen thirty-three?"

"I see you weren't doing advanced electronic research in that year. Yes, they did. Would you believe they had something almost like it in eighteen ninety-seven?"

Ginny went on showing him what he was expected to do with the equipment; the way she talked about it, it didn't sound particularly hard. And maybe he didn't yet believe wholeheartedly in the reality of all that she was telling him, but he remembered everything she said. He also lost track of how much time was passing. When he began to get overpoweringly sleepy, she calmly sent him back to his room to rest.

Lying on his bed, he tried to think. But too much had happened to him today; he couldn't think straight about any part of it. . . .

He awoke with the feeling that he might have slept for half an hour. The phone at bedside was chiming musically. When Norlund answered, Ginny's voice invited him to come downstairs for dinner.

It was still daylight outside, and Norlund's wrist-watch indicated seven o'clock. He washed up and put on a clean shirt, choosing one of several that he now found hanging in the room's closet. He didn't think they had been there when he came upstairs, but he had been so sleepy he hadn't even noticed what time it was. Ginny had said that everything was going to be provided for him, and he decided to take her at her word.

Had he been dreaming Andy Burns?

It was just a few minutes after seven when he located some stairs and went down them. They brought him to the ground floor in sight of a rather ordinary dining room, with a table big enough for eight or ten. Only three places were set, and two of those were occupied by Ginny and Dr. Harbin.

They both looked up as Norlund approached. Ginny asked: "How're you feeling, Alan?"

"Pretty good, after that siesta. I don't know what happened. I don't usually . . ."

"Common reaction," said Harbin, clearing his throat as if it were rusty with disuse, "after a learning session like the one you had. Sit down."

Norlund sat. A casually dressed young man Norlund hadn't seen before appeared in the capacity of waiter, outlined some limited choices in the way of food, and went casually away.

Norlund looked at the doctor. "Are you the one who's treating Sandy?"

The man's expression did not change, nor did he answer, but went on chewing methodically. Ginny said quickly: "That's not an answerable question right now. Do you want to call the hospital, Alan? You may, of course."

"And then call again in the morning?"

"Yes, certainly. Use the phone in the next room there. Or the one in your room, if you prefer." As Norlund started to rise, her eyes held his. "Alan? Don't give any hints. About this. It's getting more important hour by hour. It could wreck everything right now."

"I won't."

He used the phone near the dining room, punching out the never-to-be-forgotten hospital number. There was more than one way to learn something indelibly. Sandy's oncologist was naturally not at the hospital at this time of the evening, nor was Marge on hand. But the nurse on the floor—one who, after the long struggle, Norlund thought of as something of a friend—reported that the patient was better today, eating well and resting comfortably.

Norlund announced this when he got back to the dinner table. Ginny and the doctor smiled to show that they were pleased; neither was in the least surprised.

The food, brought by the casual waiter, was okay: roast beef, mashed potatoes. Plain home-cookin', folks. Norlund, retreating into his thoughts, tested himself silently, determining that everything Ginny had taught him before he slept was still clear in his mind, as available as if he were reading it from a printed page. There wasn't much talk at table, and none of it about anything more consequential than the weather. Norlund had coffee again, and enjoyed it, though he was reasonably sure that they had drugged his coffee earlier. If they wanted to drug him again they'd find a way, as long as he stayed here. And he was not about to jump up and run out. Not as long as they kept their word on Sandy. . . .

That was true, but it was also rationalizing. Actually, and it surprised him to realize it, on some deep level he was starting to thoroughly enjoy all this.

But he was also tired, in spite of his nap. He turned to Ginny. "Have we got anything else planned for tonight?"

"Not at all. Wait a minute and I'll walk you upstairs. I want to get something in my room."

When the two of them reached Norlund's room, Ginny said, "I think all your new clothes have probably arrived by now," and walked in with him. She looked at the garments hanging in the closet, and checked the dresser drawers, which Norlund now saw were stocked with clothing too.

He took down the coat of the gray suit now hanging in the closet and tried it on. The mirror mounted on the bathroom door showed him it was a good fit. Though the suit was clean it didn't look new; it looked used as well as old-fashioned, a little baggy at the elbows. Of course men's suits didn't age much in terms of style. On a hunch Norlund reached for the hanging gray trousers and examined the fly. Sure enough, buttons and not a zipper.

Ginny was at the door. "I'll let you get settled in."

"Okay. See you in the morning."

He was sleepy again; it had been a day not easily matched in any lifetime. No need to hypothesize more drugs to explain his tiredness, he thought.

His room had a small television and a radio, but he didn't feel a need for noise. He was down to his underwear, looking out into the night from a darkened room and not seeing much, just about ready to turn down the bed and retire, when a light tapping sounded at his door.

There sprang to mind the image of Ginny coming back, wearing something filmy. . . . It had been a day of miracles; why not? "Just a minute," he called quietly, and pulled on his pants again. Then he switched on a light and opened the door.

Nineteen-year-old Andy Burns was standing there, dressed as he had been when Norlund saw him in the afternoon, with the sling still supporting his altered right arm.

Andy said: "Al? It is you, ain't it?"

"Yeah," said Norlund, letting out a sigh. He had the feeling that he was dreaming, though he knew that he was wide awake. He stood back from the door. "Come in," he told the kid waiting outside.

Young Andy Burns entered, looking ill-at-ease. He peered around as if he expected to find someone else. "Ah wanted t'talk t'you," he said. "Ah'm still tryin' to get it straight in m'mind. They've told me what happened and all, how they caught me right outta the air, and Ah gotta believe 'em. . . . You mind if Ah smoke? Ah mean, here, maybe you want one?"

"No." Norlund had quit decades ago, and declined the offered pack. "But you go ahead. Here, sit down."

"Thanks." Andy dug out matches and lit up, the flame making his face look, to Norlund, quite incredibly young. Then he located an ashtray, and threw himself into the one padded chair.

Norlund sat down on the edge of the bed.

Andy gave him a look in which nervousness, fear,

and recognition were all mixed. "You're really . . ." He didn't know quite how to say it.

Norlund nodded. "Alan Norlund. Yes. Not the same one you remember, not by forty years. But it's me."

Andy nodded, obviously relieved to have his reaction understood, his doubts accepted.

"Andy, tell me. For you, how long has it been since we—were in that plane together?"

"Oh. T'me it was only three weeks ago. Three weeks today. Ginny Butler and them caught me outta the air, Ah dunno exactly how. Ah don't remember that. I do remember bein' in the Fort, and knowin' that Ah was hit, real bad. They say you put me out the waist."

Norlund spoke slowly and softly. "I was afraid that if I waited any longer I couldn't get you and myself out, both. I thought any minute we'd blow up or go into a spin. I figured the krauts took care of wounded prisoners, Americans and limeys anyway, so. . . . As it turned out, we made it home. I had a shell fragment in my leg, too. Yeah, I put your hand on the D-ring and put you out."

Andy nodded solemnly. "And then," he said, exhaling smoke, "Ah woke up in a kind of hospital these people got. It ain't here, in Eighty-four. Ah think it's somewhere in the future but they won't say where. You been there?"

"No."

"It's quite a place. All these hah walls like a prison but. . . . Anyway they been breakin' it all to me gradually these three weeks. About time travel and how Ah'm never gonna be able to go home and all. They fuckin' tell me that Ah . . . 'scuse me . . . " Suddenly Andy looked flustered, almost as if he were home on leave and had forgotten and used foul language in his mother's hearing.

Norlund told him: "You can swear if you want. We both of us used to swear a lot." My God, he thought to himself, did I look as young then, in Forty-three, as this kid does? Of course I did, I must have. "I guess I kind of got out of the habit," he concluded, "when I was raising a kid myself."

"Ginny an' them have kinda started hinting that Ah oughta get outta the habit too. That, and smokin' butts." Andy looked at his cigarette, then back at Norlund. Still marveling, he shook his head and blurted: "You sure do sound like him." Confusion. "Ah mean . . ."

"I am him," said Norlund. "As far as I know," he added in deference to the lately re-demonstrated insanity of the world. "What're they going to do with you now? They say you can't go home?"

"Too many problems, with timelines and all, if they tried to send me. They tell me Ah'll have me a choice of jobs, once Ah get through orientation. Ah'm in a different kinda fix from you, see. You'll work a little while and then go home, that's how they've told me it is. Ah dunno what kinda job Ah'll have, but it's better'n bein' dead. Tell me, did Graham ever get outta the tail?"

"Ah." It had been years, or maybe decades, since Norlund had thought about Graham. "Yeah, that was after you got hit. He did come forward from the tail, I remember, because both his guns back there were out. We were all shot to hell. Damned old Forts. They sure could take it."

The years were blowing away like clouds; for a moment everything was clear. "Graham came forward and took your gun. Another FW made a pass at us . . . they had everything up after us that day, one-oh-nines, one-nineties, everything. I was hit in the leg myself." The immediacy of it all faded. "They sent me home, and I became a gunnery instructor."

"What about Graham?"

"Oh yeah. I think he flew two more missions after that, and his tour was up. Never got a scratch, as far as I know. I lost track of him a long time ago."

Andy was once more looking at Norlund oddly—or perhaps he had never stopped looking at him that way. "For me all that was just three weeks ago."

Norlund couldn't seem to find a good answer to that. Andy ground out his butt in the ashtray and lit another. Norlund felt no desire at all to smoke again. Finally he asked: "How's the arm?"

Andy brought it slowly out of the sling, moving it mostly under its own power. Norlund could see that the fingers moved a little. "It's okay. It's pretty good, they say it'll be real good soon. That's another thing— if Ah did go home, Ah couldn't keep it." Now Andy rotated the forearm gingerly and made the gloved fingers clench, a slow but natural movement. "Actually it's pretty keen," he said without too much conviction. "Ah cain't feel nothin' in it yet but Ah kin do things. Later it might even be better'n mah own arm. Later they can fix th' skin so's it looks more real."

"That's good. That's great."

Andy was looking at Norlund intently. As if repeating a lesson learned, Andy said: "Arm's good and Ah'm glad t' be alive. Ah just ain't never gonna see any of mah family again, that's all."

Shortly after that, Andy broke off the conversation fairly abruptly and took his leave. It was not as if he were upset or even tired; more as if his mind was suddenly busy elsewhere.

Norlund could sympathize. But he himself was

yawning. Something was running through his mind about Scrooge, confronted by the ghost of Christmas past. Trying to really think about anything had become hopeless. . . .

In the morning, his first impression was that of having been awakened by some kind of alarm. But whatever it was must have ceased its signal in the second before he became fully conscious of it.

Now the room was quiet, and looked quite ordinary. Norlund lay still for a while, trying to fit the strange experiences of yesterday into some kind of pattern of reality that could be trusted. During the night there had been strange dreams, but he could no longer remember them.

Andy Burns. That had been no dream. And Ginny had said that he, Alan Norlund, was the main reason they had gone back forty years and somehow plucked Andy to safety out of the aerial inferno over Regensburg. It had cost them to do that, she said, and Norlund could well believe it had. So it would seem that he, Alan Norlund, truly was important.

But Ginny hadn't said why.

Norlund got up and went to the bathroom. He remembered Ginny telling him how he should dress today, and he followed her instructions. He picked out clothing they had issued him, letting his own garments hang in the closet against his return. Sort of like leaving the barracks to fly a mission, he thought. Though in this case the special clothing was not high-altitude stuff. Here instead he got cotton drawers, and a white cotton undershirt with thin straps across the shoulders. The business shirt was white, wrinkly cotton also, lightly starched in collar and cuffs—he'd forgotten how the starch felt when you wore it. The

pants of the gray suit with the used look were, as he'd
expected, just a trifle baggy in the knees. There was a
matching vest, and a red tie.

Beside his own reading glasses on the dresser had
appeared a different pair, in an old clamshell case,
and he put them on and slipped the case into his
pocket. The glasses worked beautifully. Also on the
dresser was a small tray that he was sure hadn't been
there last night. The tray held the potential contents of
his Thirties pockets and a wristwatch, leather-strapped
and ticking. Norlund gave the winding stem of the
watch a few turns and put it on, leaving his own
quartz model in its place.

Then there was a leather billfold, slightly worn. It
was packed with what certainly looked like real US
money, circa nineteen-thirty. Norlund counted two hundred and twenty dollars in assorted bills, some crisp
and new-looking, some old and worn. None of them
were dated after nineteen-thirty two. Thoughtfully
Norlund rubbed the money in his fingers before he
replaced it in the billfold. The money bothered him—
whether because it might be counterfeit or because it
might not be, he wasn't sure.

The billfold also held some business cards, with
Norlund's own name on them—someone must have
been sure of his recruitment. The cards gave a Wheaton
address for the Radio Survey Corporation; he wasn't
sure whether it was the address of the building he
was standing in. No zip code, of course, but the cards
did bear a phone number—he'd have to ask what that
connected to. There was a New York driver's license,
looking new but old-fashioned, also made out to
Norlund and dated nineteen thirty-three. He wondered
why there was no Social Security card, and then he
recalled that in the year he was supposedly visiting,

no one in the world had yet seen one of those.

Something made of cloth was folded up on the dresser beside the tray. It was an old-style money belt, the kind that you wrapped around your body under your clothes. Snapping open the belt's pockets, Norlund discovered two thousand dollars more. God, if the unimaginable really happened, and he found himself living in the depths of the Depression, he'd be able to buy himself a house and a small farm and settle down. . . .

When he'd gotten the belt on, and his clothing readjusted, he inspected the modest handful of coins that the tray held. Holding up a quarter dollar, he saw that the coin was of real silver, its milled edges of the same brightness as the faces. The quarter was dated nineteen thirty-two, and it was hardly worn at all. Also mostly unworn were the Liberty-head silver dimes, the buffalo nickels, the bright copper wheat-wreathed pennies. There were no Indian cents in the assortment; to the best of Norlund's recollection the early Thirties would be a little late for them to appear in common circulation.

Dropping the coins into his left-hand pocket, Norlund absently ran a finger up his fly, checking that all the buttons were fastened. Old habits returned quickly. Now, fully dressed except for the hat that still waited on the dresser, he looked at his reflection in the mirror. The old clothes made him look older in some way . . . not like his father, no, he'd never looked much like him. But in another odd way he felt that he was younger, returning to the days of youth. Buddies again with Andy Burns . . . no, never again really that. Suddenly he wondered what Ginny Butler really thought of him, of old man Norlund.

He tried on the fedora, which fit perfectly, and now

the image in the mirror reminded him somewhat of his own grandfather. And reminded him also of how as a kid he'd always looked forward to being able to wear a grown-up hat.

A leather traveling-bag was in the closet. Norlund put it on the bed and packed it with clothes from the closet and drawers—shirts, underwear, socks, a sweater, a couple of pairs of pants. He found and packed a new old-fashioned shaving kit and toothbrush. He reminded himself to get a haircut soon after arrival. . . . God, but he was taking this thing seriously! He really thought that he was going to—

Struck by a sudden idea, he got out his newly acquired driver's license and looked at it again. The date of his birth was given as eighteen seventy-three, and, yes, there was a place where he was supposed to sign. Getting out the fountain pen that had been provided on the tray, he took care of that detail.

He was all ready now, as far as he could tell. He stood for a moment looking at the modern bedside phone, then picked it up and punched out the number of the hospital. It was Sunday morning; he just might catch one of the first-team doctors making rounds.

This time he got through directly to Sandy's room, and it was Marge who answered. "Our girl is looking pretty fine this morning, Dad. Maybe that little set-back is all in the past." And Marge's tone was even happier than her words.

"Can I talk to her?" And he did. Sandy sounded chipper, very good indeed. Then he had Marge back on. "She sounds like she's getting well," said Norlund to his daughter. "Jeez, I hope so. Hey, I love you guys."

"Well then, Dad, I think you ought to hurry back to us. Where are you now? You didn't really say."

Norlund cleared his throat. "I hope I'll see you soon. Tomorrow I'll be back in Chicago, I think. Maybe the day after that."

When he arrived downstairs in search of some breakfast he found the dining room deserted. Finding his way into the kitchen, he discovered a pot of coffee on the stove, but no other signs of activity. He poked around in cabinets, getting out a few utensils and some instant oatmeal, and made himself a bowl of it. If they wanted him they could find him, and he was a touch hungry; breakfast was usually his favorite meal. He made two pieces of toast and then discovered he could eat only one. Again he thought vaguely that today was like the morning of a combat mission. Fear was present, but something else too, something to be savored. And where was Andy Burns this morning? Already out on the ramp and loading ammo?

He finished eating and cleaned up after himself a little, as much as he felt like cleaning up. Then he picked up the traveling bag that he'd carried downstairs, and headed in the direction of the garage housing the old truck. He'd thought he'd heard a voice or two from that direction while he was in the kitchen.

The first thing he noticed on entering the garage was that the Dodge truck had somehow been turned, so now it faced the overhead doors. It was still the only vehicle in sight. A hunched, white-coated form that looked like that of Dr. Harbin was doing something inside the cab while Ginny, in worker's coveralls this morning, stood outside talking to him.

She saw Norlund as soon as he entered, and came over to him. Her manner as she looked him over was all business. "You look okay," she decided.

Norlund asked, "What's been decided about my partner? Who do I get?"

"You'll hire someone there. Follow the rules we gave you yesterday in choosing someone. None of our people here can be spared—Andy with his artificial arm is certainly not a candidate. Now let's run through some of the procedures on the machinery again."

Norlund still hadn't forgotten anything from yesterday's lessons; he had no trouble in playing back to Ginny his operating knowledge of the gear in the back of the truck. As for the ultimate purpose of it all, he hadn't been taught anything and he didn't ask now.

Ginny was unfolding a paper. "Here's a map of the approximate route that you should drive once you get there. I think you might be able to finish the job in one day. Here are shown the approximate locations where the recording devices must go. Of course, you have to use the equipment to decide on the exact best positioning."

Presently Harbin came to take a turn at catechizing Norlund. From time to time Harbin or Ginny would drop other tasks and go over to the wall at the far side of the garage, where there was a phone. Whatever they learned in their brief phone conversations didn't do their morale any good, for Norlund could see strain growing progressively in their faces.

Then Harbin, returning from one of these conversations, had suddenly acquired a gunbelt strapped round his waist, over his long white lab coat. The doctor silently handed a similar belt to Ginny, who accepted it without comment and calmly put it on. Norlund thought that the weapons in the holsters looked something like Israeli machine pistols that he'd seen on television or somewhere; not that he was an expert on any kind of modern firearms.

He waited for a moment, but when it was clear that they weren't going to volunteer any explanation of the weapons, he commented: "Doesn't look good, hey?"

Ginny looked up from a checklist that she was going over. "Doesn't feel too good, either, Alan. But you know I never promised you that this job was going to be perfectly safe."

"I never really suspected that it would be all that safe. And I know exactly what you promised me and what you didn't."

She was about to answer, but Harbin—on the phone again—was gesturing violently, calling her into conference.

In a few moments she was back. In a voice more tightly controlled than ever she ordered: "Here, Alan, take these pills." Her smallish hand held out two yellow capsules in front of him, and then produced from somewhere a styrofoam cup of water. "For launching we want you at peak alertness."

"Instead of at peak learning ability."

"What was that?"

"I said"—he swallowed pills and water—"I have to be not quite so impressionable now. Or when I get there. Someone might tell me to do the wrong thing. Not so damn suggestible."

And Ginny surprised him by being briefly delighted, as if she were rooting for him personally. "You're right. Oh, beautiful, Alan, you're with us, I know it for sure now. This is going to work."

And Norlund, even knowing that he judged from an abyss of ignorance, felt pleased that he thought so too.

He was up in the driver's seat of the big old Dodge, fumbling briefly for a seatbelt that of course did not exist, when some kind of almost silent hell began to break loose just outside the doors of the farthest bay of the garage. And all at once those doors were rolling up by themselves, moving to the accompaniment of slow warbling sound effects. The light that came in from outside was not a normal light; it was mottled, and though at moments it might have been acceptable as normal, it changed swiftly. It did not look like ordinary daylight, or moonlight, or even any kind of artificial lighting that Norlund had ever seen before.

The doors were not yet fully open when the odd sounds stopped, and to Norlund's astonishment a large old-fashioned black sedan, a car that Cagney or George Raft might have driven through a gangster movie, came rolling in under them. Ginny and Dr. Harbin, looking as much surprised as Norlund felt, jumped back out of the car's way.

The old-fashioned sedan entered the garage bouncing on stiff springs, as if it had had to negotiate some kind of large hump just outside the doors. From where Norlund was sitting in the Dodge it was impossible to see outside through those doors, but now the entering light was going mad, putting on a syncopated disco show. And the instant that the sedan was fully inside, the doors came rolling down, this time with the slamming speed of a guillotine.

Men were already piling out of the black sedan. Not Raft or Cagney, but these characters' clothes would have fitted them: all three of them were wearing dark topcoats, along with other winter garments, and two of them were carrying the third. On second glance Norlund was sure that he saw snow melting on the black car's roof, while mist formed on its windows as they warmed.

The first man out of the car was a beefy character

about thirty years old. Before he was completely out he was shouting excitedly at Ginny and Harbin: "When do we transship? He's got two creases on 'im!"

Harbin raised an authoritative voice "We're in the middle of a launching here—"

The two new arrivals who could stand stood holding their helpless comrade who might have been dead for all that Norlund could tell. They responded to Harbin in what quickly became a shouting match.

"—attack's going to diffuse this far—"

"—pack-year has precessed out of range—" At least that was one set of words that Norlund's ears seemed to be recording.

"—transshipment clockwise is not an option—"

Abruptly Harbin turned back to Norlund. Leaning in through the truck's open window, the white-coated man spoke with superbly controlled haste. "We're going to have to launch you immediately. Roll up your window till you get clear of the garage. When you drive out, you'll be in nineteen thirty-three. We're all depending on you to complete this mission properly; if we should lose this—"

A klaxon interrupted, deafeningly loud. It had to be some kind of alarm. The doctor backed away from the truck, motioning for Norlund to raise his window and get moving. Norlund, cranking up the glass with his left hand, noted that the window on the other side of the cab was closed already, and reached with his right for the gearshift. The shooting had started. Well, he'd never believed that this goddamned survey they were sending him on was as simple as it sounded. This was war. Well, he'd survived war before. . . .

The doctor was still yelling final words toward him, but the words were lost and Harbin's tense figure obscured behind a red translucent wall that was condensing like moisture out of the air in the garage. The red wall was hot; Norlund could feel its radiance on the left side of his face before he got his window up, the heat coming and going in waves like the light that had come from beyond the doors. Now Norlund had closed his window and a lid of the same translucent red had clamped down across the truck's flat windshield. That, as Norlund remembered perfectly from yesterday's briefing, was the signal for him to start his engine. The four-cylinder plant under the hood turned over, coughed once, and settled into a vibrant purr that had the feel of dependable power.

Now, put it in gear. Now, foot ready on the clutch . . .

The red lid on the windshield was darkening toward purple, growing more opaque. Through it Norlund saw that the garage doors directly ahead of him were starting to open. They rose revealing brilliance. Norlund eased in the clutch and drove slowly forward. Then for a moment he was almost blinded, as they had warned him he might be, by the shifting light of a rainbow that surrounded his vehicle, making it impossible for him to see anything else. The world was silent but for the sound of the truck's engine.

Then he was driving into bright but perfectly natural summer sunshine. Exterior sound came back. He could hear the crunch of his tires on a cinder drive, and the lazy drone of a cicada in one of the tall trees nearby.

Increased warmth engulfed the truck, the sun shining down on it from high in a clear sky. The truck was rolling slowly along a cinder drive, which just a few yards ahead entered a country road, hardly more than a single lane of hard-packed clay and gravel.

Norlund glanced behind him. He had just driven

out of a garage attached to an isolated farmhouse. It was a narrow garage, big enough for only one car, and its single set of doors were already closed.

He looked to right, to left, and forward. In every direction weedy meadows and shabby cornfields stretched into the distance.

1933

Norlund fought back his first impulse, born of shock, to slam on the brakes. True to his brief training he kept on driving, and turned left out of the driveway. At thirty miles an hour he followed the otherwise deserted narrow country road, in what was supposed to be an easterly direction. Glancing back once again, wildly, he saw the old farmhouse receding behind him, looking abandoned, altered, shrunken.

Now oncoming traffic appeared on the narrow road, in the form of an old Ford, and Norlund automatically steered past it. When the dust raised by the Ford had settled, the road ahead was empty again. Norlund drove through a deserted crossroads that displayed road signs of forgotten types. A little farther on, another intersection was also empty of buildings, but marked the beginning of paved streets. Now there were narrow, weed-rimmed sidewalks bordering empty fields—doubtless some housing development had been started here during the prosperous Twenties and abandoned when things fell apart. Another quarter of a mile and Norlund drove past a filling station with antique pumps, advertising twelve-cent gas.

It was about at that point that the shock of it all overtook him. It hit him so hard that he gave up and pulled off onto the shoulder of the road. He just sat there. His hands were shaking, and he put his head down on them as they gripped the steering wheel.

It wasn't so much the shaking hands that had forced him to stop, though that was bad enough. It felt as if his mind were shaking too, in danger of giving up on the effort to keep track of swiftly altering reality. Reality was what could kill you, and he feared that if he went on driving he ran a risk of careening head-on into a truck, like that big square-nosed whatever-it-was approaching now. A sanely fearful part of Norlund's mind knew that he had no seat belt, and wasn't even sure that the big flat windshield in front of him was safety glass. But the demonstrated mushiness of reality had evoked another component of his mind, and with it he felt no more apprehension about crashing into the truck than if he had been watching a movie or playing some damn video game.

Jesus. Jesus Christ. He didn't know if he was praying or swearing, but he did know that he had to rest for just a minute. He clenched his eyes shut against his knuckles. He had to think.

I think you'll fit right in when you get there. With just a minimum of preparation before you go.

Sounds foreign to me.

To me it would be.

But to him, to Alan Norlund, it wasn't foreign at all. He clung to the thought that he had lived in this strange country as a child, that he was—or ought to be—acquainted with its natives. This fact of his origin was, he supposed, one of those important qualifications that Ginny Butler had been so sure he had.

The truck naturally had no air conditioner, and it was growing hot inside. Norlund moved mechanically to crank down both side windows. After that he felt a little better, a little more in control. He looked around.

Everything around him was still nineteen thirty-three. And, somewhat to his own surprise, he found himself already beginning to cope with and accept that fact. The sudden fancy came to him that the half-century he had lived through following this year had been one vast dream . . . but judging from the appearance of his hands, still locked on the steering wheel, it was a dream that had aged him pretty severely.

Norlund drew a deep breath. He was still a long way from calm, but ready to drive again. This time he didn't even fumble for the non-existent seatbelt. Did he need to consult his map? No, not yet, he decided. It had been fixed quite firmly in his memory.

Half a mile or so ahead of where he had pulled over, he could see some buildings clustered among trees. It looked like, and probably was, the tail end of some suburban residential street. He was heading east, toward the city, and the countryside would soon come to an end.

Norlund got the truck going again, proceeding with what seemed to him more or less normal care. Here was another gas station. But he had almost a full tank.

He had been warned that one of the first things he must do upon arrival was to check the date, make sure that he'd reached the target day or was at least within

the window extending a few days on either side. A
newspaper was the recommended way. He was coming in among the houses now. Here the streets were
decorated with someone's collection of old cars, many
of the specimens not very well kept up. The houses
were a little strange also—that one, good God, had an
outhouse behind it. There were no television antennas
to be seen. Paint tended to be peeling and fading. Still,
not counting the outhouse and the old cars, Norlund
might have accepted this scene as current if he had
run into it in nineteen eighty-four.

At the first stop sign he came to, he turned left onto
a larger street, not forgetting to hand-signal for the
turn. Now, a couple of blocks ahead, there appeared a
block of stores, a modest business district; Norlund
saw it first framed through a gothic cathedral arch of
elm trees, and somewhere in one of the trees a mourn-
ing dove was moaning a soft lament.

At the block of stores the street was wider, painted
into diagonal parking spaces along each curb. Norlund
pulled into an empty space—there were a lot to choose
from, and no parking meters. Slowly he disengaged
his fingers from the wheel—his hands were cramped
from the way he had been gripping it. He turned off
the ignition.

No one in nineteen thirty-three appeared to be taking any notice of his arrival.

On the side of the street that he was facing from his
driver's seat, two of the stores were empty, and their
FOR RENT signs appeared to have been up for a considerable time. The next thing that caught Norlund's eye
was the small movie theater halfway down the block
from where he'd parked. The theater was open this
summer afternoon, and there were black letters on the
white marquee:

SHE DONE HIM WRONG
MAE WEST

Turning to the other side of the street, Norlund spotted a small newspaper and magazine stand opposite the theater—and, sure enough, next to the newsstand was a barber's painted pole.

He got out of the truck, setting foot in territory that, he kept telling himself, ought to be basically familiar to him. He crossed the street and entered the barber shop, interrupting a conversation between two old cronies. One of them, in a white coat—Norlund kept trying to see the elderly man as Dr. Harbin—came to help Norlund off with his jacket.

"Yessir. What'll it be?"

"Trim it all the way around."

He heard talk about baseball. The Cubs were in second place. He saw brass spittoons, and lazy flies. The calendar on the wall, as it should, said July of nineteen thirty-three. He checked the time on the majestically ticking wall clock, and reminded himself to reset his wristwatch later.

He also looked over the list of prices posted on the wall. And presently, trimmed, brushed, and redolent of bay rum, he gave the barber a quarter and told him to keep the change.

From the barber shop Norlund stepped next door to the newsstand and picked up a paper off a pile, meanwhile handing another quarter to the old man tending the stand. The old fingers trembled back his change, two silver dimes, two pennies. Norlund, struck by a sudden thought, delayed, staring impolitely at those fingers and their owner. He couldn't help himself. The man he was looking at had perhaps been born in eighteen sixty. As a child he might well have seen

Lincoln, and his father had as likely as not fought in the Civil War. . . .

Norlund got hold of himself, and made himself walk away, giving his attention to the paper he had just purchased. Yes, right on the money, Saturday, July 22, nineteen thirty-three.

WORLD FLYER ON HOMEWARD LAP
Wiley Post Hops off for Edmonton
STAGE SET FOR ROOSEVELT SON
TO WED TODAY

He'd read more of it later. He returned to his truck and got into the rear seat, taking off his coat and loosening his tie. It was time to get some of the electronics up and running on battery power. With the equipment running, he calibrated it according to instructions, and took some preliminary readings. Curiosity about what he was really doing began to nag him. The readings he took were recorded somewhere, he was sure, perhaps also transmitted somewhere. They hadn't told him anything about that, or even explained to him exactly what it was that the machinery was supposed to be recording. Well, as long as he got paid . . .

The preliminary session completed, Norlund turned the electronics off and went back to the driver's seat. There he got out his map and spread it on his knees. The areas where he was to install recording units were not marked on this map, or anywhere but in his newly strengthened memory. But having the map in front of him helped Norlund to visualize the pattern that those areas made. They formed two lines, with ten units in each, each line several miles long and not quite straight. The lines converged upon a point of intersection on the Lake Michigan shoreline, right next to downtown Chicago. Ginny Butler in her teaching had never mentioned the existence of any such convergence point. Nor was it marked on the map. But it obviously had to be right on the peninsula called Northerly Island, that had been built out into the lake by landfill as a site for the Century of Progress—the site shown in the photographic blowup that Ginny had on the wall of her conference room fifty years in the future.

It was a job, and the thing to do was get on with it and finish it. Looking up and down the quiet elm-arched street, Norlund could see no roaring black sedans, no men staggering with the burden of wounded comrades. Well, most of war was always dull. If Ginny hadn't issued him a gun she must have figured that he wasn't likely to need one. He was an important man—at least until he finished his job for her.

His next step was to pick out someone suitable and hire him as temporary helper. The choice could not be very long delayed. Fanning himself with his hat, Norlund again looked up and down the street, but saw no one at the moment who looked like a likely prospect. But after all this was nineteen thirty-three. He didn't think for a moment that he'd have a hard time finding someone to take a job.

Jerry Rosen, trudging eastward through the weeds lining the highway slab, thought he could feel at least two blisters starting to develop, one on his right foot, one on his left. He was heading back for the big city, slowly making his way home. With every step, another drop of sweat trickled down from under his cap. What a day for hiking. Still, he kept trying not to think about the heat and the blisters. It was Jerry's firm conviction that if your willpower was great enough you could do anything. Well, almost anything. Maybe anything at all except find a job.

Each time he heard another eastbound car approaching, overtaking him from behind, Jerry paused, smiled and turned, sticking out his thumb. So far he was striking out every time. Each car's passage hit him with a blast of hot air, momentarily cooling, as he faced east again and prepared to trudge some more. If no one gave him a ride, eventually he would walk all the way to the western edge of Chicago, where the streetcar lines started, and there he would spend seven cents and be able to ride most of the rest of the way home. Maybe he'd spend a whole dime and get a transfer. Hell, he knew he would, if he had to walk that far.

What a goddamned waste of a day, not to mention the carfare coming and going. Not that Jerry really had anything better to do with his days than waste them, and it had got him out of the house, at least. Maybe Judy and her mother could sit there in the heat listening to the baby crying, and the radio, all the goddam day when they weren't doing housework, but he couldn't. And then in the evening when Judy's dad came home from the factory . . .

Jerry could and did feel guilty about wanting to get out and away from his own wife and kid, sometimes telling them he'd been looking for work when he'd just been going through the motions, or just sitting somewhere doing nothing. But what else could a guy do? And today he really had been looking. He'd packed a sandwich, and had eaten it for lunch in an opportunely discovered suburban park, washing it down with water from a drinking fountain there. He could tell old man Monahan that he'd really tried hard today, and look him right in the eye when he said it. And old Mike would believe him; he nearly always did. He pretty well had to. Everyone knew that there were no jobs.

If Jerry couldn't really believe in the possibility of finding work any more, after a year and a half of trying, well, he couldn't really stop believing in it either. Some guys, like Judy's dad, were working. If one out of four workers were unemployed, like they said, well, that meant that there were still jobs for three of four. And once in a while one of those jobs just had to open up.

Even this morning Jerry had felt real hope when a friend had suggested to him that chances in the suburbs might be a little better than in the city. His friend had been able to get a couple of days' work landscaping, that kind of thing, at a cemetery out in Westchester. It was certainly worth a try, Jerry had thought this morning, and even worth the investment of a couple of dimes in carfare. Even if things in the suburbs really weren't any better they sure as hell couldn't be any worse, and at least they ought to be somehow different.

Another car was approaching him from behind, this one not coming very fast. No, judging from the sound of it, a small truck. Jerry turned, with automatically extended thumb and created smile. Clipping along toward him was a black panel truck, what looked to Jerry like about a '27 Dodge. The truck started to slow down. The sign painted on the side was poorly contrasting and hard to read, but Jerry made out RADIO SURVEY CORPORATION.

Gratefully he grabbed at the sun-hot doorhandle as soon as the truck stopped. He yanked the door open and climbed aboard. The truck pulled back onto the narrow highway, a cooling breeze generated through its open windows as soon as it got moving.

"Thanks," said Jerry.

The gray-haired driver nodded. He was compactly built and sort of intense-looking, one of those lively little old geezer types. The coat of his gray suit was draped over the back of his seat, and his tie was loosened as you'd expect on a day like this. Obviously a businessman of some kind; he was too well dressed to be simply making deliveries.

"Welcome," the driver replied, not wasting words. And that was all the old guy had to say for a little while, though he kept shooting glances over at Jerry every few seconds as he drove. Jerry soon got the feeling that he was being sized up with a more than casual interest, for what purpose he couldn't tell.

"How far you going?" the driver asked him at last.

"All the way into the city. If you're going that far." And meanwhile Jerry's attention had been captured by all the equipment that was racked in the body of the truck. "Radio survey, huh? I bet your tubes jar loose a lot."

"Not so often as you might think. We use special locking sockets in a rig like this. Know anything about radio?"

"Not much. Hell, really nothing, I guess. My wife's folks have one. I'd like to have one myself."

"What d'you do for a living? My name's Alan Norlund, by the way."

"Jerry Rosen." They shook hands, Norlund sparing one hand from the wheel for a quick grip. Jerry went on. "What do I do—I look for work. Today I been out around here, looking at golf courses, cemeteries, any place I could think of that might have work. Until my feet started giving out. A guy told me there might be jobs out this way, but . . . it's the same as in the city. Not even any cooler. Farther from the lake, I guess."

Jerry leaned back in the high truck seat and closed his eyes.

"You live with your wife's folks, do you? I guess it saves a little bit financially if you can do that."

Jerry opened his eyes. He watched the alien suburban treetops pass between him and the sky, making the sun blink. "It don't help. There's just nothing else we can do. And now we got a kid. And . . . I dunno. My wife's family's Irish." He glanced toward Norlund. "Not that I got anything against the Irish. Or anyone else. It's just . . . "

"And you're Jewish? Rosen, you said?"

"My family is." Jerry's tone added: If it's any of your business. "I don't work at being anything."

The old man drove on for a little while in silence. He appeared to be thinking. Then he asked: "Got a driver's license?"

Jerry looked over at him, blinking. "Yeah. I used to drive a delivery truck sometimes. Why?"

"Want a job?"

Jerry's eyes popped wide open, even before, it seemed to him, his brain had had time to fully understand the words. In a moment he had completely forgotten his sweaty hike, his blistered feet. During the couple of seconds before he could answer, the old man glanced his way again, continuing the process of sizing him up.

"You're not kiddin', are you mister?"

"Hell no, I wouldn't kid about a thing like a job. It starts right now. Thing is, my regular partner's not available. I got to tell you it would be just temporary, for no more than a day or two."

"Hell yes, I'll take a job. What do I have to do?" Even as Jerry spoke an idea struck him, and he glanced back at the racks of radio equipment. Something about the way the setup looked suggested fake to him. Maybe just because there was so damn much of the radio stuff. He lowered his voice slightly. "I already done a little bootlegging in my time. It wouldn't bother me at all."

"No." The old man calmly shook his head. "Nothing like that. This is completely legit, just like it says on the side of the truck. We're taking a survey. Measuring how strong the broadcast signal is from certain radio stations, at different points on the map. That helps the companies judge how many people are listening to 'em, that kind of thing. I'll pay you a dollar an hour."

For a few seconds Jerry's breathing was reverently suspended. Then: "What do I have to do?" he repeated.

"I'll show you. It's not that hard. We're mounting little gadgets, call 'em radio markers, in certain places. Little units I got in a bin back there. You'll climb up a wall or tree or something and attach 'em, while I take readings on this equipment in the back of the truck, and tell you exactly where they have to go. I suppose you can use a hammer and a screwdriver?"

"Yeah. Sure."

"That's about all it takes. I got all the tools and fasteners we'll need. Our first installation ought to be about a mile up this road." The old man briefly concentrated on his driving, meanwhile humming under his breath some tune that Jerry didn't recognize.

Then he looked across at Jerry again, more sharply this time. "Oh, and one more thing. I expect you to keep quiet about what we're doing. I mean, you can tell your family you got a job. But don't tell anyone any details, not even your wife. There's a lot of competition, you know. Other companies would give a lot to know about signal strength and so on. I mean the methods of how we measure it."

"Jeez, yeah, I will. I can keep quiet about anything."

"Good. Why don't you just reach back there and we'll see what we can get on the radio now? See that first brown knob? Then the second one over is the tuner."

Jerry twiddled knobs. A speaker right over his head came to life. First he got some dame singing, with piano music in the background. It was right at the end of the song, and now some man's voice came on telling everyone how healthy their skins would be if they used this soap. Jerry estimated Norlund's expression, and turned the dial for another station. This one had two women's voices, engaged in a fake-sounding argument with stagy pauses, over whether someone's long-lost daughter was ever going to come home.

"My wife likes this one," said Jerry. "She's probably listening to it now. . . . Jeez, I'm on the payroll now?"

Norlund consulted his wristwatch. "It's just about two o'clock. Starting at two, okay?"

"Jeez, yes," said Jerry. And he made a mental note to himself to make sure that this nice-sounding old guy actually paid him for this first half-day's work when quitting time came around.

Presently Norlund pulled over to the curb. Now he let Jerry take over the driving. Jerry eased the truck ahead, block by block, going slowly at Norlund's direction, while Norlund sat in the chair in the rear of the truck and twiddled dials and read things off and called out orders. Jerry couldn't really see what Norlund was doing back there, but then he wouldn't have been able to understand it anyway. He wished for the millionth time that he had a real education of some kind. But he didn't have one, and that fact wasn't about to change. Not having much school just meant that you had to be that much smarter than you'd have to be

otherwise, use willpower and determination, and look
out for yourself every minute.

"Now take it across the street, Jerry. Stop by that
vacant lot on the corner. That should be about it."

"Okay, Boss."

They were still well out in the suburbs, but the
houses were gradually getting closer together and the
streets busier. The empty lot beside which Jerry stopped
the truck was crisscrossed by paths worn in the grass
and weeds, and littered with a moderate amount of
junk. In the middle a few trees were growing, and in
the largest tree some kids had once put up a treehouse.
It was now collapsed—like a lot of other housing
plans, thought Jerry.

The old man was sweating when he emerged from
the hot back of the truck to squint in the sunlight
toward the lot. "Tell you what, Jerry, put it right up in
one of those trees. Here, I'll help you get the ladder
out."

The ladder slid out from a long storage compartment in the back of the truck under the electrical
stuff, and then unfolded. Like the other tools Norlund
now brought out, it appeared almost new. Norlund
brought out some dull gray coveralls, too, with the
company name on them as it was on the truck, in
letters that didn't stand out very well.

Jerry found a pair of coveralls of the right size and
pulled them on, meanwhile pondering to himself: Why
have a name showing at all, and then tell me to keep it
a secret? Something was not quite kosher here. Maybe
his first suspicion about bootlegging was right. Maybe
the racketeers now needed fancy radio communica-
tions systems to keep ahead of highjackers and the
Feds. Well, that was all right with Jerry; everybody, or
almost everybody, had something to do with boot-

legging, and right now a job was a job. Just make sure, Rosen, he cautioned himself sternly, that you get out of sight before the highjackers show up and the shooting starts. Not that he thought that was really likely.

Presently Jerry was standing atop the ladder, his head among tree branches, a modest assortment of tools and fasteners stuffed into his coverall pockets. Norlund had gotten back into the truck. He stuck his head out every few seconds to call directions to Jerry, saying move it right or left a little, or up or down. If any of the neighbors were at all curious about what was going on, none of them bothered to come out and ask—anyway, Jerry thought, the whole thing looked pretty official.

"That's it right there! Take some screws and put it in tight now. Do a solid job of it." Norlund got out of the truck again and came to stand right beside the ladder, supervising this first effort closely. Jerry, as soon as he had the little banana-shaped thing fastened to the treetrunk, took a grip on the device and wobbled his whole weight back and forth on it, demonstrating solidity.

Even so, Norlund had to climb the ladder and take a close-up look himself before he was completely satisfied. That was all right with Jerry, who had done a good job; he always liked to do a job well, if he was going to do it at all.

Norlund had to stand on tiptoe atop the ladder, to get a good look at what the taller Jerry had been doing. "Good," the old guy said at last, and came down briskly. "Well, on we go. Only nineteen more to put in." And he looked at his watch.

Jerry was pleased, too. Nineteen more would mean that the job was certainly good for one more day at least; obviously Norlund was concerned that it be done right, and there'd evidently be a lot of driving in between.

They loaded their tools back into the truck, and Jerry drove on, at Norlund's direction. They were entering a different suburb now.

"We're probably not gonna get lucky with too many more empty lots," Norlund mused aloud, studying his map as Jerry drove. "Well, we'll figure out something." He looked up. "Seen the Fair yet?"

"Hah, you kiddin'? Who can spare half a buck for a ticket, just to get on the grounds? I wouldn't mind gettin' a look at Sally Rand. But I hear they charge extra for that."

"Well, I can't promise you Sally Rand. But it looks like we'll be going on the fairgrounds at least, toward the end of this job."

"Great. Hey, Mr. Norlund? Would you mind if I stopped someplace and phoned home? Just to tell 'em I'm working. I'll keep all the details quiet like you told me. But otherwise they're gonna start to wonder what's happened to me."

"Sure. Stop somewhere when you see a phone." And Norlund, staring at his map again, was wondering privately if getting onto the fairgrounds, where the last units had to go, and working there, was going to pose a problem. He'd have to bring the truck with its equipment on too, to determine the exact placing of those last units. There'd have to be a service gate of some kind, and he could probably bluff his way through that. He'd hand out a few bucks if necessary to smooth the way.

"There's a phone booth right over there, Mr. Norlund."

"Okay, stop. Make your call. Just don't take all day." The youngster pulled the truck over. He hesitated, then fished in his shirt pocket and pulled out a metal matchbox that proved to hold not only matches but a couple of cigarettes. He made a gesture of offering one to Norlund, and when that was refused quickly lit up himself.

Looking after Jerry as the wiry kid went trotting off to the phone booth, Norlund found himself reflecting on youth and its eternal difficulties. Jerry was a strong kid, with a head of wiry, almost-blond hair. After people had learned his name, he probably often heard from them that he didn't look Jewish. A tough young guy, thought Norlund; well, Jerry was headed into years when toughness was certainly going to be an asset. Of course, if you thought about it, that was the predominant kind of year in human history.

This kid Jerry must have been born in nineteen ten or thereabouts, and was therefore chronologically—if that was the right word—somewhat older than Norlund himself. And on the tail of that thought came another one, that brought with it a fresh sense of logical vertigo: There might be, in fact there probably was, a septuagenarian Jerry Rosen alive somewhere in that distant land of nineteen eighty-four—an aged Jerry Rosen who probably reminisced from time to time about his weird experiences during the Great Depression.

Just as there was now a ten-year-old Alan Norlund only a few miles away. . . .

Norlund didn't even want to think about seeing that kid or his young parents. There was only so much that the psyche could take at one time.

The Time Machine, thought Norlund wryly. H. G. Wells. When Norlund was younger he had read a fair amount of science fiction.

Here was Jerry, still moving at a trot in the baggy

coveralls, coming back from the phone booth before
Norlund had really expected him.

"Hey, Mr. Norlund? I'm supposed t' bring you home
for dinner. If you can come, that is. They said if it was
at all possible."

Norlund was on the verge of making some easy
excuse. But then he thought, why not? He'd have to
eat dinner somewhere, and there was nothing in his
orders against fraternizing with the natives. And
anyway, he felt a need for human society, to fix him in
this version of reality.

"Okay," he said. "Sure. If it's no trouble with the
women folks."

"No trouble. They're the ones who told me. Whenever we get there is fine."

Jerry got behind the wheel again. They drove on,
soon nearing the place where the second unit would
have to be installed. The instrumentation in the back
of the truck indicated to Norlund that the ideal place
for this device was right in the middle of a large
suburban house. Well, forget that ideal place. One
part of Norlund's job was to overrule the machinery in
a case like this, and force it to come up with a suitable
compromise.

Coaxing the instruments as he'd been taught to do,
Norlund got them to admit as an acceptable alterna-
tive the mounting of this unit in a large tree overhang-
ing the sidewalk directly in front of the house. Once
again Jerry climbed the ladder and went to work. If
people saw him, maybe they thought that he was
trimming trees.

On to the third site. Here the perfect location would
have been in someone's back yard, and here Norlund
directed Jerry to mount a telephone pole in the adjoining alley.

Norlund was working back and forth between the converging lines in the planned pattern, filling in both of them from west to east. The truck, with Jerry driving most of the time, zigzagged north and south, gradually working its way east.

By the time they had the first eight units planted, darkness was threatening. They had worked right through what must have been Jerry's regular dinnertime, and through lunchtime by Norlund's biological clock. At last he noticed that he was hungry.

"Jerry, I think we got to knock off for the day. No way we can go on doing this after dark. Tell you what, I'll drive you home and pick you up again in the morning."

"Great. Sure." And Jerry watched avidly as Norlund counted out dollar bills into his hand, one for every hour that they'd worked together. "Hey, don't forget, you're having dinner with us. Judy and her old lady are really expecting you."

"I'm looking forward to it." And strangely enough he really was. Usually Norlund didn't particularly enjoy meeting strangers. But right now he had the sensation that if he closed his eyes and relaxed for more than a second, the world of the Thirties might evaporate away from around him, leaving him God knew where. Contact with other people might make a web to hold him in.

They had already reached the western boundary of Chicago, and now they drove on into the city. The only immediately apparent indication was in the design of the street signs. Norlund continued to let Jerry do the driving, while he himself sat in the right seat, observing and contemplating.

"Where you from, Mr. Norlund?"

"New York. The company's based there." If he'd

told the truth, that he was a native Chicagoan, efforts to pin him down further would have followed.

"Yeah? My Mom lives in New York now. My Dad's still over in the old country. He went back a few years ago."

Norlund did not respond, and conversation died for a time. He found it easy to fall into his own thoughts. Watching the twilight streets go past, the old-fashioned streetlights coming on, mile after mile of houses and stores and shops and small factories, lights everywhere coming on against the night, he beheld a half-remembered city. The buildings were mostly smaller and dingier than those of the Chicago he thought he could remember from his childhood. There were the street names, time-proof incantations he had used and lived with for most of his life.

With each block he traveled, the sensation was stronger of imminent return to a childhood home, though his own neighborhood had been some distance from this one. This world was saying to him that yes, he could go home again. . . .

So familiar were the endless blocks of working-class houses, mile upon mile of them. And yet, so different was this from the childhood world that he had thought he remembered. Even now, with darkness fully fallen, he could see how many FOR RENT signs were on houses, apartments, stores. There was furniture, piled on a sidewalk, a human figure in a rocking chair beside it with blanket over knees. Eviction, nowhere to go; it happened. This year the hard times of the Depression were at their hardest. The people Norlund saw were generally shabbier than he remembered people being, the children more ragged . . . and it struck him now, as it had never struck him in his childhood, that he had yet to discern a black or an oriental face among the thousands to be seen along these streets. Chicago's black ghettos in nineteen thirty-three, he seemed to recall, would be limited to the south side, and form only a comparatively small part of that vast region. And nobody in America would call a black slum a 'ghetto' yet — a ghetto was still a European Jewish quarter.

"What's your wife's name, Jerry?"

"Judy. Her family name is Monahan. Her folks are Irish, I told you that. Norlund's Scandinavian, ain't it?"

"Yep."

A streetcar, a lumbering rectangular dinosaur of wood and metal, groaned around a corner nearby, steel wheels fighting with screams of rage against unyielding steel tracks. The single eye of the dinosaur glared at them, the overhead trolley threatened them with blue-white lightning as it stuttered along its wire.

Now Jerry was driving past a huge brick Catholic church, St. Something-or-other, Chicago pesudo-Gothic. Norlund had gone to a Lutheran church early in life, when he'd been made to go to church. He had alternated between feeling rather superior to those who were led from Rome, and vaguely envious of them for some reason he couldn't quite pin down.

On the next intersection, each corner building held a storefront. One small bakery, one barbershop with painted pole, a placard in the window advertising LEECHES. Two other stores with whitewashed windows, closed and FOR RENT.

Now down a side street Norlund glimpsed an enormous factory building, fairly new, eight or ten stories high and a block square, almost completely dark now and grim as a prison. There were probably ten thousand potential workers within walking distance, among these blocks of houses, two-flats, and small apartments. The factory reared up among them as Norlund imagined that a medieval cathedral might have risen from its town or village. And suddenly another eerie twinge went through his spirit—the realization that as far as he knew, travel into the past was not limited to only fifty years. . . .

Jerry turned a corner, and Norlund saw the factory again. One entrance of the huge building was a cavelike door big enough for trucks, and from this mouth a small body of workers was now issuing. Norlund could see them plainly under the garish streetlight that guarded the factory entrance. They had, almost to a man, lunch pails under their arms, cloth caps or battered hats on their heads. Their feet were dragging now, their movements slowed by what must have been a long punishing shift at whatever machines they served inside. These men were the lucky ones, the employed. Norlund wondered if Jerry's father-in-law might be among them.

Jerry swerved the truck suddenly. He swore at a passing horse-drawn wagon, illegally lightless and hard to see in the dark street. Some junkman or peddlar, crying his daily chant no more, quietly heading home.

And then Jerry was pulling the truck over to the dark curb, parking in front of a close-packed row of small houses. There was no problem in finding a parking space.

On the front steps of the nearest house sat a figure mottled by leaf-shadows from the nearest streetlamp. A stocky, graying man rose to greet them as they alighted from the truck. He had a quart beer bottle on the step beside him, and a glass in hand.

"Mr. Norlund, this's Mike. Judy's dad."

Mike Monahan was muscular, going to fat. As his evening leisure suit he wore a white cotton undershirt with narrow shoulder straps, over his work pants. His handshake was firm, and his greeting hearty, though most of it was drowned out by the shrieking of children going up and down the sidewalk on roller skates. Their noise was very little different from that of their grandchildren half a century away.

Monahan still shook Norlund's hand. "Sit down, have a beer."

"Be glad to."

But it was not to be, not yet. The two women of the house had been watching for the arrival and had come out, and now Norlund was going to have to go into the house and be welcomed properly. Mrs. Monahan was small, mousy, and apologetic as she insisted on having her own way. Judy looked worn and brave. Her prettiness was of a type that Norlund thought might fade quickly. Several half-grown children that Norlund took for Judy's younger siblings also milled about, indoors and out, taking off roller skates and wanting to know if this was the weekend they would at last get to go to the Fair, and when the ice cream was going to be opened. The two girls were in dresses, the two boys in knickerbockers with largely destroyed knees—school's out for the summer, save your good clothes was evidently the plan. Norlund had completely forgotten knickers, though he'd worn them often enough himself, God knew. How things were starting to come back now. . . .

At last he was able to get back out of the house, full glass of beer in hand, to rejoin Monahan on the cooler front porch . . . but the women had faked them out; it was now time to go back inside and eat dinner. Since the arrival of the eminent visitor, Mrs. Monahan had been in open debate with herself as to whether the kitchen would do for him to eat in, or whether the cloth-covered table in the dining room would be required. Norlund now settled the matter by plunking himself down at the kitchen table, establishing his beer glass on the worn oilcloth there, and letting those who would come and join him.

Everyone besides he and Jerry had already eaten dinner, but there were two pork chops apiece being kept warm for them—Norlund suspected that Jerry would have gotten only one if he hadn't been bringing an employer home. There were mashed potatoes with butter—it was real butter, naturally—and fresh peas with the irregular look and fine taste of having just come from someone's garden.

Judy had damp brown curls, and a graceful way of leaning sideways as she moved about helping with kitchen tasks while balancing her baby on one hip. She paused, standing over Norlund, in the act of giving him his knife and fork. "Jerry didn't say much on the phone about what kind of work it is."

"I asked him not to." Norlund spoke loudly enough for the other people in the room to hear; he had no doubt that they were interested. "So you can understand if I still want to keep it confidential."

Mrs. Monahan went into another low dialogue with herself, the burden of this one being that no one was listening in on any business conversations, or had any intention of prying.

Jerry looked up, chewing on a pork chop. "I did tell 'em it was Radio Survey Corporation."

"That's okay," said Norlund. He'd gotten rid of his coat and tie and hat, and sat with his sleeves rolled up, eating hungrily.

"Them big corporations," began Mike, evidently triggered by a key word; and then let the rest of his sentence drown in a gulp of beer, as if at the last moment he'd had second thoughts about speaking his feelings on corporations to this particular guest, who after all had to be some part of management.

"They do a lot of things they hadn't ought to do," Norlund supplied. Then it occurred to him to wonder if Mike might be confusing his fictitious firm with RCA, which was certainly big. Well, Norlund wasn't going to try to straighten him out.

The subject of baseball came up, as if from nowhere, safe and comfortable for the men to talk about. It was Jerry's contention that in a few years night baseball was going to become a reality; there was a lot of talk about it already. Monahan couldn't see it happening— star players would be beaned, hit on the head with fly balls coming down out of the night, and the owners would see that their investment was being damaged. Norlund managed not to take sides—actually he couldn't remember when night games had really started.

Now the kids were leaving the kitchen, taking dishes of ice cream with them, heading for the living room where Norlund could hear someone turning on the radio.

"The world's gonna change in a few years," Jerry was asserting. He spoke with assurance, like a man who had a job, even if temporary. "There'll be more than night baseball happening. You'll see. This Depression'll come to an end like nothing you've seen before."

"You been reading too many of them damn magazines," Mike grumbled. But he was smiling lightly and there was no force in his crabbing. Having another job in the house probably took some strain off everybody's nerves.

A steam or hot-water radiator at one side of the kitchen was serving as a summer catch-all table. Among the old magazines that were lying on the radiator, Norlund discerned some science fiction pulps. On a cover he picked out the names of H. P. Lovecraft, and Clark Ashton Smith. *Astounding Stories* with SALVAGE IN SPACE, by Jack Williamson.

"God damn," said Monahan, unable to keep entirely away from disputatious subjects. "Roosevelt is doing something, at least."

His wife murmured expostulations at his language, but they were automatic and went unheeded. Her small form was bent in front of the wooden icebox, trying to do something difficult at floor level. The two men native to the house were just vanishing toward the living room, glasses in hand, to listen to the radio. Norlund realized suddenly what Mrs. Monahan was about.

"Here, let me help you with that." And he bent beside her to lift out the heavy pan of melt water from under the appliance. He manhandled the pan over to the white enameled sink, and poured it out. The lady's nervous chatter thanked him, and informed him that some day she wanted an electric refrigerator, or maybe a gas model like one of those new Electroluxes.

Norlund put the drain pan back under the icebox. Then from the cold radiator he picked up a piece of cardboard about a foot square. An advertisement was printed in the middle of it, and at each edge was a two-digit number in large bold numerals. Each number appeared upright when its edge was up. If they had sent someone younger, Norlund thought to himself with satisfaction, how would that person have managed this? Would they have been able to deduce what this card is?

"How many pounds, Mrs. Monahan?" he asked.

"Seventy-five, if you don't mind." Apologetic, as if she were asking Norlund to carry it in himself. "In this heat it goes so quickly. Put the card right here in the kitchen window, if you please; the ice wagon comes down the alley."

Norlund propped the card up in the window, so the large 75 was right side up and visible from outside.

Now the kids were calling to them from the front room that Amos n' Andy was coming on. The two women in the kitchen responded as if to an offer of paid work.

Awarded a place of honor as guest, Norlund in the living room sat back in one of the better chairs, while the other adults took chairs and sofa and the kids sprawled on the floor. Presently Judy had to take the squalling baby away and change it. Norlund sat back, listening comfortably, closing his eyes. The taxicab company and its problems came back as if he had last heard about them only yesterday.

He could feel himself putting out mental and spiritual feelers, tentacles, reconnecting himself to his earliest memories. Here. He lived here. Not really in this particular house, no, but if he were to leave this house and walk down the street, his own house would be there somewhere. Or it could be. It really could. . . .

Amos n' Andy concluded in organ music. The adults adjourned back to the kitchen to consume coffee, beer, or just plain water, according to taste. Norlund chose water for this round. Judy was getting milk out of the icebox, to mix up a bottle for the baby. She had to shake the quart milk bottle first, to blend the cream back into it. Of course she wouldn't be breast-feeding. These people would consider themselves too modern and well-educated for that.

"Whaddya think about Repeal?" Monahan suddenly demanded of Norlund.

Norlund considered. The beer they had been drinking this evening had been legal now for several months. He knew that the rest of Prohibition couldn't have long to go, though he couldn't remember the exact date of its demise.

"Oh, I think it's coming," he answered cautiously. They hadn't told him, back in Eighty-four, that he had to be wrong every time someone in the past asked his opinion of the future.

They had cautioned him against setting up as any kind of seer or fortune teller. And had added something like: "Don't rely, even for your own purposes, on your knowledge of history being correct in every detail. You may remember perfectly who wins the big game, or on what day a war began, and you may be quite wrong. The past is no more immutable than the present; of course not, it *is* the present while you're living in it. What we're doing now is history to other people. Life in any year is reality, and people can act on reality and change it."

The more Norlund had thought about it, the more his mind had seemed to knot in paradox. "Look here," he'd said. "Suppose I'd gone back and—and—"

"The usual form of the argument you are trying to formulate" (this was Dr. Harbin speaking) "concerns one who goes back in time and shoots his or her own grandparent, before his own parent is conceived. This supposedly precludes the time-traveler's own existence, creating a paradox. There are different answers, on different levels of profundity. The answer on the practical level, the one you need, is that shooting the grandparent in early youth has no more or less effect on reality than shooting the same person in modern times—what you consider modern times. If you're there to pull the trigger, you'll still be there afterwards, unless the shot goes through your own body. After the shot there may be another world in which you don't exist, but that's hardly startling; there may be an infinity of such worlds anyway. You didn't exist in this one, either, for most of its history."

Now, seated at the Monahan kitchen table with his glass of water, half-listening as Monahan argued with the big corporations, Norlund was enjoying himself. No, he wouldn't want to live in this household, but right now as a place to visit it was fine. He could hear the radio in the front room being retuned to a different station. A half-familiar voice came at him out of memory, that of some old news commentator. Walter Winchell? Boake Carter? Gabriel Heatter? He'd forgotten their exact respective time-frames. He heard the voice mention the word Repeal.

Mrs. Monahan, not one to let a guest remain for long content with water, came fussing toward him, coffee cups in hand. Norlund nodded wisely, and agreed with her opinion that sometimes when it was hot drinking hot coffee could actually make you feel a little cooler.

This idea was soberly debated by the other people sitting round the table. In the background Norlund heard the sound of the radio changing again. Not simple music or talk now. Sound effects? he wondered vaguely. Maybe one of those early mystery programs.

There were two sounds in alternation. First a short one something like *eeeh*, and then a long, polyphonic *ahhhh*, deepening toward the end and seeming to break down into its myriad voices.

The big corporations, said Monahan, were going to own everything when the Depression was over. Jerry disagreed. Mrs. Monahan fussed. Meanwhile that radio sound kept nagging at Norlund's attention. It went on and on, and he found himself listening to it as if it were something he ought to recognize. He even thought of making some excuse and going into the living room.

But he was still listening from the kitchen when the voice on the radio began to speak. It began almost too quietly for Norlund to hear it from two rooms away, but it soon grew louder. It rose and fell, contorting itself as if there were obstacles that it must squeeze past or overcome.

Norlund soon recognized that the voice was speaking German. Norlund did not understand German, but when he recognized the language, a light dawned.

He felt a chill that had nothing to do with the possible effects of hot coffee.

He sat there, staring unseeingly at the coffee cup in front of him, losing track of what was being said around him. The voice paused, and someone else, probably a translator, came on speaking English, though Norlund could not make out many of the words. And then the cheers again. It wasn't really *eeeh* and *ahhhh*, though. It was *Sieg . . . heil. Sieg . . . heil. Sieg . . . heil. . . .*

And soon Norlund, more or less abstractedly, was saying goodnight to his hosts. Yes, he was going to have to be on his way. He'd come round in the morning, Sunday morning, and pick Jerry up on the corner, and he'd be sure to phone ahead so Jerry would know what time to be out there waiting for him.

Three-fourths of the family came outside with Norlund to see him off, waving goodbye from the sidewalk as he got into the truck alone and drove away. At the first cross street he turned east, just exactly as if he knew where he was going. All he really felt certain about was that he was going to be sleeping in the truck tonight. It had been suggested that that would probably be the wisest thing to do, barring unforeseen complications. And the truck had been designed with this in mind; the operator's seat in the rear folded down into a narrow cot that Norlund thought would probably be fairly comfortable if you weren't too big. So all he had to worry about now was where to park.

When he came to a large diagonal street he read its name as Lincoln Avenue, and turned southeast onto it, heading in the general direction of the center of the city. Within a block he had passed another big church, this one of stone and true cathedral size, though it served only a neighborhood. In front of the church an illuminated signboard gave the schedule of services in both English and German.

In the four or five blocks after that were three or four movie theaters. Lincoln was mostly a business street. Some of the stores were open on Saturday night, and one or two of them even looked busy. This was a working city, and a majority of its people were still employed. Except for teachers and a few others, those employed would have been paid.

Lincoln Avenue went on for miles, cutting diagonally across everything else. The continuous flow of it brought Norlund into a state of mild exhilaration. He felt half hypnotized by the endless array of neon lights, antique cars, groaning streetcars, costumed people. The women's summer dresses hung to within a few inches of the ground; their short hair was often so tightly curled that it fit their heads like caps. There was another pile of furniture on the sidewalk, with hopeless-looking people standing guard.

There were hot-dog carts and ice cream carts on the street, all powered by bicycle mechanisms or by the even more direct push of the owner's muscles. There was a blind man selling pencils, and there a legless man doing the same. On one corner a man sold apples, or tried to, from his outthrust hat. The legs of a derelict protruded from under a pile of newspapers. There were shoeshine boys and paper boys too numerous to try to count, and there a young woman who looked as if she were peddling something else—the areas of family trade were falling behind Norlund now. He now drove among places where harder business was transacted. Not an openly labeled tavern, of course, to be seen anywhere, but he guessed there'd be a speakeasy at least every couple of blocks.

Abruptly Lincoln Park was just ahead of him. Had he subconsciously selected it as destination? Already, with the proximity of the lake, he could feel a touch of coolness in the air. Other people, a slow, trickling throng moving mostly on foot, were entering the park ahead of him. The Fair was miles to the south of here, and probably about to close for the night; they must have some other goal. Looking at the pillows, blankets, and baby equipment that many of them were carrying, it didn't take much thought to figure out that they were planning to escape the heat by sleeping in the park. A single strolling policeman looked on benevolently. No one appeared to be worried by the thought of camping out all night amid big-city shrubbery.

Norlund drove on slowly into the park, following a curving drive under streetlamps shaded by tall trees. Vehicular traffic was light. He was almost at the lake before he parked, in a small open lot that was evidently intended primarily for daytime beachgoers. There were only a couple of other cars parked in it now.

When he shut off the truck's motor, he could hear the lake's recurrent waves working, irregularly and methodically, on sand and stone. The lake itself was invisible, a huge gulf of utter blackness just beyond the shoreline's concrete wall and the tumbled boulders that had been put there to break the surf on rougher days. Norlund left the truck and walked over to the top of the wall, trying to see out into the night. A couple of small and lonely lights were visible out there—some kind of boats.

Every minute, with regular timing, the whole sky was swept by the Lindbergh Light, from its place atop the tall Palmolive Building to the south. Norlund remembered watching that same beacon when he had been small, lying in his bed. . . .

Other powerful beacons shone in the clear night sky from farther south. Those of course would be from the Fair itself. Norlund realized that he was looking forward to going there tomorrow, like a kid. He wondered what it meant that the lines of recording devices—or whatever—that he was constructing converged on the Fair. He would be wondering about it more, he supposed, if he didn't have so much else to wonder about.

How was Sandy doing tonight? Why, tonight Sandy wasn't doing at all. Sandy wouldn't be born for a long, long time yet.

Were they recording devices? If so, what did they record? Well, he'd go on thinking of them that way. That made as much sense as any other explanation that had yet occurred to him.

Not many yards away along the seawall, someone laughed in the darkness. Lovers, maybe. Or just friends. There were a few dots of lanterns in the distance, illuminating small groups of people out to fish or just to relax in coolness amid the sound of waves. Along the miles of lakefront, Norlund realized, there was not a portable radio to be heard—oh, that people might realize their blessed state while they had it. There was a trustfulness in the night, thought Norlund, and in the occasional human voice that could be heard in speech or laughter.

With the sound of waves as background, Norlund did what he had to do to get ready to sleep, opening his folding bed inside the truck. The strain of the day was overtaking him and he was tired.

The waves were in his ears as he drifted off to sleep. They might have been of any year, a thousand in the past or two thousand in the future. . . .

Churchbells woke him from some deep dream of youth, and he found himself in the gray coolness of early morning. He lay there, listening to the bells and the patience of the waves. Last night, he thought, I heard the voice of Hitler on the radio. And not on some old recording, either. Not until now had Norlund been able to try to think about that fact.

Norlund moved the truck to a space just outside the nearest park toilet. Inside the building were cold-water sinks and metal mirrors, and with these aids he washed and shaved as well as possible. He had never been a fussy shaver, and the process went reasonably well. Once Norlund was up and moving he felt hungry, and surprisingly energetic. More benefits from the yellow pills? Even his bowels had moved on schedule. While perusing the graffiti in the stall he reflected that some things seemed to change very slowly or not at all.

Dressed with fresh underwear and a clean shirt, Norlund drove out of the park to breakfast at one of the middle-sized hotels nearby. He splurged, and for thirty-five cents enjoyed pancakes as well as eggs and bacon. Putting down a nickel tip, he stood up feeling like a plutocrat. Before he left the hotel he found a public phone and dialed the Monahan's number. As he had expected, his helper sounded wide awake and eager to go to work.

Jerry was waiting on the corner near his house when Norlund drove up. The young man's face lighted up as soon as the truck hove into sight.

Norlund continued to fill in both legs of his pattern at the same time, zigzagging the truck from north to south and back again, slowly working his way east. This morning he found himself actually whistling, sitting in the sweaty rear compartment, taking readings that he only half understood. Whatever the work ultimately meant, it was something to do, and important because it helped Sandy if for no other reason. From time to time Jerry in the driver's seat turned his head, glancing back at his whistling boss with discreet curiosity.

Putting in place one unit after another, they worked their way steadily into and across the city. Jerry in his company coveralls climbed utility poles and scaled, to modest heights, the sides of buildings. So far none of the units had actually required placement indoors, for which Norlund was grateful. Jerry fastened one, with considerable difficulty, to a girder of a railroad bridge spanning the Chicago River. Another went under a bridge abutment, right above a miniature Hooverville.

The huts of the unemployed here were fabricated of old auto carcasses, scrap lumber, tar paper and sheet metal. Stovepipes stuck out of packing boxes. A pole was flying, for some reason, a torn black flag.

Nobody in the city objected to any of the activities of the Radio Survey team, though some of the Hooverville inhabitants fled. The more people there were around, thought Norlund, the less conspicuous workmen became. So far, he thought, all was going very well.

He bought lunch for himself and his work force at a Greek place on Halsted Street, the sandwiches Judy had packed in a brown bag being reserved for afternoon snacking. Not far to the east of this restaurant rose the Loop's tall buildings, and not far beyond them the lake terminated the city, and right there on the lake shore the job would presently end. Norlund, in an almost-euphoric state, was toying with the idea of buying some souvenir for Sandy at the Fair, or maybe in one of the downtown stores, Marshall Field perhaps. No one up in Eighty-four had said he couldn't bring back something.

Jerry, seated across the table, had plainly enjoyed his lunch. But now he was fidgeting. "Mr. Norlund? Think you'll have another job like this sometime? Or maybe some other kinda work?"

"It could be, Jerry." Norlund found himself wishing that it could. "You've been a good worker."

"You got a phone number where I could get ahold of you? Here in Chicago?"

Norlund felt torn between the urge to hold out hope and the thought that in the long run it would be kindest not to do so. He let himself be swayed toward the former, and reached into his pocket for a card. He got out one of the business cards he'd put into his billfold, giving the address of the old Wheaton farmhouse, and a phone number. He had been assured that anyone dialing that number in the Thirties would get only a busy signal or a sound of endless ringing. He had also been urged to use discretion in handing out the cards, but now seemed like the perfect time if he was going to use them at all. A card once separated from its fellows, he had been told, would wear rapidly. A couple of months in pocket or purse and it would be illegible. In less than a year it would be little more than dust.

Norlund handed one of the cards across the table. Jerry looked at it, brightened a bit, and put it in his pocket.

They left the restaurant and got into the truck, and began the job of putting the final units into place. By midafternoon there were only two more to go, and these were going to have to be placed right on the Fairgrounds. This near the convergence point, Norlund's equipment was becoming increasingly hard to satisfy as to the location of the devices. Now each unit was taking longer to position.

They drove east on the long bridge that carried Twenty-third Street over the Illinois Central railroad tracks, approaching one of the main entrances to the Fair. The tall multicolored buildings and the brave banners could be seen from some distance, against the lake. The Skyride towers, each the equivalent of sixty stories or so, by far overtopped any other building within the city. They were mostly openwork girders. At what Norlund estimated as about the two hundred foot level, cables bore cars filled with sightseers back and forth between the two towers, over the Fair's central lagoon.

The Fair entrance was crowded, with lines of people

waiting to buy tickets and more lines forming to get through the gates.

"Sally Rand draws 'em", Jerry commented knowledgeably. "Streets of Paris is almost right inside this entrance. That's where she does her hootchy-kootch. Hey, you really think she's not wearin' nothing behind those fans?"

"I'm getting old, kid, my eyes are not too good. I'll have to get a front-row seat to know for sure."

And Jerry laughed.

Sure enough, there was a service gate close to the one for paying customers. Norlund pulled in line behind a small telephone company truck, and when it was waved through he pulled up to the gate.

The uniformed guard who came to his window was a small, intense-looking man. Immediately he impressed Norlund as a frustrated dictator. He challenged in a raspy, almost quacky voice: "What's this? You can't come in this way."

Norlund looked back with what he hoped was a properly outraged stare. "They didn't tell you we were coming in today?"

"Nope. Nobody told me nothing like that." But the aggressive edge in the guard's squawky voice had now been dulled by caution.

Norlund had a five dollar bill ready in his hand. It was folded so that just a numbered corner would be visible to the intended recipient. In sixty years, Norlund thought, you learn to do some things pretty well. He said: "Oh hell, it's not worth it to me to have to wait around while you check." There was another uniform in the background. "Treat your partner to a little something, too."

Five dollars might well be more than either guard would earn today. Resistance vanished. As he drove the truck in, Norlund muttered thoughtlessly: "That guy sounded just like Donald Duck."

"Like who?" Jerry was honestly puzzled, though he'd been listening carefully.

"Someone I used to know." A slip there, thought Norlund, but no harm done. And he grinned faintly to himself, thinking of the hard times that guard was going to have in a few years, when Disney's creation began to walk the movie screens.

Jerry was quickly absorbed in the splendors of the Fair. There was a lot to see; that black-and-white photo blowup of Ginny Butler's didn't begin to do justice to the reality. The buildings had been deliberately constructed in a variety of colors; there were varied shades of green, blue, yellow, red, and orange, with black, white, and gray in a minority. Masses of flowers grew beside the broad walks. A sightseers' bus, passengers sitting facing open sides, drove slowly ahead of Norlund's creeping truck. There was a goodly crowd in attendance, mostly well dressed by the standards of the day. The weather was fine, and the lake, visible between buildings—there was the Chinese Lama Temple, there the Colonial Village—was sparked with white sails. Avenues of brave, multicolored banners snapped briskly in the breeze.

Stopping to change drivers, Norlund observed a plaque nearby: ONLY A HUNDRED YEARS AGO CHICAGO WAS A HUDDLE OF HUTS, CLINGING TO THE SHADOWS OF FORT DEARBORN FOR SAFETY FROM THE INDIANS. FOUR YEARS AFTER ITS INCORPORATION AS A VILLAGE IN 1833, ITS POPULATION, CONQUERING PATCHES OF DREARY SWAMP, HAD REACHED 4,000. TODAY IT IS NEARLY 4,000,000—3,376,438 FOR THE SAKE OF ACCURACY, BY THE CENSUS OF 1930, AND GROWING AT A RATE OF 70,000 A YEAR.

Glancing once more at Jerry from his own seat in the rear, Norlund thought that the young man's thoughts were not on the hundred years past. The future was a likelier bet. Or Sally Rand.

ON THE MIDWAY — — LIVING WONDERS
Largest collection of strange and
curious people ever assembled.
Human mistakes and mishaps.
Siamese Twins
GIANTS FROM
THE FOUR CORNERS OF THE EARTH
Adults, 25 cents   Children, 15 cents

* * *

OLD PLANTATION
SHOW
60 hand-picked
Colored Entertainers
Hottest colored band from Dixie
Singers, Comedians and Dancers
Fastest moving, fastest stepping
Show ever put together.
Adults, 25 cents   Children, 15 cents
Both shows operated by
THE DUKE MILLS CORP.

"You think people will ever get to the Moon, Mr. Norlund?" Obviously Jerry was not much interested in minstrel shows and freaks. In his mind science and industry were on the move, and great things were to be expected from them just over the next hill of years.

"A lot of people think I'm crazy when I say that. But I can picture that. By—by a hundred years from now there'll be guys landing on the Moon."

"I dunno, Jerry." Norlund supposed that the kid would have picked a closer year than two thousand thirty three except for his concern for the sensibilities of conservative age. "What's all that over there? General Exhibits Group. I think we may wind up putting a unit inside one of those buildings."

The outside wall of one of them turned out to be preferable. One unit left to install. Norlund, looking alternately at his instruments and out the window, realized suddenly that the convergence point of his two long-drawn lines had to be right at the eastern Skyride tower, the one on the outer peninsula and closest to the lake. What that might mean, he couldn't begin to guess.

As location for his last unit, his instruments opted for somewhere inside the House of Tomorrow—which was, he supposed, appropriate enough.

In brief moments when Norlund's attention wandered from the job he thought about Jerry and the kid's wistful eagerness for the future. Jerry had said that he was twenty now. He'd still be possible draft bait in nineteen forty-one, by the standards of the World War II selective service—even in America where no one was fighting on the local soil. Not that he'd waited around to be drafted. I was gung-ho in those days, he thought; and then he cautioned himself not to say gung-ho aloud. He'd get another of those funny looks.

Trying to plan tactics, Norlund picked up a small brochure on the House of Tomorrow.

A circular glass house, incorporating possible indications of what the future may bring . . . built around a central mast which contains all utilities. Exterior walls are of clear glass, and there are no windows. Privacy is obtained by drapes and roller and Venetian blinds. The most modern equipment available has been used, including everything from an airplane to electrically controlled doors. The furniture is especially designed. The ground floor includes the airplane hangar in addition to the garage; the roof above forms an extensive deck terrace, opening from the living room floor, and there is a similar deck around the drum-shaped solarium on the third floor. Ventilation is provided by filtered, washed, heated or cooled air, recirculated every ten minutes. There are no visible light fixtures, as the necessary artificial light is indirect, from hidden sources. There are no closets, but movable wardrobes are used . . . the house is frankly declared to be a 'laboratory' house, for the purpose of determining the attitude of World's Fair visitors to the idea of an utterly different home . . . price has been no object . . .

Jerry was still inside the House of Tomorrow, Norlund watching his instruments in the back of the truck, when a slight sound came from the front, and the whole truck shifted slightly as if someone's weight had come aboard.

Norlund's right hand, concealed by equipment from the intruder's gaze, moved to scramble dial settings, wiping all sense and purpose from the panel. With the same motion he turned his chair. "Yeah?"

There was a uniformed head and shoulders leaning in through the open window on the left side. The face that came with the uniform looked baked, as if by sun bouncing from city pavements. It had dusty-looking eyebrows and in general a hard, unhappy look. The voice was gritty, also suggesting streets and pavements. "Let's see your working-on-the-grounds permit."

Norlund put on an expression that he hoped looked like controlled arrogance. He moved forward through the narrow aisle, and threw himself into the driver's seat with an air of exasperation. With one hand he further loosened his tie, at the same time managing to call attention to it as a badge of social authority. "Who sent you guys around now? If you don't want to make trouble for yourselves, better butt out and let me get some work done."

"Just lemme see the permit, please," said the hard face a few inches from his own. That last word represented a concession, but Norlund got the feeling that bluster on his part was unlikely to accomplish more.

Peering out past the man, Norlund demanded, "Who's in charge here?" He could see now that there were at least two more uniformed figures in the background, and just behind them the gray unmarked car in which they had evidently driven up.

And where was Jerry? He still had to be inside the House of Tomorrow, some yards away across a concourse. Norlund was careful not to look in that direction.

At a nod from one in the background, the cop who had been peering into the truck now yanked the door open. "All right, buddy, step out."

Norlund wasn't sure if these were city cops or some of the Fair's own security force; he noted that they were wearing guns at their belts as the regular city policemen did. Their uniforms were of police type, but otherwise uninformative. Norlund got out of the truck—he realized he'd be dragged out if he didn't—and moved toward the two men in the background. They stood waiting for him. One of them was leaning, arms folded, against the gray car behind him. This man was thin but strong-looking, a little taller than average, and Norlund instantly picked him out as the authority. His fair coloring suggested Nordic ancestry, but something in his cast of features suggested an unusual combination, perhaps black or Indian. Norlund didn't consider the incongruous effect handsome, but it was certainly striking.

This man, still leaning against his car, spoke to Norlund in a voice of authority. "We have to see your driver's license as well as the permit." There was more than enough authority for a police sergeant in that voice; well, these days a lot of former big shots were glad to have any kind of a job.

Being careful to move his hands slowly, Norlund got his billfold. He fumbled with it for a moment, then drew forth a business card along with his license. When he handed the card and license over, there was a folded ten-spot pressed between them . . .

. . . and Norlund knew at once that bribery wasn't going to do him any more good than bluster. The pale-faced sergeant—or whatever he was—carefully and at once separated the money from the card and license, holding the bill in plain sight between two fingers while he studied the documents carefully. The expression on his face was one of faint amusement.

Then he handed the three items back, separately. "Mr., ah, Norlund, you're going to have to come along with us. Just until we can get this straightened out." He managed to make that last sentence sound almost reassuring. He held out an empty hand. "The keys to the truck, please."

One of the other uniformed men had gone to poke around a little inside the truck, and had evidently not found any keys. Jerry must have taken them with him. Norlund's hands had already gone to his own pockets, under an almost hypnotic compulsion to look for keys where he knew they wouldn't be found. He stood silent.

"Look in his pockets," said the sergeant abstractedly, as if more important things were on his mind, and pushed past Norlund to go take a look inside the truck for himself. Meanwhile the other two uniforms grabbed Norlund.

Passersby, people who had come to the Fair to have fun, stared briefly at the search and moved right on. This, recalled Norlund, would not be a great year in which to complain about police brutality. Nobody was going to worry about their slapping you around, not unless you were a person of some power and importance yourself.

Norlund was handled roughly. At least he wasn't slapped. The necktie and a general air of respectability, he thought, saved him from that. His billfold was looked into. "Wow, what a roll!"

"Let him keep that for now," said the leader, who had come back from the truck. He stood frowning, eyeing the passing throngs, the nearby buildings.

At last the invading hands left his pockets, ceased to poke and prod. "He's got no keys at all on him, chief. Wearing some kind of money belt under his shirt."

Chief? Norlund turned his head to get a better look at the man he had been thinking of as a sergeant, but his arm was jerked and he was made to face the other way.

"Okay," soothed the one who had been called chief. "We can take him all apart later." He paused thoughtfully. "I don't want to try to move that truck without the keys." Pause again. "We'll come back for it later. Put him in the car."

Norlund's arms were brought behind him, and he experienced something new in his sixty years: the hard bite of handcuffs. Then the leader opened the door of the gray car for him, as if with politeness, and the other two put him in. One of the men got in the back with Norlund, and the other drove. When the leader turned his head from the front seat to gaze at Norlund with satisfaction, Norlund noted that the shoulder patch on his uniform said nothing at all. It was only a decoration.

There was no conversation inside the car as it eased into motion. It edged courteously past strolling Fairgoers, who no longer bothered to stare. After all, they had more interesting and pleasant things to look at. Now the car had gotten onto a service drive, and now it was approaching a gate. Yes, the same gate where Norlund had bribed the guard to let him in. Donald Duck was not in sight at the moment. Screw you too, Donald—but of course it might have been something else entirely that had brought down the fuzz.

The gray Packard was waved out through the gate with hardly so much as a glance from the guard currently on duty. And presently the Twenty-third Street Bridge was flowing under Norlund again, this time in a reverse motion, east to west. Like time travel into the past, he thought. The Century of Progress was being left behind. Dark Ages ahead. . . .

And then Norlund roused himself from the cumulative effect of the shocks of the past few days to wonder at last why they were taking him off the Fairgrounds at all. There, standing in the street directing traffic, was a regular city cop. And he wasn't wearing the same uniform that these characters had on.

The blond leader turned again to study Norlund. Could it be the pre-Conquest Indians of Mexico that the slope of his brow and nose suggested?

He said to Norlund: "Now, let's see. You are from — ?"

"New York. You saw my license."

"No, no." Slight amusement, a little shake of the head. "I'd say . . . about nineteen-ninety? How is Ginny Butler getting on these days?"

Just inside the front door of the House of Tomorrow, Jerry Rosen stood looking out through a small gap in the drapes that covered most of the glass walls, watching the abduction. Jerry's hand was in his cover-all pocket, clutching the truck keys. When he'd gotten out of the truck to do this last installation he'd brought the keys along unthinkingly . . . well, almost unthinkingly. There just might have been some half-thought-out compulsion to make sure that his final day's pay was going to be forthcoming after his final day's work. Not that it had seemed at all likely that Norlund would try to stiff him on it, but years of hard times made people suspicious, almost a little crazy sometimes.

The three flatfeet had driven up in their gray car just as Jerry was about to go outside and report that his job was done. Instead he waited and watched while, sure enough, they went for Norlund. Jerry supposed that they were some kind of special Fair cops. Whatever was wrong, they were really pinching Norlund for something, shaking him down and everything. They looked in the truck but they didn't leave a man with it when they drove away.

If they'd been smart . . . but Jerry had learned long ago that most cops, like most other people, were dumb and clumsy most of the time, and if you relied on them to be half asleep you'd come out ahead more often than not. Of course there was always the time they weren't asleep and they surprised you. You had to consider what the stakes were, whether the risk was worth it.

Jerry no longer held to the theory that Norlund was a bootlegger. Jerry knew something about that business, and what Norlund was doing didn't really seem to connect with it. But the old guy was up to something besides a radio survey. Or else the radio survey business was a lot different than Jerry would have imagined it to be. But whatever game Norlund was really into, he obviously had plenty of money behind him, and in Jerry's book he was a good man and an employer who deserved loyalty. Growing up on the streets of New York and Chicago, Jerry had acquired a fierce sense of loyalty, as long as he considered it deserved.

And this was the moment when he had to consider what the stakes were, and the risks, and then act.

He could, of course, simply abandon the truck. Shed his coveralls and drop his tools here inside the building, and stroll off the Fairgrounds with the thousands of visitors—not a chance in a million that he'd be caught if he did that, assuming they were even looking for companions of Norlund who might be around. He would, of course, be leaving without collecting an earned day's pay.

On the other hand, there was not only his day's pay, but that truck, with what had to be a fortune in fancy equipment inside it. Norlund had to have friends, and they had to have a strong interest in that, as well as in hearing what had happened to their man.

Jerry acted. The gray Packard—and what kind of police force sent those out as patrol cars?—was hardly out of sight before he was out of the House of Tomorrow and down its front steps. When he reached the truck he pulled out the keys and hopped in. Now was the moment for the hidden plainclothesman to pop up out of hiding and pinch him. If that happened, Jerry would be surprised as hell, just an ignorant worker with no idea of what his boss had been up to or where he came from. The business card that might have suggested otherwise was a small, crumpled ball of waste up inside one of the indirect lighting coves just inside the House of Tomorrow's supermodern entrance.

Jerry's first instinct, as he started driving slowly away, was to look for a different gate to exit from the grounds. The truck might be more likely to be recognized at the gate where they'd driven in, if the gate people were supposed to be looking for it.

He got onto a service road, and decided to follow it north through the Fairgrounds. He thought he ought to be able to get out at the Twelfth Street gate . . .

. . . and the more he thought about those three cops, the more he wondered about them. Driving very carefully and slowly, Jerry shivered a little and looked in his rearview mirror. Capone had been put away in the Federal pen in Atlanta by Uncle Sam, and anyway it wasn't St. Valentine's day. But other guys could have picked up the idea of putting a rub-out squad into police uniforms. Something about those three birds who'd picked up Norlund just wasn't kosher.

When the service drive came out from behind a building, Jerry suddenly got a clear view of the Havoline Thermometer in the middle distance. Two hundred feet high, with electrically switched neon tubing up and down its sides instead of mercury—he'd read about it somewhere—it showed eighty-four degrees right now. A mile or so inland, the city would probably be really sweltering. Coming in sight of a clock now, Jerry noted that the time was just a little after four.

Sure enough, there was another service gate at Twelfth Street. He drove right up to it, and was motioned right through with only a casual wave of the guard's hand. As Jerry had expected, they didn't give a damn who they let *out*, as long as they hadn't been told to watch for some person or vehicle in particular. Maybe in another five minutes they'd be alerted for the truck. He wondered how far Norlund had been taken. Probably just to somewhere on the grounds. If those were really the Fair police. . . .

Jerry drove inland. He was worried, and using all his eyes and wit to try to make sure that he wasn't being followed. There was a lot of traffic here near the Fair, and it was hard to be sure.

He was just crossing Michigan Avenue, going west, when he saw something ahead that took his mind for the moment off the possibility of being followed. A gray Packard, and, son of a bitch, it looked just like the one they'd hauled Norlund away in. He couldn't get a good look at who was inside, but he thought it might be uniforms. No police force that Jerry had ever heard of gave its men Packards to drive around in. He found himself sweating in a way that had nothing to do with the weather.

Would he dare to try to follow them, just to see where they went? The idea crossed his mind. But no, the truck he was in felt painfully big and conspicuous; a sign was painted on its side. Jerry was sometimes a little too cocky about what he could get away with, but he wasn't crazy. He'd gotten away with the truck, it looked like, and that was enough. He switched lanes, getting ready to turn down a side street before the guys in the Packard spotted him in their rearview mirror.

When he turned, the gray car passed out of his sight. He kept watching for it as he drove north for a while, but it did not reappear. At last he turned west again, toward Wheaton. The address from Norlund's business card was firmly in Jerry's mind. Whoever the boys in Wheaton turned out to be, he'd bring them back their truck, and word of what had happened to their man Norlund. Jerry didn't doubt they'd appreciate the information, and maybe they could even do something for the old guy.

When he saw a handy-looking phone booth, he pulled over. He had the phone number from the card firmly in mind too.

The number was busy. He got his nickel back, paused to slip out of the labeled coveralls, threw them in the back of the truck, and jumped back into the driver's seat.

As he drove he kept checking the time, whenever he caught sight of a clock. It was about five when he reached Wheaton; the day seemed to be getting hotter, if anything. Jerry located the road named in the address, and drove slowly west along it, looking at the numbers on houses and stores and shops.

Now open countryside was just ahead, and he felt on the verge of giving up. But wait, there was something up ahead, an isolated building. An old farmhouse, he thought, but maybe it wasn't used for farming any more.

As Jerry approached the turn onto the driveway of the old house, he became aware of a car behind him. It wasn't the gray Packard, and he had no special reason to believe that it was following him, but he couldn't shake the feeling, the fear. The car was gaining on him now.

Should he drive on past the farmhouse and then loop back? The car behind was accelerating now, catching up faster. And there, half a mile ahead, another car turned out of a drive as if it possibly meant to block the road.

Jerry didn't always make right decisions, but he was willing to make them quickly. He turned on suddenly, sharply squealing tires, and went plowing up the long cinder drive in front of the old farmhouse. The place looked deserted, but he saw with a shred of hope that it did have a big garage, roomy enough for several cars, looking as if it had been recently added on.

Jerry had the truck halfway up the drive, still moving at a good clip, when something struck him. For an instant he thought he had been shot, and then he knew he hadn't. The striking force was not a bullet, but something intangible and soundless. But it was real, like a wave of dizziness thick enough to be thrown like a net and stun a man. Could a guy possibly be shot, and never hear the bullet passing through his car?

And now the air around Jerry was flashing, turning impressive colors. Just ahead of him the garage doors were swinging open by themselves—a good thing, because he didn't know if he could find the brakes— and inside the garage everything was color. . . .

And now the whole damn building seemed to blow up, carrying him away. . . .

1984

The dream was vague, but no less terrible for that. In it people were arguing about Jerry, while he lay helpless. Some of them wanted to do away with him entirely. Later he was unable to remember any of their words, but the sense of their purpose remained horribly clear.

In a physical sense, too, the argument was over him. Men and women were actually shouting at each other across his prostrate body, as he lay on some kind of bed or stretcher. And he knew that, just out of his range of vision, some kind of horrors were walking past.

Then at another time he was being carried on a stretcher, or something like one. There followed a ride in some peculiar vehicle. It wasn't Norlund's truck; it wasn't quite like anything else that Jerry had ever seen. During this ride a woman who was sitting near bent over him to whisper in his ear, words that were meant to be reassuring, and then she pulled a cloth up over his face so he couldn't see or hear what was going on around him, and he wondered if he was dead. Had he been able to move his arms, he would have pushed the cloth aside. Had he been able to worry, he would have worried like hell. As matters stood, he couldn't do either one. Even fear was gone, so that was that.

Then in the dream Jerry started to laugh, and he laughed and laughed at all the things that were just too damn funny to worry about.

Until, in the midst of laughter, he almost choked. The choking lasted for a while, with the cloth pulled back from his face again and anxious voices and people fussing around him.

Then he was able to breathe easily again.

But by that time, all he wanted to do, all he really cared about in the world, was to be able to go to sleep. . . .

Until a time came when he was trying to wake up.

Jerry had a headache. It wasn't a killer, but it was enough to let him know that he must have hoisted a few too many last night. That didn't happen to Jerry very often, especially since he'd been married. But on special occasions it could happen. Trust old Mike, when there was a wedding or some other really special reason, to get out one of the bottles of real Irish whisky, a family legacy kept hidden in the cellar. And then old Mike might want to prove that he could still drink the young guys under the table. Even a young guy who was good enough to marry Mike's oldest daughter, and especially a young guy who was Jewish, and . . . and . . .

Jerry's efforts at thought, such as they were, dissolved back into muddle. And headache. And maybe the headache was going to be a killer after all.

Jerry groaned. It probably hadn't been the good old Irish, then. That had never done anything to him like this. What had he been drinking, bathtub gin?

With his forehead still buried in the pillow, his eyelids still uncracked, Jerry reflected that this time Judy was really going to be pissed off at him. Judy's mother would put up with Mike's drinking, though she grumbled. But Judy's husband had to—wait a minute, it *was* a weekend, wasn't it? Not that it mattered to Jerry, he didn't have a job—hey, wait, *like hell he didn't*.

Now memory was returning in great chunks that tumbled over each other in a confusing rush. Norlund. The Fair. The House of Tomorrow. Norlund being bundled off in a car, Jerry following in a truck.

And the old farmhouse. Nothing after that, except the dream.

Sitting up quickly, in a spasm of anxiety, didn't do the headache any good at all. A fiend armed with a can opener took a close interest in the victim's brain. For long seconds Jerry's eyes remained clenched shut.

When at last he could see, he was in a room that, to the best of his recollection, he had never seen before.

He was in his underwear, lying between pink sheets. . . . He looked at them again. Yeah, that's right, pink instead of white. And the small bedroom was utterly unfamiliar. It was high-class, with a kind of feminine flair about the strange decorations.

For a little while Jerry just sat there, unable to make any kind of connection between this situation and his last waking memories. All he could think of at first was that he might somehow have wound up in a high-class whorehouse. He hadn't been in one of those places, high-class or low, since he'd married Judy, not even once. Somehow he must have got hold of some really rotten booze, yack yack bourbon or bootleg jake.

Oh Christ, his head. How was he supposed to think?

By this time he had progressed as far as sitting on the edge of the bed. The bedroom had one window, the fancy blind of which was closed against bright sunlight. The thinnest possible needle of the sun, coming in past the blind's edge, was enough to make Jerry wince. He observed that there were two doors in the bedroom, besides the closet door. One of them was closed, the other partly open on a bathroom with weird fixtures, yellow instead of white. With relief Jerry recognized his own clothes, piled more or less neatly on a chair near the bed. His shoes were under the chair.

In another moment Jerry was on his feet, ignoring the headache, lunging for his pants and going through the pockets. Goddamn it! He'd been cleaned out, every nickel. Even his pocket comb and his handkerchief were gone. Oh, the sons of bitches, he was going to, was going to. . . .

Fact was, he still didn't even know who *they* were, or even where he was. Dimly he groped toward the start of an explanation: he'd reached the headquarters of Norlund's people, and something had happened to him there, a fight, a drugging, an accident. They were keeping him on ice until he woke up and they could decide what to do next. This place he was in might be some kind of hotel or whorehouse that they ran, a handy place to let him lie. It didn't really look like a whorehouse, though. He didn't know what it looked like.

Never mind what it was, for now. He was going to get himself out of it and head for home.

But another urgency took precedence, even over that. Jerry barely made it into the bathroom in time.

He was still in there, starting to feel a little better, when the oddness, the real strangeness of this place started to sink in. The fixtures, the lights, everything in its own way was funny-looking. There was no window at all in the bathroom, but you could hear a ventilating fan come on somewhere when you flicked the peculiar light switch by the door. The switch moved almost silently. And the sink, the washbasin, whatever you ought to call it, was of one piece with the countertop surrounding it, and it was made out of—well, it looked like marble, but it didn't really feel like any kind of stone.

No window. Huh. This sure as hell was not the all-glass House of Tomorrow.

Back in the bedroom he grabbed up his pants again, now happy to have them even if the couple of dollars he'd had in his pocket was gone. He'd get home somehow, and then he'd try finding out what had happened to Norlund. Eventually he'd work things out with these people, explain to them that he'd just been trying to help by bringing back their truck.

Cautiously Jerry eased the blind on the bedroom window sideways a little, and peeked out into the sun. What he saw only added to his confusion. He was no longer out in the suburbs, he was looking down from some hotel or apartment building so high that it had to be located in the middle of the city. There were treetops, well below him, and other tall buildings were standing around—now what in hell was he supposed to make of this? How long had he been knocked out, and why? And why had he been brought here and left in this bed?

He didn't know what time it was. Jesus, he didn't even know what day. Suppose he'd been gone from home all night. Judy would kill him, and Mike . . .

nobody would believe a story like the one Jerry was going to have to tell.

While he was pulling on his shirt and stuffing the tail of it into his pants, his eye fell on a telephone. Yeah, dammit, that had to be a phone there on the little bedside table. He'd missed it at first, because the instrument was a funny color instead of black, and an odd shape too. Maybe he ought to call home right this minute, from here, just to let them know that he was still alive. But maybe, on the other hand, he ought to just scram out of here without wasting a second, while he had the chance.

He put on his shoes, tying them quickly. Right beside the telephone on the little table was a funny little box made out of some smooth material. On the front of this box was what Jerry, desperate to know the time, at first thought might be a clock face. But it wasn't a clock. Instead, the numbers on it were almost like those on a radio dial. Next to one row of numbers were the large letters FM, with AM beside the other row . . . instead of AM and PM? It didn't seem to make sense.

There were more urgent things than strange gadgets to worry about. When, a moment later, Jerry did see a clock atop the dresser on the other side of the bed, he didn't even recognize it as a clock at first. But it displayed what might be a time — 10:18 — even though it had no face or hands. There were just the numbers, glowing like a little neon sign. Jerry couldn't see any neon tubes, though. Just the numbers themselves, in what looked like pure orange light. And now the last digit melted away, changing instantly to a 9.

He was fully dressed now, and he was getting out of here. One stride from the closed bedroom door, he obeyed a last-moment impulse in a way that he thought must mean his nerves were shot. Changing directions, he grabbed up the telephone after all. At that point, Jerry's finger, poised to dial his home number, found itself aimed at a neat little rectangle of pushbuttons instead of a dial. Well, he could push buttons, too. The receiver beeped musically into his ear as he did so.

Then came clicking and buzzing noises, and then a woman's voice: " — suggest you hang up and dial again. If you feel you have dialed correctly — "

Jerry tried several times, with increasing urgency, to interrupt the operator's spiel. But she droned on as if she were completely unaware of his existence. Snotty bitch! And then to top it off she just pulled the plug on her switchboard and cut him off, damned snotty bitch!

But he had no time to waste on her. As Jerry put down the phone, one more thought struck him, and he hastily pulled open some of the dresser drawers and poked around in them, wondering if his money and stuff might have been put there. Or he might find a little loose change that he could use for carfare. What he discovered was piles of various feminine garments, and that was about it.

At the bedroom door at last, he tried it cautiously, and found to his relief that at least it wasn't locked. When he opened the door he found himself looking out into the hallway of what appeared to be a small apartment. Jerry stood still for a moment, listening. As far as he could tell he had the whole place to himself.

Across the hallway was the small living room, with blinds drawn shut on both its windows. At first glance the living room furniture was more or less ordinary — a sofa, a couple of big chairs, a low table with some newspapers thrown on it. But the lamps looked odd.

And in one corner of the living room a big radio sat on a low chest . . . but maybe it wasn't a radio. It was some kind of cabinet with metal prongs sticking out on top like insect feelers and most of its front surface a single panel of dull glass. At the other side of the living room in a small entryway was a door that ought to lead out of the apartment. Another door, to a tiny coat closet, stood ajar, revealing garments hanging within.

A few feet to Jerry's left down the hall was another bathroom. And beside that a second bedroom—or was it? On tiptoe he moved closer and looked in. It was another small room, with a single bed or cot crowded into one corner. The center of the room was given to a worktable holding a kind of elaborate, deformed typewriter. This machine was flanked on the table by another glass-fronted box, this one small, and a couple of other devices Jerry found equally unfamiliar. All were connected by wires covered with strange, smooth insulation. More radio stuff, Jerry guessed. Spies? Secret messages to company headquarters? Any guess he made might be as good as another. There were some rolls and scatterings of paper on the table, but he wasn't going to hang around to try to read them. In this room, too, the window blind was closed.

Moving in the other direction down the short hall, past the room in which he'd awakened, Jerry came to a small dining alcove. The table and chairs were framed with bright metal tubing, making them look as if they might have come right out of the House of Tomorrow.

Beyond this alcove was the kitchen, in which things were . . . very odd. By now, that hardly came as a surprise. The stove top was a single panel, the burners looking as if they'd simply been painted onto it. But it was obviously a real appliance. On one wall of the kitchen hung a calendar, and on another a peculiar phone—and there at last, between blinded windows on a third wall, a clock of more or less normal design. It read ten twenty-four, which more or less agreed with the odd clock back in the bedroom.

At the far end of the kitchen a closed door of solid wood was fortified with two locks and a chain. It had to be the back way out of the apartment. In a moment Jerry was standing in front of that door and undoing its fastenings. A moment after that he was outside the door, on a small concrete-floored landing. It held a pair of garbage cans that, like so many things in the apartment, appeared to have been made of something like hard rubber. From this landing a service stairway went both up and down, in tight rectangular turns, concrete and steel inside the unpainted concrete of the building's outer wall.

Jerry took the downward stair. His feet moved quickly, skipping steps, passing the rear entries to other apartments. Maybe when he got outside he could bum money for carfare from somebody. He passed several exterior windows on his way down, but they were all obscured by bars and heavy screens and grime. He could see enough, though, to tell that his descent had reached the level of the treetops outside; and then, that he was almost all the way down.

Then he was at ground level. The exit door at the bottom opened easily. And then he was outside.

1933

The gray Packard was creeping west through Loop traffic. The man in the passenger seat turned around again, and said to Norlund, "It might even be that you are innocent, Mr. Norlund—and I suppose that might even be your right name."

"It is."

"When I say innocent, I mean of course in the sense of your intentions. You are not innocent legally. Butler probably recruited you with the throw that what she wanted you to do for her was perfectly legal. Is that in fact what happened?"

The throw? Norlund wondered silently. His hands were still held behind him by steel cuffs. He thought about Sandy, and said nothing.

"Ah well, you'll tell me soon. First I want to make sure you understand that unauthorized, unlicensed time travel is very much against the law."

Norlund felt a compulsion to speak. An innocent

man ought to be able to say something. "What are you talking about?" he asked.

His interrogator smiled faintly, as if he had gained a point by getting Norlund to ask that question. "I am talking about the laws of human history. I have the honor to help in their enforcement. No time, no place in human history, stands outside our law. You will learn." The man nodded at Norlund, his attitude seeming to say, I am allowing all I can for ignorance, restraining my personal anger at lawbreakers such as you.

"Kidnapping is illegal," Norlund said. And then, seeing the instant reaction in the other's eyes, he was much afraid.

Before the chief could respond to Norlund, the driver beside him interrupted. "Sir, it's that truck. Behind us."

The chief's gaze shifted past Norlund, out through the rear window. Again something altered in his eyes, and Norlund, who had been frightened, was abruptly terrified. The chief said only: "Get him."

The driver reacted instantly, displaying a virtuosity that had not earlier been required. He twirled the wheel, expertly changing lanes in traffic. The Packard accelerated, braked, spun into a U-turn. Norlund, having a hard time keeping his balance with his hands useless, saw the truck. He lunged awkwardly toward the open window next to him, intending to get his head out of it and cry for help.

The chief hit him on the bridge of the nose, a backhand blow. If it wasn't a gunbarrel that landed, it felt like one. Norlund, half-stunned, his eyes suddenly streaming water, slumped back into his seat. Meanwhile, through his pain, he was raging inwardly at Jerry—what did the damned young fool think he was doing, trying to follow this way? It was the same truck all right; there was the dimly painted sign on the side of it. Silently Norlund cursed the young guy for an idiot.

The Packard's driver continued to be frighteningly competent. More so than Jerry. Norlund, still half-dazed, in pain, and trying to see through streaming eyes, missed many of the details of the chase. When his vision cleared they were still somewhere in the downtown area, with the truck only half a block ahead. A light was turning red — but both vehicles got through it. The truck had lost another car-length now.

The chief, ignoring Norlund now, looked forward, grunting with satisfaction. The uniformed man in the rear had Norlund by the collar with one hand, ready to apply a choke if necessary.

The fleeing truck had turned down one side street after another, and now it chose to dive into an alley. Norlund groaned aloud, viewing this as evidence of Jerry's panic — there were too many ways to be delayed, or stuck, down one of these one-lane passages between buildings.

And there, round the first bend of the alley, the truck was stuck indeed, having chosen a blind ending. The Packard screeched to a halt some fifty feet behind it. The chief had his door open instantly, and jumped out with weapon in hand, crying triumphant orders to his men. The driver, on his side, was only a second behind him. Ragged forms that had been bending over nearby garbage cans straightened up in scrambling flight. Norlund, his head twisted sideways by the grip on his collar, could just see that one of these was a young man, slight of build, with short brown hair that was just growing out of a crewcut. The youth's eyes met Norlund's, and with a tense sideways nod he indicated that Norlund should get the hell out of that alley, back in the only direction that was open.

It wasn't that Norlund was unwilling, but—

Something that was not gunfire or any conventional explosive blew up, sizzled, blasted again. It was issuing from the truck, and the air around the Packard was filled with frying noises. The chief and his companion, their bodies glowing but apparently unharmed, were diving for cover behind loading dock and garbage cans, firing back.

And now something else was happening at and around the car door to Norlund's left. The uniformed man beside him let go Norlund's collar and started to turn that way, away from Norlund. There was a staccato shrieking in the air, suggesting a wind of hurricane force being turned on and absolutely off at intervals of a small fraction of a second. First the car door, then the uniformed figure beside Norlund, disappeared and reappeared in multiple staggering images, flickering in time with the hurricane wind. Norlund saw the door open, the door closed, the man in this position, the man in that. Grabbing for Norlund, falling down, reaching for the door, drawing his gun, lying back slumped, sitting there alert. As if segments or frames from three or four different sequences of events had been chopped up and randomly spliced back together.

Norlund could feel himself, even see himself, being sucked into the maelstrom too. Forces he had never known sawed at him. Mutually exclusive pathways opened simultaneously. He could feel himself being sliced as by a camera's whirling shutter, divided and subdivided, minced, multiplied and integrated again. Norlund Descending a Staircase.

The guard was gone from beside him, the car door was open. He lunged for it.

Norlund found himself rolling out of the Packard onto the ground. He was afflicted with dirt and grit and terror, and the blasts that were not of bullets or cannon still raged in the air nearby. But he felt essentially unhurt, and the world around him had regained stability. With steel still clamping his hands behind him, he got his legs under him and ran, trying to stay in a crouch. Already he was gasping but he ran as hard as he could, heading back down the alley. The noise behind him suddenly abated, as if a heavy door had closed, but one quick glance backward showed him both truck and Packard still enveloped in special effects. Two bodies, one uniformed, one ragged, lay anonymously on the ground.

Norlund pounded around the corner in the alley, breath sawing in his throat. He was just approaching the alley's mouth, wondering which way he was going to turn out of it, when a green taxicab with a broad stripe of checkerboard pattern round its body pulled up in front of him on the street. A rear door of the cab opened, and Ginny Butler leaned out beckoning.

Norlund, stumbling forward as fast as he could, gasped with dismay when he saw that the car was starting to roll before he'd reached it. He lunged. Ginny's hand caught him by the upper arm and pulled. He was in safely and the door slammed as the cab leapt forward.

Ginny, dressed in clothes of the Thirties, her short hair rearranged, helped Norlund up to a normal position on the seat. Harbin, dressed as a cabdriver, was up front behind the wheel. The taxi shot down the street and around a corner as if expecting close pursuit. It slowed down somewhat after that, but still kept moving right along, putting distance between its occupants and whatever might be happening back there in the alley.

In one hand Ginny was now holding what looked like a giant Brillo pad of coiled wire. She began to pass this like a sponge over Norlund's body, touching him quickly, gently, working from head to toe. She used her free hand to turn him this way and that, careful not to miss any spots. The process, whatever it was, was complete in a matter of seconds, and he was allowed to lie back gasping, his eyes closed. He was too old for this kind of nonsense, he told himself.

"I never promised you it would be a safe job, Alan." Ginny was reaching behind him now, with some other kind of instrument in her hands. There was no sound, not even a tug, but one after another the bracelets fell free of his wrists.

He opened his eyes. "You said that before." He wished that he could stop gasping. "What about Andy Burns?" Gasp. "I saw him back there."

"We have some good, experienced people there with him. Chances are they'll do all right." Ginny, putting tools away, rubbed her forehead wearily. "Andy is working for us willingly, you understand. A lot of things have been explained to him, and he's accepted combat assignment."

"Wish I could say the same, about things being explained. What happened to Jerry Rosen? Has he enlisted in your commandos, too?"

She shook her head. "He wasn't in the truck when we sent it after you; he's safe for the time being. We can't send you to safety, but we've got to try to keep you safe. You're becoming rather important."

"The job's done," said Norlund, not without pride. Ginny didn't answer. She was looking back through the rear window of the cab as if checking for pursuers.

"Always liked to think of myself as important." Norlund got in a few more good breaths and decided that maybe he wasn't going to faint after all. "What's the news on my granddaughter?"

Ginny turned back to him, and looked at her watch — at least at some device that she wore on her wrist. "As of two days after your launching from Eighty-four," she declared, "Sandy is doing just fine. You don't have to worry any more about her having our continued support; you've earned that."

"Thanks." Norlund breathed a sigh. "Naturally Sandy's mother is wondering where I am, if I've been gone two extra days."

"I suppose she is. Alan, I have to tell you that I don't know when we're going to be able to get you home. I thought it would be two days. But the whole situation has changed drastically since you were launched."

Norlund nodded, feeling almost no surprise. A little, at himself, for taking the announcement so calmly, as if he'd been expecting it all along. "In the army they used to say that your enlistment was being involuntarily extended. That was the official term for it, anyway."

Ginny was watching him carefully. "The job really isn't done yet. I'm glad you can understand."

"When you're sixty, you realize that you're never going to understand very much. But you do start to have a certain feeling for how the world works." Norlund rubbed his newly freed wrists. Then he started trying to brush some of the alley grit from his clothes. Ginny helped him. "I'd like to hear a guess, though, at when you might be able to get me home. Not that I'd necessarily believe it." He'd lost his hat in the . . . but *that* looked like his hat. It was sitting atop his traveling bag at Ginny's feet. Next to it was another bag that must be her traveling tool kit. From the latter she now withdrew another appliance, to help Norlund remove a streak of grime from his coat sleeve.

Ginny sighed. "I'm reluctant to make such a guess. You should realize, Alan, that right now you're rather lucky to be alive at all. Alive and coherent. However." She paused, raising her eyes to the driver's rearview mirror as if to consult with the silent Harbin. The cab was still in the downtown area, turning corners frequently; Norlund had no idea where they were going.

Ginny looked back at him. "A new timeline is being created here. I don't think we've ever really discussed timelines with you."

"I only had one day of basic training before you shipped me overseas."

She continued to consider him. "We chose well, I think. You're a pretty tough man."

"Thank you, ma'am." Oddly, he really felt honored. And that she was telling him something she really felt.

"And again, I'm sorry, but getting you home as I promised isn't possible."

"I've grasped that point. By the way, you also promised me that what I was going to do was legal."

"What's that supposed to mean?"

"I've just been told that it isn't."

Harbin spoke up unexpectedly from the driver's seat. "By that man who just now kidnapped you? I suppose he mentioned me."

Norlund met Dr. Harbin's eyes in the rearview mirror. "Actually he never mentioned you at all. He did ask how Ginny Butler was. Said she goes around convincing people to break the laws . . . of human history,

I think he called them. Her kind of time travel does that."

Ginny asked quietly, "Did you think he might be right?"

Norlund's head still ached from the backhand blow. He could still see the blond man's eyes. "If I have to choose between you, you're still ahead."

"You do have to choose. That man's name is Hajo Brandi." Ginny spelled it out for Norlund. "Sound like a funny name?" She wasn't smiling. "I hope our people back there have managed to kill him this time. That's a faint hope, but at least getting him out alive will cost his side a great deal—energy, time, and other things. That's something. I'm not going to try to tell you about him now; he deserves a whole chapter and we haven't time. But he's a mass murderer. And he likes to torture people."

"Well." Norlund sighed. He could believe it.

Ginny was looking at her watch impatiently. At the moment the cab was stuck in traffic. She switched subjects briskly. "If we do arrange to get you home, Alan, it won't be for weeks or months. Maybe longer. Meanwhile, it's *possible* that we can work out something, sometime, on the telephone."

Norlund considered this as he held his aching head. "You mean I might be able to phone home? From one year, one decade, to another?"

"It might be possible. If you think your relatives would be comforted more than unsettled to hear from you that way. You'd have to plan what you were going to say to them. You couldn't tell them what you were really doing, of course, or where you really were."

"Wow."

"Think about it."

"I'll try. Where am I going now?" Even as he spoke

he realized that they were now in a line of other taxicabs, working their way slowly toward the curb in front of a giant building—a railroad station, he realized.

"You're going to your fallback position. I'm sure you remember what that is."

He did; it was one of the things they had engraved upon his memory. If something had gone wrong in Chicago, if Ginny hadn't contacted him and he hadn't known what to do next, he had been ordered to make his way east, to New York, as best he could. "All right. The Empire State Building lobby, at noon. Who's meeting me?"

Ginny gave him a look, but that was all.

"All right, so you won't tell me. It seems absolutely insane to me, the things you insist on keeping secret and the things you don't care about—my name for instance."

No reply. The line of taxicabs was momentarily stalled.

"All right. Tell me instead how you did that switch with the truck back there. Maybe the other side will try it on me some day. When Hajo Whatsisname wants to arrest me again, he shouldn't have much trouble finding me."

That got a response. "Oh, his people will know approximately where you are, and when. Getting at you will be another matter. You'll be safe for a while. As for the truck, Jerry drove it back to Wheaton, and inadvertently took it clockwise—that is, forward in time. We knew Brandi had already seen it, so we loaded it up and brought it back anticlockwise to the same day, trying to trap him. But you won't see a stunt like that very often, from either side. It's too costly and too risky. In this case we decided that the costs and the risks were justified."

"To save me. Because, as you say, I've become rather important."

"You have. But I must admit that might not have been enough. When there was also a chance of trapping Brandi . . ."

She let it trail off. The other taxis ahead of them were moving and now Harbin had his chance to pull up to the curb. Just ahead of and behind them, other cabs were letting out passengers and taking them in, redcaps and drivers shuffling baggage.

Norlund delayed getting out. "What about Jerry? You said he wasn't in that truck just now."

"We're doing what we can for him, Alan. He's not hurt. But he's in a time-bind situation. That means we could have trouble sending him home."

"Like me."

"We know there's a problem in your case. I'm not sure yet about him. When he showed up in Eighty-four and we realized what had happened, we put him to sleep with drugs, to keep him from learning too much, and just to keep him out of the way until we can deal with his case."

"Learning too much?"

"Sometimes, in this crazy business, knowing too much can be as bad as knowing too little. So I've got him stashed away in my own place in Eighty-four Chicago. The condominium I usually live in when I'm there. I hope to be able to get back to him within a couple of hours after I left him. There was just no one to spare for baby-sitting."

"Brandi's side is keeping you all busy."

Ginny ignored that, except for a small sigh. "Now to business, quickly. You'll go into the station here and get yourself a compartment on the *Twentieth Century*. That's a crack train on the New York Central railroad,

and it departs for New York in about twenty minutes."
She handed Norlund a scrap of paper. "Use this name
until you reach New York. Then use your own."

"What if there's no compartment available?"

"There will be. If not, get to New York some other
way."

Harbin was already out on the sidewalk, in his
character of taxi driver holding the rear door open for
Norlund.

"Okay," said Norlund, and got out. His hat was in
his hand, and now he put it on. He took the traveling
bag from Ginny's hand and nodded to her and Harbin.
His feelings were a curious mixture. Relief at being
rescued, anger at being put in a situation where res-
cue became necessary. There were other feelings in the
mixture too. Somehow, and this was the odd part, he
just wasn't as outraged as he might have been about
the way these people had treated him—drugging him
and sending him into danger for some unexplained
purpose. Was he drugged now? He didn't think so. It
was as if, from the start, he had really been looking
for some kind of all-out test.

Harbin was getting back into the driver's seat. Now
all the cab's doors slammed and it pulled away, frus-
trating the efforts of a woman who tried to flag it
down.

Norlund stared after it, but only for a moment.
Then he straightened his rumpled garments as best he
could, hoisted his bag, and strode into the railroad
station, along with an intermittent stream of other
weekend travelers.

Inside, the station was a temple of light-colored
stone. Dim and lofty, like a museum, but smelling
faintly of disinfectant and cigars and coal. Obviously,
some people were not suffering from the Depression;

Norlund saw no signs of poverty among the people entraining, with their expensive-looking luggage.

He stood briefly in line at one of the several ticket windows that were open in the vast marble concourse, and without any trouble bought the ticket that he was supposed to buy. Glancing at the scrap of paper given him by Ginny, he reserved the compartment in the name of Earl Greenidge. Briefly, Norlund wondered if that man still existed, or ever had, and what had happened to him. *A new timeline is being created here. I don't think we've ever really discussed timelines with you.*

Someday she would, though. As soon as she really wanted to get around to it.

Bah. They kept manipulating him. Yet here he was, still following orders. And, yes, looking forward to what might happen next.

Consulting the timetable he'd been given with his ticket, and looking at a poster or two displayed in the station, Norlund confirmed that the train he was about to board was one of the crack specials. According to the schedule it should take him only about twenty hours to reach New York. Briefly he wondered if regular airline service between the two cities had yet been established. He doubted there was regular passenger service but he wasn't sure. Too bad Ginny hadn't arranged for him to go by air—that would have been something of an adventure.

His train was boarding already, a giant's voice booming almost unintelligibly over the station loudspeakers to announce the track number. Still moving with a trickle of fellow passengers, Norlund showed his ticket and was allowed to pass the gate. Moving from a temple of light marble into an even vaster cavern of steel girders and tracks and steam, he passed along a broad concrete walk, stretching into an invisible distance. There were tracks to right and left, and gray, grimy skylights far above. An engine bell was clanging, and the hiss and smell of steam hung in the air, along with the psychic electricity of a sooty airport. Norlund's bag was snatched from his hand by an insistent porter, who carried it on ahead, leading him to his Pullman car.

1984

Later, much later, when Jerry had been granted the time and a platform of relative sanity from which to look back, he could not remember in which direction he had turned first on leaving the tall apartment building. Nor could he recall exactly what had influenced his decisions at the time, or what he had been thinking. Nor which shock was the most decisive, among all the shocks that he was subject to within the next few minutes. Nor just how far he had walked, nor on what erratic course, before he came at last to a halt.

When he did halt he was on the lakefront, leaning his elbows on a low concrete wall that ran just inland of a broad paved walk. Just beyond the walk were piled boulders and low wooden pilings and lapping waves. To Jerry's right, as he faced the lake, there began a border of sand beach.

Farther south, perhaps a mile away in the same

direction, a building of glass and black steel went up to something like a hundred stories, dwarfing the recognizable Drake Hotel in front of it. Jerry knew, he knew damn well, that there was no building anything like that black monster in Chicago. Yet here was the lake, and he'd seen some familiar street names. And down there was the Drake, a footstool now instead of a tower. . . . Nor ought there to be so many buildings of the size of those surrounding the black giant. And their grouping strongly suggested to Jerry that they were only the front ranks, that more like them would be massed behind them to the south, around the Loop.

Jerry stood there for some time, leaning on the wall. For a while he would gaze at the tall buildings, and try to think about them. But his ability to think seemed to exist only intermittently, and he'd find himself staring at something else, not thinking about anything at all.

Just in front of Jerry, a little complex of concrete game tables adorned the strip of parkland that separated the lake and a wide, busy street. The wall that Jerry leaned on was part of this table complex, which was shaded by trees and more concrete. Game boards were inlaid into the tabletops, and there were concrete benches for the players to sit on. A couple of chess sculptures of the same material, almost life-sized, looked on over the players' shoulders just as Jerry did. Most of the boards were currently in use, and kibitzers had accumulated from the trickle of people passing on the walk. Most of the people nearby were wearing beach clothes, hot-weather clothes, clothes that looked quite strange to Jerry.

Among all the thousands of people Jerry had seen on the street and in the park since leaving the apartment, he couldn't remember anyone who had been dressed very much in the way that he was dressed. On the other hand, no one had really appeared to think his clothes were odd. There'd been such diversity that maybe it just didn't matter.

A good number of people were out today, enjoying the park and the beach and the nice weather. Most of them were young adults, or maybe high school kids. Some cruised along the broad lakefront walk on bicycles. Some, whether biking or walking, wore earphones, as if they might have little radio sets hidden in their handlebars or somehow concealed on their bodies, and faraway listening looks on their faces.

Not all the radios were connected to headsets and inaudible to others. Jerry could hear music ... of a kind. Mostly it sounded like little kids whining, unable to sound grown-up, while instruments banged with the monotony of punch presses.

On the beach Jerry could see niggers, playing around and stretched out on the sand, mixed right in among the white people, who seemed to be paying them no attention at all. Jerry might have stared longer at this phenomenon, but he was distracted by the girls. Most of the girls on the beach, white and colored, were wearing about as little as Sally Rand probably had on behind her fans. And no one but Jerry seemed to be paying much attention to the girls, either.

And now he momentarily forgot even about the girls. An airplane had come along; there seemed to be quite a lot of airplanes, and Jerry raised his head to gape at it. The sounds these aircraft made were like their shapes, smooth and quick as bullets—but again, nobody cared.

Jerry removed his elbows from the wall and slowly turned around. He took off his cap and ran his fingers through his hair. He could see no other caps like his anywhere. No regular fedora hats, either. Most men were bareheaded, and needed haircuts. There were a few straw hats and odd caps. So there could be another cap like his around here somewhere. . . .

Here came a young guy walking by, wearing a kind of undershirt with short sleeves, colored yellow. Across his chest like advertising a message was emblazoned in blue: SPOCK LIVES. And a picture of a hand, raised in what Jerry Rosen thought looked like an old Jewish prayer sign. Whatever in the hell . . .

And now a pair of young men walking by together. Their hair was so long that you'd think they had to be fairies—or at least something very odd, like violin players. God, they must be fairies; one of them was wearing a necklace, a thin gold chain round a tanned, brawny neck. But nobody even looked . . .

Between the moments in which he took in all these marvels, Jerry's eyes kept coming back to the chess players. They were doing something that he could understand. They were being calm about it, once in a while getting quietly excited, just like the chess players he'd known when he was a kid. Jerry's father played, and when he was a little kid living with his father, Jerry himself had gotten quite good at it. Good for a little shaver, anyway. Right now chess was one of the few things in this new world that Jerry felt able to recognize with any certainty. The lake was another. Maybe that was why the sight of chessplayers beside the lake had brought him to a halt.

A blond girl on the beach screamed something, throwing a beach ball, and one of her tits almost fell out of its tiny halter—chalk up one more thing recognizable, unchanged. Even if Jerry wasn't capable of enjoying it right at this moment.

Now another fancy undershirt came past, this one reading DRACULA SUCKS. Jerry got the point; he'd seen *Dracula* just last year when it first came out. And now a guy could put on a shirt like that, that made jokes about cocksucking, and walk around in public with it on and not be arrested. Nobody even looked up from their own concerns to notice him. . . .

One of the chessplayers was a nigger, wearing a gold wristwatch on one brown arm coming out of a short-sleeved pink shirt. Nobody cared what color the player was, or his shirt either. The pieces that brown arm reached for and picked up were just the same shape, the same style, as those that Jerry's father had taught him to play with. Except maybe these pieces were not real ivory. Or maybe they could be.

Jerry watched the chess games. He began to get interested, following their progress, switching his attention from one board to another. Leaning on the wall again, he was able to become absorbed in the play for long seconds at a time, thereby dulling his awareness of other problems, and maybe incidentally keeping himself from going nuts.

His problem was not that he didn't know where he was. Or that he hadn't grasped what must have happened to him. He had grasped those things all right; he had gotten the basic fact, though he didn't begin to understand it. And despite the fact that, in his science-fictional imaginings, Jerry had never pictured it this way.

No, he had never pictured it like this.

And now Jerry found the craziest goddamn thing happening to him. Leaning there against the wall in the sunshine, watching the sailboats playing out there on the calm lake, and the girls walking by in G-strings, and the sleek airplanes cruising overhead and the giant buildings and the calm chessplayers—watching all that, Jerry Rosen began to cry.

He wasn't noisy about it. He usually hadn't been noisy about crying, as a kid. The tears just oozed and trickled out, and he had the old childhood tight, burning feeling in his throat. The people around him, used to ignoring marvels, ignored this one, too: a grown man standing here and blubbering.

The chessboards blurred now when he tried to look at them. And Jerry was mad as hell at himself for crying, and madder because he didn't even know what he was crying for.

Was it for Judy, who might be dead and gone by this year, whatever this year was? No, he had no gut feeling that Judy was lost to him. However he had arrived here, she was waiting for him at home. And if he had been able to get here, he would be able to get back.

Maybe he was bawling for all those great big beautiful buildings, for the guys who had built them all and now nobody cared. Maybe for the girls on the beach, who had taken almost everything off, and now nobody bothered to look. Maybe for the kids who wandered around with earphones on so they could listen to punch presses. As if they wished that they were somewhere else, as if they were still living in the Depression instead of having all of this. . . .

"Sir, are you all right?" The blurry forms of two women, one white, one colored, had stopped at Jerry's side.

In an outrage of shame he tried to clear his vision, to wipe tears from his face. More still oozed and trickled. To stand here crying like some goddamned baby. . . . The two women were probably in their thirties, Jerry thought. Dressed in blouses and shorts, dressed younger than their age, though they were not in G-strings.

"I . . ." In his hurt confusion his first impulse was to snap some obscenity at the two women and drive them off. But he choked on the words and could not get them out.

"What's wrong?" This, the second to speak, was the colored one. They both sounded alert and practical. Schoolteachers maybe, or nurses, off duty.

"I said I'm all right. All right. Just lay off me. Forget it." Jerry had started to pull himself together. He thought that his face must still look strange, but give him a minute. He was making progress.

" . . . stoned." This was from the white woman, speaking in a low voice toward her companion's ear, meanwhile tugging gently at the colored's arm. And Jerry, not understanding, for one imaginative moment could imagine a crowd suddenly forming around him—except for the chessplayers, who would go on playing—and gathering up stones to hurl at him, Jerry, the outsider, as soon as these women gave the order.

The two women retreated slightly. Had he scared them off? No, they were just making room in front of him for someone else.

This was a younger woman, with dark hair and blue eyes, blurrily familiar to Jerry. Not from his own world, but from somewhere earlier in this mad aventure . . . from the dream. She was wearing blue jeans and a blue shirt, and was looking haggard and relieved at the same time.

"Jerry? We've been looking for you."

"Oh," he said. And was suddenly wary. When the people in his dream had been arguing about his fate, which side had this woman been on?

"Oh, good," murmured one of the first pair of

women, half to herself, half to the newcomer. "We were wondering. . . . "

The blue-eyed young woman leaned closer to Jerry, putting a hand on his arm. "Jerry? Come along with me now, won't you?"

"Okay." He sure as hell didn't have anyplace else in mind to go. He let go the concrete wall that had been supporting him.

With the young woman holding Jerry's arm, the two of them walked inland through the park, following a paved path. Not very far ahead, the path descended into a pedestrian underpass. Now Jerry could vaguely remember coming through the underpass earlier, to get out here to the park. Waiting for them just where the path started to dip was a young man, who also appeared relieved at the sight of Jerry. The young man had longish hair; Jerry could see he was going to have to stop noticing hair. He wasn't sure if he could recall the young man's face or not, from that interval he had once taken to be a dream.

With Jerry in the middle the three of them walked down into the pedestrian tunnel that burrowed beneath what a glimpsed street sign said was Lake Shore Drive. Yeah, Jerry reassured himself again, this was Chicago.

The young woman had a firm hold on his arm. "Jerry, do you remember my name? It's Ginny, Ginny Butler. Now we're going to take you to where you can lie down and get some rest. After that I'll be able to explain things to you better. We're your friends. Everything is going to be all right." Her voice was full of soothing tones.

"Can I go home?"

They were already at the end of the short tunnel, emerging from under the multi-lane drive of traffic into bright sunlight, amid tall apartment buildings.

Ginny replied carefully. "We're going to work on getting you home right away. As soon as you've had some rest. You did a good job with Mr. Norlund, by the way. He's told me so himself."

"He's here?"

"Unfortunately, not right now. But he was okay when last I saw him."

Jerry's hands were in his trousers pockets. "What happened to my money? I had a buck and a half."

"We were intending to return that to you, with your other things. You can have them all as soon as we get back to my place. You see, I didn't realize you'd wake up so soon."

"Oh." Her place meant that he'd awakened in her bed. He looked at her again, more closely, but he still couldn't remember anything else.

The young man explained, "We had to look at all your things, see, to try to make sure of who you were."

Jerry nodded. His head was swimming and his eyes ached, as if he'd been staring for a long time into the sun. Maybe that was from the crying. He wasn't crying any longer, but to rest his eyes he walked without raising them from the sidewalk just ahead of him.

He asked: "Anybody got a cigarette?"

"Afraid not," said the young man.

"Sorry, I don't," said Ginny Butler. Without a pause she continued. "Jerry, it must have been something of a shock for you, waking up like that, in a strange place. What have you been doing since you woke up?"

He got the impression that much might depend on his answer to that question, though she had put it casually enough. He thought his answer over carefully. "Walking," he said at last.

"Talk to anyone?"

"Hardly anyone. Just those two women, I think. Couple of words."

Now the young man was unlocking the door of an automobile, one of a line of low vehicles parked along a curb. The young man held the door for Jerry, who had to bend his head way down to get in. It was a painfully cramped vehicle inside, though on the outside almost as bullet-smooth as the aircraft Jerry had just been watching.

A tiny female voice spoke from the mysterious dashboard, telling Jerry to put on his seatbelt, please. The young man had to show Jerry how the belt worked, and help him to fasten it. Then they were on their way, with Ginny driving. The gearshifting arrangement, Jerry noted, was strange. Even with seatbelts on they didn't go very fast, or very far for that matter. Presently they were nosing down into an underground garage beneath a tall apartment building. Jerry assumed it was the one he'd walked away from.

They led him into an elevator at one side of the underground garage, and a minute later they were all back in the apartment, entering this time by way of a fancy hallway and the front door. An old man with white hair, unfamiliar to Jerry, was sitting in the living room as the three of them came into the apartment; he got to his feet, looking at them as if he'd been expecting their arrival. He was taller than Norlund, and even older-looking. So far no one had told Jerry either of the men's names.

After a brief whispered conference with the old man, Ginny led Jerry into the kitchen, and marched him right up to face the calendar on the wall. He hadn't really looked at the calendar before, not to take in any of the numbers.

She held his arm and spoke to him gently. "Do you

understand what you're looking at, Jerry? Does it start to explain some things for you?"

"I understand. Nineteen eighty-four." And he repeated the year to himself, under his breath. "But I already figured it out. I didn't know exactly what year it was, but . . . nineteen eighty-four." He said it to himself again, and nodded as if with satisfaction.

Ginny studied him for a moment. Then she pointed a red fingernail at one square in the monthly chart. "This is today," she told him softly.

The particular day she had pointed at didn't really stay with Jerry. He didn't really take in the month, either. He was still looking at the year. "That's fifty years," he said, in a wistful, abstracted voice. "Fifty-one years, really."

"Yes," said Ginny encouragingly. She and the old man, who had come into the kitchen after them, exchanged what looked like hopeful nods. "Yes, it is," she repeated.

"Holy cow," said Jerry. Somehow in this situation he felt reluctant to swear, and not just because there was a lady present. It was because the situation went beyond any swear words that he could possible have come up with.

He moved away a little, to the nearby dining alcove, and sat down in one of the funny metal-tubing chairs. Ginny presently came to stand over him, holding out money. It was, he realized, the dollar and a half that he'd been missing. Jerry took it, and the young man came, holding the other items that had been in Jerry's pockets. He stowed the stuff away, except for one cigarette, which he lit up. Someone brought him a small ashtray.

Then Jerry realized that he was still wearing his cap in the house, and he took it off. Not that it mattered at all, but . . . he lost the train of his thoughts, and just sat there looking at his cap, twirling it slowly in his fingers.

He looked up to see Ginny and the old man looking at him. The young man was now nowhere to be seen.

"My kid," Jerry said at last, "will be grown up. Grown up, hell—he'll be a paunchy old man probably. And Judy . . ."

The two people were listening to him with sympathy, he thought. But he realized with a shock that they were not interrupting him with soothing protests and telling him that everything was certain to be all right.

"I gotta get back," said Jerry, with an edge of panic in his voice. And he got swiftly to his feet.

"We want to help you do that." Ginny reacted at once, like a kind nurse, and stood beside him patting his arm. "That's one of our highest priorities. And the first step toward helping you is giving you a little test. Unless you'd like to take a rest first?"

Jerry fought down incipient panic. "No. Let's get on with it." Still he held back, irrationally reluctant, when Ginny tugged gently at his arm. But after a moment he let himself be steered down the hall and into the second bedroom, where the deformed typewriter waited on a table. The old man was already seated in front of it, doing something with it.

"This won't hurt," Ginny assured Jerry brightly. "It won't even tickle. It'll help you remember certain things better, and it may cause you to forget a few things too—just sit down here, will you Jerry? But the things you forget won't be anything you care about. And there won't be many of them anyway."

Jerry, reluctant again, momentarily hung back. But what else was he going to do? He sat down. The old man—Ginny now called him Dr. Harbin—came and helped adjust bands on Jerry's wrists and forehead, connecting him to the machine.

"Like a lie detector," Jerry muttered. At least it was like a version of the lie detector that he'd seen in movies.

"Something like that," Ginny agreed cheerfully.

With his eyes Jerry followed the smoothly insulated wires that connected him to the typewriter. Now the glass screen on the little box came alive with rows of letters and numbers; Jerry caught just a glimpse of it before Dr. Harbin turned the box away from him.

Then the old man raised his hands over the keyboard and began to type.

When next Jerry looked up, he felt disoriented. Ginny and the old guy were already rolling up wires, putting things back into boxes, and he realized that the test must be over.

"How'd I do?" he asked.

"Just fine," said Ginny. "Lean back and rest."

Eventually it had grown dark outside, and only he and Ginny were left in the apartment. The old man, like the nameless young one, had departed without Jerry noticing exactly when or how. Now Jerry was sitting in a deep chair in the living room, while Ginny moved around him, turning on lights. "Come into the kitchen and talk to me," she said, "while I fix dinner."

He came along, and sat nearby in the dining alcove, on one of the tubular chairs turned backwards, while Ginny bustled about in the kitchen. She had a neat shape, Jerry thought, watching her turn and move. But right now he couldn't really get interested. There was too much else on his mind. Including Judy.

He tried to distract himself. "Boy," he said, "I used

to read in magazines, you know, about the future. I didn't think my first day in the nineteen-eighties would ever be like this." Jerry paused, then in a different tone added: "Hey—"

"What?" Ginny gave him a quick smile in passing.

"It just hit me," Jerry said. "I mean, to wonder whether I'm still alive around here somewhere? I mean, I could be walking around out there—" he gestured toward the darkening windows, "—seventy years old. Am I? I mean . . ."

Ginny paused with the refrigerator door open. Outside of its funny color, Jerry thought, the appliance didn't look all that different from the one Ma Monahan was hoping to buy. "I understand what you're asking. But it's not a question I'd want to answer for you. Even if I knew the answer, which at this minute I don't. In this game it's sometimes dangerous to know things."

Jerry chuckled suddenly. "I played games like that before, doll." He wished he felt as confident as he now sounded.

Ginny got moving again. "I hope you like chicken."

"Crazy about it."

While the chicken was cooking she kept bustling around, getting other things ready. Meanwhile they talked, mostly about him. What magazines he'd liked to read in the Thirties, that had given him his ideas of what the Eighties and other decades might be like— stuff like that. And how he'd met Judy, and what objections her family had had to her marrying someone outside the Church. What kind of jobs Jerry had worked at—he decided not to mention the bootlegging just now. Maybe later, when he knew more about what kind of an operation was going on here. How he'd met Norlund, hitchhiking. . . .

Then dinner was ready, which was fine with Jerry, who by now felt starved. The food was served in what he considered a very fancy style, with a glass of wine, good-tasting wine, beside each plate. Ginny had the knack—hell, she was a genius at it—for making a guy feel at ease, ready, eager to do whatever she wanted him to do. Jerry had now and then encountered other people with the same skill, his own sixth grade teacher especially. But never before anyone who could do it as smoothly as this.

When dinner was over, he even found himself volunteering to help with the dishes. Wow, if Judy could have heard him say that. . . . He'd volunteer to help Judy too, yes by God he would, as soon as he got back to her.

Actually the kitchen clean-up didn't take long. When Ginny had the coffee started, she asked, "How about if we watch some television?"

"Great." Maybe, thought Jerry, at least the television would be the way it had been in some of the stories.

"Let's see what's on." She led the way back into the living room.

Jerry seated himself with a good view of the screen. Sure enough, the picture came in sharper than on a movie screen, and in bright, real-looking colors. Ginny could switch from one station to another just like that, without any fumbling around trying to tune them in. She settled on some kind of story in which people were frantically chasing each other around, while in the background waves of laughter ebbed and flowed, evidently coming from some unseen studio audience. Actually Jerry couldn't understand what they all thought was so funny, but then he supposed he'd missed the early part of the story.

Ginny brought in the coffee. He was sitting at one end of the sofa, but she sat in a separate chair. Don't worry, lady, I got enough on my mind without. . . . It was safer to watch television than to start thinking of Judy.

He wanted to get interested in the story, such as it was, but ads kept breaking in. Jerry was reminded of one summer when, as a kid, he'd visited relatives in a small Illinois town. On clear Saturday nights, movies sponsored by local merchants had been shown, free to anyone who wanted to sit on the grass in an empty lot. There were breaks for slide-projected ads—not as many breaks as this. A lot of these television ads looked like cartoons, but Jerry couldn't figure out how anyone had ever managed to draw them.

After a while, Ginny looked over as if checking on him. She found Jerry watching her intensely.

Jerry said, "Look, if you send me home, I'm gonna keep quiet about all this, if that's what you want. I swear it."

"I know you'd keep quiet. You don't have to swear to that."

"Hey, no, I mean it."

"I'm sure you do. But it doesn't really matter whether you do or not. Because if we do send you home, we'll insist on treating you to a little forgetfulness therapy first. You won't remember where you've been. You couldn't talk about this if you wanted to."

"Whaddya mean, *if* you do send me home?"

She remained calm. "I mean if. It's not at all a certainty. You should understand that. There are a lot of things that have to be taken into consideration, and the final choice isn't up to me."

Jerry tried digesting this. "What about that test you gave me? I thought that was what decided."

"The results of that test will have a lot to do with the final decision. And one of the things we were testing you for was how well you'd take to the forget- • fulness treatment. On some people it doesn't work too well."

"So, how did I do?"

"The results aren't in yet. We'll hear when they are." And with an appearance of calm, Ginny turned her attention back to the television screen. She appeared to be really interested in hearing how the bubbles of gas in the intestine had some resemblance to beer.

Next thing, some woman jumped off a motorcycle and started complaining about her hemorrhoids. Jesus, this television was just too embarrassing and disgusting for Jerry to cling to it as a distraction. Suddenly feeling trapped, he got up and wandered off through the apartment. He didn't want to stay in the apartment and he didn't dare try to leave. There was literally no place for him to go if he did run out. Jesus. . . .

As long as he was passing the bathroom anyway, he went in to take a leak. Then he washed his hands and came back out to the living room. His first day in the future.

Ginny was still watching the screen as if she were interested. There was a different program on now; it looked like a regular movie in black and white. There was background music, like a movie would have, but no waves of laughter.

Ginny turned her head. "I thought maybe you'd find this more interesting."

He asked her: "What if, when the results of the test come back, the answer's no?"

"It won't be an absolutely final no. There'll still be things we can try."

"Yeah? Like what?"

"We'll see. If it becomes necessary."

"When'll we know the test results?"

"Probably in a few hours. I'll get a phone call."

Jerry nodded wearily. He wondered if he wanted to sit on the sofa again. He started watching the movie while standing. Presently he asked, "Who's this guy? The star?"

"Humphrey Bogart. This is quite an old movie, actually. Almost from your time."

"I don't remember him. I don't know who he is." Jerry wasn't sure if he remembered the leading actress' face or not.

Ginny considered calmly. "I think he's on stage, on Broadway, in Thirty-three. Not terribly famous yet."

"Yeah. Well." Jerry did sit down, then looked around him restlessly. "You got a drink around somewhere? I think maybe it'd help."

She looked at him. "Yes, perhaps it would. Then I think you'd better get some sleep, even if it's early in the evening. I don't have to remind you that you've been through a hard day."

"Yeah." But he knew he wasn't going to sleep any time soon. There was a nice soft bed in her room, where he'd spent last night—without her, by all indications—and some kind of a cot in the other. Eventually he supposed he would head for the cot.

Ginny had gone into the kitchen, presumably to see about a drink, and Jerry looked at the television. Now some guy had come on in full color, sounding very sincere, to say how the Democrats just had to be elected this year, to save the country from the awful mess that the Republicans had created over the last four years.

Ginny was back, carrying two glasses; Jerry was glad to see that she was joining him.

"Hey," he called, struck by a sudden curiosity. "You guys still got Prohibition?"

"One problem," said Ginny, "that we are spared. Cheers."

"Cheers," echoed Jerry, and their glasses clinked. On the little television screen, by coincidence, Humphrey Bogart — what a name — was hoisting his glass, too.

"Y'know," Jerry heard himself blurting out, "I never been unfaithful to Judy, anything like that. We been married more than a year now."

"You certainly were not unfaithful to her last night, if that's what's worrying you." Ginny approached her own drink as if she expected to enjoy it. "What did you get her for your anniversary?"

"Huh." Jerry felt an odd mixture of relief and disappointment at having his innocence confirmed; he could feel his ears burning lightly. "What *could* I get her? I took her to a movie, lucky I could afford that. And we stopped and had ice cream."

Ginny said something soothing. He wasn't listening. The movie had been interrupted again for ads. Another politician in full color, sounding trustworthy and honest, saying how under this Republican administration things were really going great again, and telling everybody to remember what a mess the Democrats had left everything in four years ago.

The movie came back, and Jerry was able to get involved in it, at least for short stretches as he had with the games of chess. Now someone slipped Humphrey Bogart a Mickey Finn; Humphrey put down his drink, rubbed his face a few times, his vision blurred, and down he went. Then a runty, nasty-looking little guy kicked him in the head.

Jerry looked at his own drink, which was almost

finished. He was very sleepy now. But in his case, of course, feeling sleepy was only natural. Anyway Ginny Butler didn't have to worry that he was going to make a pass at her. She was out of the room right now, but when she came back he was going to ask her if anyone had yet thought about trying to get to the Moon. . . .

When Jerry awoke, he was sprawled, fully dressed, across the getting-to-be-familiar bed. This time the door to the bedroom had been left ajar. From somewhere out in the apartment there came a murmur of voices, not especially trying to be quiet. Again it was broad daylight outside the blinds, and the funny clock on the dresser read 8:34.

Reflexively Jerry checked his pockets. This time he still had his money, and all the rest of his stuff, too.

No headache this time. Actually he felt pretty good, reasonably rested and unwilling to worry over whether or not he'd been slipped something in last night's drink. Looking at himself in the bathroom mirror, he wondered . . . but it didn't matter. At least he'd gotten a good night's sleep.

But he was going to have to shave soon. Running his fingers through his hair to comb it, Jerry mooched along down the hall to the second bedroom. The cot in one corner of that room now appeared to have been used, but the two other people present were up and dressed. Ginny was seated at the worktable, along with a colorless-looking man of about forty that Jerry couldn't remember having seen before. Ginny and the man were looking at the typewriter device as if they might be studying how to work it, or maybe like two rich people at a stock ticker—not that Jerry had ever actually seen one of those. Now the machine came briefly to life, though no one was touching it, and chattered out part of a roll of paper.

"Hello," Jerry said.

Both of the people at the table looked up. "Jerry," said Ginny, "this is Mr. Schiller. He's my boss."

"Rosen," said Mr. Schiller. He had an authoritative voice, and somehow his appearance was not so colorless once he'd spoken. "Rosen. So, you're Jewish, right?"

In a cold voice Jerry gave his usual, automatic answer: "I don't work at it." And only then did he remember one conviction that he'd always held about the future, that magical world of fifty or a hundred years to come. By the time that men were getting ready to travel into space, things on Earth would have changed to the point where nobody cared any more who had a Jewish background and who did not. Maybe somewhere on the home planet there would still be people who practiced being Jews—well, let 'em. No one else would worry about who those peoples' relatives might be.

"Ginny, do you mind?" asked Schiller. He spoke without taking his faintly smiling eyes off Jerry. Ginny shook her head no, murmured something and got up and went out of the room, shutting the door behind her.

The typewriter, possessed by some ghost of science, burped out a few more lines at incredible speed. Schiller ignored it. He was still watching Jerry. "Sit down," Schiller said. Maybe it was an order, maybe an invitation. Anyway Jerry sat.

Schiller said: "I'm Jewish too, as it happens. That's one of the reasons why I wanted to talk to you myself. I do work at it, as you put it . . . though I suppose not in the way that someone of your time and place would expect. But never mind that. I want to begin to explain to you what this is all about. It is not by any means a strictly Jewish enterprise—though I think you'll agree, when I've explained, that we as Jews do have a special stake in it."

This was just about the last goddamned thing that Jerry had been expecting to hear. He was so surprised that for a moment he could almost believe that the whole time-travel business was a fake.

"All right," Jerry said. "You can be Jewish, or not, but don't expect me to. You be an Eskimo if you want; me, I'm just trying to get along. To get home. But these guys here tell me I'm gonna have a problem doing that."

Schiller faced him solemnly. "It's quite likely that you'll never be able to get home. I hope the people here made that clear to you."

Jerry felt a chill begin somewhere near the middle of his gut. It spread rapidly. "They told me they were waiting for test results."

"I've seen them. They were not good."

The chill spread further.

"But," Schiller added, deliberately, "there is, possibly, just one way."

Now Jerry could feel the relief, a great quivering wave of it that started down in his legs somewhere and came up through his stomach mixed with anger. He tried hard to keep the relief from showing in his face, but he didn't think that he succeeded. To hell with it. He ought to have known. All that crap they'd been feeding him so far about how hard it would be to get him back home, how probably he'd never see his family again, all that had been just to set him up for some proposition that they were now about to hit him with. They were just like cops in some precinct station, softening up some poor son of a bitch with threats of prison, to get him to confess or else to rat on his friends.

Jerry tried even harder to look calm. Now the hard pitch, whatever it was, was coming. He'd know in a minute what these bastards really wanted from him.

Schiller asked him, "Have you ever heard of Adolf Hitler?"

Jerry didn't know quite what he'd been expecting to hear next, but that wasn't it. He blinked. "Sure, he's . . . I mean, in nineteen thirty-three he was the new Chancellor, whatever the hell they call it, over in Germany."

"Right. And what have you heard about what he and his people were doing in that year?"

Jerry considered. "There was a lot of talk in the papers, that they were against the Jews."

"More than talk, wasn't it?"

Jerry shrugged. "If you say so. What do I know?"

Schiller nodded agreement. "Now, have you heard anything at all about Hitler since your clockwise trip? I mean, since you arrived here in Eighty-four?"

Ignorance can be a help in this game, Ginny had told him at some point. Well, he didn't have to fake ignorance this time. "No. Don't tell me he's still alive."

"I trust not. Not here and now in this timeline. Jerry, I want you to watch a little historical show. Ginny ought to be getting ready now to run it on the television in the next room. It's about the things that happened in Germany—in Europe, in the whole world—in the late Thirties and the early Forties."

Now Jerry could hear other voices, muted by the closed door. People certainly tended to come and go suddenly around here. Now there was a tap on the door; Schiller called out and it opened. A young guy of about Jerry's own age stuck his head into the room.

It wasn't the same fellow who'd come with Ginny to the park.

"Ginny says she's 'bout ready, Mr. Schiller." This one had something of a southern accent, and his brown hair was just growing out of a crewcut.

"Right." Schiller got to his feet. "Jerry Rosen, meet Andy Burns. We picked up Andy in Forty-three, and he works for us now full time—how's the job suit you so far?"

"Jes' fine, sir." It sounded like it might possibly be the truth.

"Andy will be able to confirm parts of what we're about to show you, from his own experience. But he doesn't really know the whole story himself as yet, so I want him to watch also. It'll help fill in the picture for him. Eventually, of course, you'll both be able to confirm all of it from other sources." Schiller motioned them out into the living room, and followed. "If you're ready, Ginny, let's start the show."

Afterward Jerry estimated that the show could have lasted no longer than half an hour. While it was going on, though, it seemed longer than that, though it was not what he would have called boring. Sickening would be more like it. When it was over, he got to his feet from the sofa as if he were about to leave a theater, feeling somewhat shaken. Looking at Andy Burns, he could see his own feelings mirrored in the other's face.

The others, perhaps by design, almost at once left the two of them alone. They sat down again, looking at each other silently. Then Andy got out cigarettes, and offered one. They lit up.

Jerry began. "You believe that, what we just saw? The shower baths with poison gas, and the ovens, and all that?" Again he felt an awed reluctance to use swear words. In his mind's eye he could still see the piles of babies' toys and clothes. "You believe six million people, or eight million, or whatever in hell the number was?"

Andy, looking back at him, was thinking it over very seriously. "Well, Ah gotta believe part of it. Ah was in that 'ere war they're talkin' about. In fact Ah was damn near kilt in it . . . and we knew Hitler was doin' some of that stuff." Andy paused. "Shit yes, Ah guess Ah gotta believe it all."

Schiller had re-entered the living room. "I'd like to talk to Jerry alone again."

Andy took his cue and left. But at the same time Ginny reappeared from the kitchen, looking over Schiller's shoulder. Schiller, Jerry realized, was not very big.

"Did you understand your job with Mr. Norlund very well?" the graying, smallish man asked Jerry.

"No. I didn't have to. I just did what he told me."

"What did you think those little units were, that the two of you were installing?"

"I dunno. He said we were taking a survey. They were to record signals or whatever. I don't know nothing about radio."

Schiller nodded as if satisfied. "Would it make you feel better to know that you've already done a lot to keep Hitler suppressed in a new timeline?"

Ginny put in quietly, "We haven't had a good opportunity to discuss timelines with Jerry yet."

Schiller gave her a look that subtly conveyed dissatisfaction. Then he addressed Jerry. "Say that there are worlds, universes, in which Hitler is successful—in some of them, beyond his own wildest dreams of world domination. And there are other worlds in which he's cut off early, forced into total failure. There are

Europes where World War Two is fought, and the death camps that you just saw really exist—and there are other Europes where humanity is spared all that."

"I can imagine that," said Jerry, the experienced reader of science fiction. "Yeah, all right. I'm glad I did my part against Hitler." And he waited warily for what was coming next.

"You've contributed a lot, as I said," said Schiller slowly. "But I don't think your job is quite over yet." He paused, waiting for a reaction that did not come. Then he proceeded. "Suppose it should be up to you, Jerry, to decide: which kind of world, of the two I've mentioned, do you want your wife to live in and your child to grow up in?"

"I want the one where I'm going back to them," said Jerry stubbornly.

"The only one in which you have a chance of going back to them, is the one in which you work for us."

"And what would I have to do?"

"It would work like this," Schiller said, choosing his words slowly. "After you've been given some training, I would send you back to Chicago, in nineteen thirty-four."

"Thirty-four? That'd be a whole year I was gone."

Schiller held up an appeasing hand. "Meanwhile, you might possibly be able to communicate with your wife, let her know that you are coming back . . . but the big point is this. That you must be willing to do a job for us in the Chicago of that time, before you rejoin your family. Not a long job, maybe a day or two. But a dangerous one, I won't lie to you about that. If anything should happen to you, we'll look out for your wife and kid. And if you come through okay, you stand to collect a pretty good reward yourself. How about it?"

"If that's the only way I can get home, you're really telling me I got no choice." And then Jerry belatedly remembered something.

Schiller saw his expression alter. "What is it, Jerry?"

"I was just remembering. My Dad," Jerry said at last. "He went back to Germany, in nineteen twenty-nine."

1933

For Norlund, who could remember long train rides from his youth, this one began pretty much as expected: a promise of early boredom, and a hint of motion-sickness, flavored with a little soot from coal-burning locomotives. There was no pretense of air conditioning on his train, but fans did keep the air circulating in his compartment, and it was otherwise comfortable enough.

The black porters who served the Pullman cars were professionally jovial, if not quite convincingly cheerful. Norlund wondered if any of them might live in the horrendous south side slums, which were almost the first scenery that the train encountered after it pulled out of the station. He decided that they probably did not. Even false joviality would have to be impossible, he thought, to a dweller in the acres of firetrap ruins and rats. Feeling the guilt of the lucky, he made a mental note to himself to tip the porters well, and continued to watch the slums with a grisly fascination.

Presently the worst blight began to give way to more habitable housing, dingy but endurable, looking very much like the working class realms on the north side. From exclusively black, the inhabitants were again exclusively white. And everywhere was the weedy summer greenery that always sprang up all across the city, wherever pavement or cultivation failed by an inch to cover the earth.

The train was picking up speed now, the clicking rhythm of the wheels accelerating. Now it was gradually emerging from the inner-city tangle of the world's largest railroad yards, making its direction clear, proceeding more and more on a clearly defined and separate line.

We haven't had a chance yet to talk about timelines. At some point Ginny had said that to him. When would the chance come? Whenever she was ready. And what exactly was a timeline?

A few more miles of travel across the south side, and industry was taking over. Meanwhile the tracks were curving gradually from south to east, preparing for their passage round the south end of the lake. Norlund caught one glimpse of the lake, blue and startling between brick factories.

South Chicago, the Indiana border. Calumet City. Gary. Miles of gigantic constructs, visions out of some cartoonist's fevered nightmare about industry, were interspersed with rows of workers' houses. Here in the midst of the Depression, production must be low, and most of what normally ran must be shut down now, on Sunday. Yet what looked like a permanent pall of soot and smoke, from kilns and blast furnaces, hung in the air. A blend of exotic industrial fumes infiltrated the passing train. The lake with its almost uninhabited sand dunes would be just over the horizon here, but along the tracks the world was a parody of power and pollution, a zone of factories incredibly filthier and uglier than it was going to be in fifty years.

The people, Norlund noticed, also looked different from those of fifty years in the future, even allowing for the changes in clothing styles and relative poverty. He could see a difference in the faces of those who stood here and there to watch the train go past. These people had no less anxiety than their children and grandchildren of the Eighties, but these, perhaps, were more willing to be hopeful. These people of the Thirties obviously still saw a train bound to faraway places as a symbol—more than that, a concrete expression—of hope and promise. Children black or white stood almost reverently at grade crossings to observe the flying passage of the *Twentieth Century*, and waved impartially at those who rode it into the future. Each time Norlund tried to wave back before his speed carried him away.

—and then without warning his view was wiped out by a passing freight. Car after car flew past, at doubled speed. He was granted instantaneous glimpses into open boxcar doors. As in detached, flickering frames of film he could see ragged men, hobos, looking back at him, or staring to one side at something he could not guess.

Then the freight was gone again, nonexistent, as if it had never been. The industrial heart of America flowed on, seemingly without end.

It was, in a sense, a scene that Norlund had never seen before. Only time travelers, he thought, could ever see this; not an old movie but reality, rerun with half a century of experience augmenting the perceptions of the beholder. It was a vision of power and beauty, horror and junk, ruthlessness and hope. . . . Norlund knew, for almost the first time in his life, a wish to be a composer or a novelist.

He was roused from reverie by a porter passing in the narrow corridor outside his compartment, whanging a melodious gong.

"Fust call t' dinner . . . fust call t'dinner . . . "

Looking at his watch, Norlund decided that they must be starting to serve early. But he was hungry; lunch in the Greek restaurant with Jerry seemed a very long time ago. And he hadn't been ordered to stay locked up in his compartment for the duration of the trip. He checked his appearance in his private mirror, made sure he had his compartment key, and went out into the corridor.

In the dining car he found linen tablecloths, silver, and flowers in vases on the tables. The menu might have been that of a good restaurant, though the prices, for the time, were high.

Norlund was early enough to have a table to himself. He ate with his thoughts elsewhere, coming back to himself now and then with a start, realizing how rapidly he was becoming accustomed to the change of time.

After dinner he went to the smoking car, and treated himself to a cigar. He sat reading a newspaper, listening with half an ear meanwhile to traveling salesmen nearby complain about business and exchange jokes. Norlund had heard all of their jokes before.

The newspaper was of some interest.

ROOSEVELT DRAFTS MESSAGE
DETAILING PLAN FOR PARLEY
TO INCREASE WORLD PRICES

NEW DIPLOMATIC APPROACH
TO NAZIS URGED

SOVIET RECOGNITION
SEEN IN SEPTEMBER
Provisional recognition of Soviet Russia, at
least to the extent necessary to permit
unhampered trade, is a distinct probability
within the very near future ...

HITLER ALTERS AIM, SEEKING 'EVOLUTION'

ITALIAN FLEET OF 25
SEAPLANES TAKING OFF
... bound for the Century of Progress ...
gesture seen as improving relations with
the Fascist government ... *Graf Zeppelin*
to visit US in October ...

TWO-CENT POSTAL RATE
GOING INTO EFFECT
Letters to cost three cents if sent outside
local districts ...

The salesmen were passing a flask around now,
taking no particular care to conceal it. Booze was of
course still illegal, except for beer. Norlund wondered
if the dining car would have served him a beer if he'd
asked for one; he had no yearning for whatever might
be in that flask.

He thought of law. Whose laws ran here, besides
those that the inhabitants themselves might have passed
and were aware of? Hajo Brandi had invoked the laws
of humanity, as if it were his perfect right to do so.

Norlund at once decided that anyone who spoke so confidently in the name of the People, or of God, was his enemy.

Ginny Butler had invoked no authority, only friendship. Friendship of a precarious sort, and not one that Norlund had had a whole lot of choice about. Well, by their fruits ye shall know them. Ginny had healed his granddaughter, Brandi had slugged him in the face when he was handcuffed.

All this was getting Norlund nowhere. He looked at his newspaper again.

VIENNA DIET
OUSTS ALL NAZI DEPUTIES

JAPANESE CONSOLIDATING
GRIP ON MANCHURIA
Further conflict in north China likely . . .

Ginny Butler didn't claim to speak in the name of anyone, except her boss, whoever that might be. Was that why Norlund tended to trust her and believe her, even after he knew she'd drugged him? Or was he still drugged into doing so? Or because she sent him out on a mission that he was really, deep down, enjoying?

Norlund returned to his compartment to find that his berth had been made up for him, sitting space converted to sleeping space with a surface of taut white sheets, and a blanket that probably would not be necessary. The porter, of course, came and went with his own key. He'd have to remember to tip the porter. . . .

Norlund dreamed that he was riding a train across Manchuria. Japanese soldiers, fugitive characters from the war movies of the Forties yet to come, were charging as cavalry against the train windows from outside. To repel them Norlund had as weapon his old waist gun from the Fortress, a fifty caliber Browning, swivel-mounted. There was supposed to be some modern attachment on the machine gun to keep it from jamming or overheating, and he was pouring out a stream of tracers against the enemy, who for some reason could not seem to break in through the *Twentieth Century*'s glass windows. Norlund's only worry, but it grew and grew as the dream progressed, was that he was going to run out of ammunition before the buzz-bombs appeared, with swastikas on them. Only he could defend London, where the train was headed. And now there was going to be a wreck. . . .

Norlund awoke, luckily, congratulating himself on his good timing, just as the phase of real nightmare was about to start. He lay there sweating, feeling deep pain in his old leg wound, rejoicing in the pain because perhaps it had awakened him. The *Twentieth Century* of his present reality had stopped, somewhere in the anonymous country of the night. The train started up again as he lay there listening, then stopped again. It kept on doing that, shaking with the little jerks and hesitations of its progress. The distant whistle questioned the night. Were they changing engines? Making way for a fast freight? The passengers were never going to know.

Time for night thoughts now. They were of course unwelcome, but he had to have them.

The train was in fast motion when Norlund awoke on Monday morning. He cracked his window shade and obtained another view of a freight train passing, this time with no 'bos to be seen. Now he saw green countryside, fences and farms. He looked at his watch and timetable, and decided that he was somewhere in Pennsylvania.

With nightmares behind him, he felt good, actually eager to get on with things, though when he got up he had enough leg pain to make him limp. And he was sore all over from being manhandled by Brandi and his people, and running in the alley with his arms bound.

Breakfasting in the dining car, he was told that arrival ought to be on time, or very nearly. He thought he might be able to meet his contact at the Empire State Building today.

Arrival in New York actually took place a little after one in the afternoon, local time. Norlund alighted from the train inside another enormous station. Swift alternations of cloud and sunlight made dramatic lighting effects through vast skylights above. He handed the final porter a final tip in exchange for his modest baggage. He had remembered to tip the others, generously he hoped, but not enough to make himself especially memorable.

Avoiding the struggle for taxicabs, he walked out into the streets of Manhattan, carrying his bag. It was decades since he'd been in the Big Apple—and he didn't think anyone in this decade would call it that.

The streets and sidewalks flooring the narrow rectangular canyons were briefly beautiful in the aftermath of rain. Norlund saw people selling flowers out of pushcarts. He crossed Fifth Avenue, watching a doorman in an operatic uniform drive a derelict scavenger away from garbage cans nearby. Garbage cans were distributed everywhere, up and down the street, spoiling the sidewalks' hope of elegance.

Now, in the middle distance, Norlund could see the

Empire State, more prominent now among lower buildings than it would be in fifty years. But the time was already well after one, and Norlund was supposed to meet his contact at around noon. He decided he'd wait until tomorrow, and began to look for a hotel.

He entered a large and impressive one. Uniforms cluttered the lobby, outnumbering the visible guests — there were bellhops, elevator operators, messenger boys, a whole swarm of the underemployed somehow clinging to subsistence jobs.

Going up in the elevator the bellhop, halfway through his teens, gave Norlund a rundown on the types and qualities of bootleg liquor available. He also dropped a broad hint that it wouldn't be hard to arrange for female companionship. Norlund shook his head to both offers, considering that they represented complications that he didn't need right now.

His room was ornate. He wondered if he would be able to leave his shoes out in the hall tonight and find them there shined in the morning; but he decided not to try. He left his bag in his room and went out for a stroll. There were theaters but he didn't want to spend his time seeing old movies. Broadway? Right now, tonight, he'd rather look at life.

He had last visited New York in the early Seventies, when Times Square was already Babylon and Sodom. It was different and more human now in nineteen thirty-three, he thought, for all the beggars.

On Tuesday he got up and breakfasted, hesitated, and told the desk clerk that he'd be keeping his room for one more night. Then he went out. At the Empire State Building he entered the lobby, leaned against the marble wall, and observed the Thirties Modern decor and the passing crowd. The uniforms in the lobby were doubtless on the alert for loitering bums, but Norlund, obviously waiting to keep an appointment, was too well dressed to have to worry about that.

The crowd in Times Square had looked more human than its Eighties counterpart. But this business-hour throng was very little different from what it would be in fifty years, Norlund thought, once you allowed for change in hair styles and in dress, and that this mob was more racially homogeneous. But it was basically the same rush of people, wearing the same concentrated expressions, that he might have seen any day in . . .

"Mr. Norlund?"

The speaker was a man in his fifties, trimly built and about six feet tall. His smooth-shaven face displayed what looked like hopeful relief. Dressed in an expensive-looking summer suit and hat, he reminded Norlund vaguely of some movie actor of distinguished appearance.

"Yes," said Norlund, pushing himself away from the wall, standing up straight, ready as he could be for Hajo Brandi to reappear.

The relief in the other's face became more definite. "Good. My name is Geoffrey Holborn. Our mutual friends have said that you are to be staying with me for, ah, some time." There had been a slight pause after the name, as if the man expected it might be recognized; and Norlund, who had been thinking of movie actors, thought again. There was something about that name . . . but he couldn't manage to pin it down right away.

Holborn continued. "Have you any baggage?"

"Not much. It's over at my hotel."

"If you'd like to give me your room key, I'll have my chauffeur pick it up. We'll be staying at my place in town, at least for now, if that's all right — ?"

"Perfectly all right, I'm sure." Feeling lightly dazed, Norlund dug out his room key and handed it over. After a moment he remembered to pass on a ten-dollar bill. The room would have to be paid for.

Holborn stepped aside, making a small hand gesture. "Then shall we — ?"

"Yes. By all means."

The limousine was parked arrogantly at the curb, not far away, with other traffic picking its way around it resignedly, as if it were the type of obstruction about which nothing could possibly be done. Holborn paused to speak to the uniformed driver, and handed over the ten-spot and the hotel key.

Then he rejoined Norlund, leading him in a stroll along the sidewalk. "Griffith will pick up your things and take them home. I'd like to stop in at my office for a moment; then we'll go along home, too. Unless there's something else you'd prefer to do first — ?"

"No, not at all. You're being very accommodating, and I hope I'm not putting you to too much trouble. You say that I'm supposed to stay with you for some time?"

They had come to a corner, and Holborn indicated which way they were to proceed. "Yes, those were my instructions. There's no problem, we've plenty of space and a guest room that we hardly ever use. Look here, I presume you understand that I've been strictly forbidden to try to find out anything about you. Which would be all right, except . . . well, it does rather dampen the small talk, and so on. Don't know if I should ask if you've had a pleasant journey, or what."

"I see your point. Well, we can small talk about the weather. But is it all right if I ask you a few questions?"

"On most subjects, I should think so." A panhandler

approached, took a look at Holborn, and gave up without trying.

"How long is this 'some time' that I'm to stay with you? Have you any idea?"

The taller man shrugged, appearing unconcerned. "I got the impression that it might be weeks or months. As I say, there should be no problem. I was a bit worried, until I saw you. . . . " He let it trail off, then resumed: "I expect you'll fit right in."

"I see," said Norlund, who wasn't sure that he did. "I didn't realize I was going to be moving into someone's house for a long stay. Sorry, Mr. Holborn, I seem to have relinquished a great deal of control over my own future." Which always happens, he thought, when you enlist.

"Call me Jeff." Holborn sounded anxious to be reassuring and co-operative. "You must, under the circumstances. I'm going to present you to my daughter as someone I knew well during the War."

A daughter, but no mention of any wife on the scene. "All right," said Norlund. "And I'm Alan." They shook hands. When someone in the early Thirties spoke about the War, there was no need to ask which war they meant. They meant the Great, the World, the One to End All. Few yet realized how strong the demand was going to be for a sequel. The War to End All Wars had been over now for about fifteen years.

They entered another tall office building. At one side of the lobby a couple of elevators appeared to be reserved for use of the exclusive few, and Holborn naturally gravitated toward these, leading Norlund into one. The lift was passenger-operated, probably, thought Norlund, to afford the passengers greater privacy.

Norlund thought that they might as well take advantage of the fact. "What part did you and I play in the War?" he asked. "I mean, army, navy — ?"

Holborn gave him a look that betrayed a trace of surprise, quickly concealed. "Army. In France. I was a lieutenant colonel by the time the bloody thing was over. I should say we're about of an age, so perhaps you would have been of comparable rank."

"All right. Say that I was Lieutenant Colonel Norlund, and that we knew each other in France. I suppose we can be rather tight-lipped about the details."

"Yes, certainly. God knows everyone's used to me not wanting to talk about the War."

The elevator had reached Holborn's destination, on one of the highest floors. Norlund, before opening the door, asked, "Excuse me, but what about my current occupation? And how are we going to explain that I'm staying with you for a long time?"

Holborn looked almost offended. "No need to 'explain' anything to anyone, old fellow . . . Alan. Your present occupation, though. Hmm. You do have a point there. What would you like?"

"Say I'm in radio. How's that?"

"Good enough. Manufacturing, or what?"

"Say that I'm a consultant," Norlund decided thoughtfully. "That sometimes I work for the networks. My job entails a lot of travel, and right now I'm resting up between assignments. What do you do, by the way?"

This time the tall man's surprise was scarcely concealed at all. "I'm a designer," Holborn said shortly, and reached past Norlund and with a flip of his finger opened the elevator door. Ahead of them stretched the reception area of a large office. The decor was Modern Thirties, as Norlund thought of it: partly Art Deco, mostly something more American and mechanically exuberant. A tastefully modern sign announced HOLBORN AND ASSOCIATES, DESIGN.

And now it came to Norlund where he'd heard the name, what it ought to have meant to him. Geoffrey Holborn was one of this decade's second-rank celebrities, a War hero, to be reknowned through the Thirties and Forties for his practice and advocacy of modern, streamlined design for objects ranging from toasters to circus tents to opera houses.

With Holborn half a step ahead, they moved briskly forward into the office. But just as they were passing the first receptionist, who voiced a cheerful greeting to the big boss, Holborn tugged Norlund aside. Standing at a window that overtopped all but a few of those in Manhattan he pointed out and upward.

"That radio mast going up on the Empire State—see? That's one of mine. A good reason, by the way, for you and I to have some professional connection. To spend time in private business meetings, if that becomes necessary."

"Sure."

"Take a good look at it, Alan. That's not just your ordinary broadcast antenna, though of course it serves that purpose. It'll also serve as a mooring mast for dirigibles."

"Ah." Norlund was staring at impressive complexity, hard to distinguish in the distance.

"The extra strength, and the mechanism. Imagine unloading passengers and cargo a thousand feet above the street. Not easy to come up with ways of doing that in perfect safety."

Norlund turned. Jeff Holborn was looking at him as if his opinion on the matter were something of importance. "Very impressive," said Norlund, and meant it.

Holborn was pleased. "I've done something similar

on one of the Skyride towers, at the World's Fair in Chicago. Actually we designed several buildings for the Fair, though when the Crash came those fellows couldn't come up with the money to build 'em all."

They turned away from the window, and began to penetrate the office, passing one receptionist and secretary after another. Norlund noted that some of these were good-looking and some were not; he got the impression that Holborn hired for efficiency. Everyone they passed, unless absorbed in work, gave Mr. Holborn a good afternoon. It was a large establishment. And, to judge by the level of activity, it had no shortage of work even now in the deep Depression. A couple of rooms, one large, one small, were occupied by draftsmen. Elsewhere there were clerks, typists—not a word processor in sight, of course. Holborn returned all greetings absently—rather, thought Norlund, as a general returns salutes.

Eventually Norlund and Holborn were alone, in a room that had to be Holborn's private office, though it wasn't overly large or expensively furnished. Holborn went at once to the large desk and riffled through its litter in search of something. A drafting table stood near the window, which offered a great view out over the city. Photographs and awards hung thickly on the walls. Models—of aircraft, towers, radios and locomotives—hung from the ceiling and perched wherever shelf and table space allowed.

"Here it is," said Holborn absently, recovering some papers. He put them into a briefcase, which he left atop his desk, as if to have it in readiness to pick up when he left the office. Then he sat down behind the desk, motioning Norlund to another comfortable chair.

"By the way, Alan, something has just occurred to me. A possible difficulty. I know some people who are rather high up in one network and another. If you claim to be consulting for them, they're going to think something funny's going on."

"Ah, I see your point." Norlund thought it over, meanwhile gazing out the window. "How's this? The work I do for the networks is mostly confidential, so much so that not even all the higher-ups of the companies themselves know of it. And those who do know might not admit the fact if they were sounded out. So it would be hard for your friends, for anyone, to check up on me."

"Good idea. I think that'll provide all the explanation that we could possibly really need. We'll keep it in reserve. Cigar?"

"Thanks, don't mind if I do." It was a long time since Norlund had had a really good cigar, and these looked and smelled like prime Havana.

He was just lighting up when he heard the office door behind him opening. There had been no warning of any kind. Norlund turned. . . .

Lovely, was his first thought, as he put down the cigar and automatically got to his feet. He judged that the young lady was somewhere in her late twenties. She wore a red dress that accentuated her slim height; her hair was brown, tinged with auburn, and cut in an upcurling Greta Garbo bob.

Her blue-green eyes flicked once at Norlund, as she stood in the doorway, one hand still holding the knob she had just turned. She seemed to dismiss him as of no importance, and went on to Holborn.

Her voice was surprisingly husky. "Jeff, the damn fools over there just won't listen to me."

"What damn fools this time? Oh, I know who you mean. Dear, this is Alan Norlund. We were in France together. Alan, my daughter Holly."

"How do you do?" said Norlund.

His tentatively outstretched hand was pressed firmly, then dropped. He was again ignored. Holly was not smoking, but somehow her nervous gestures conveyed to Norlund the impression that she held a cigarette. She was wearing what appeared to be a diamond wedding ring. She was also perhaps a couple of years older than Norlund had first estimated.

"Yes," she was saying, "Damn fools." Then she really looked at the visitor for the first time. "Hello, Mr. Norlund. Sorry to barge in on your meeting. Some of my father's stuffy old friends, that's who I'm talking about."

"Associates," Jeff corrected her soothingly. "Not particularly friends. Important businessmen of the—"

"Yes, well. Damn fools whatever else they are." Holly focused on Norlund now, as if he were some kind of an appeals judge. "I've been trying to convince them that a port for seaplanes in downtown Manhattan would be a beautiful project on which to use some of this government make-work money when it starts to flow. But the idiots won't hear of it."

"Holly is an aviatrix," Jeff explained. "Sorry dear, I know you hate that word. You're a pilot."

"I see."

Holborn showed amusement. "Holly, I don't think it's been demonstrated that there's going to *be* any government money thrown around. Not for projects like that, anyway. Even if it would be fun for you to have a seaplane and be able to park it right downtown."

"I don't have a seaplane, I'm not planning to get one. But why not a project like that? It would put people to work. It would stimulate aviation, which means more jobs. More business orders. You and your friends can swear at Roosevelt all you like, but he's going to *do* things. He's got the country behind him, and Congress will have to . . . "

Something about Norlund was evidently distracting Holly, and she let the subject of the seaplane port drop for the time being. "You know, I rarely get to meet any of Dad's old comrades-in-arms. Are you free for dinner tonight, Mr. Norlund?"

"For several dinners, I'm afraid." He reseated himself on the edge of Holborn's desk, and relighted his cigar. Jeff had continued puffing on his.

Holborn interrupted, with explanations. "Alan's going to be staying with us for a while. I've invited him. He can move into the spare room."

"Oh, how nice." It seemed that Holly might mean it. "For how long, Mr. Norlund?"

"Call me Alan, please. Oh, that depends."

Jeff was on his feet now, picking up the briefcase into which he had put the papers from the desk. "Griffith is taking Alan's bag over—are we ready to go?" This was addressed to Norlund.

"Yes," said Norlund. Then he hesitated. "I'm a trifle short on clothes, actually. How formal are we going to be, at dinner and so on?"

"Generally not at all. But of course I can take you round to some shops if you like. Ah . . . "

Norlund read the delicate hesitation. "Oh, I'm solvent enough, it's just that I'm not all that familiar with New York. Exactly where do you live, by the way?"

"Overlooking Central Park," said Holly, smiling at him. "Most people are impressed."

"I'm sure I will be, too. Well then, no rush about visiting shops. I expect we can skip all that for now."

Holly continued to study him, and whatever she saw evidently intrigued her. "Mr. Norlund, do you fly?"

"Call me Alan, please. I've been up, but I'm no pilot. Why, do I look like one?"

"Yes. I'm not sure what a pilot ought to look like, but I think you do. But then, I'm quite good, and people tell me I don't look the part. Anyway I admire you for flying; a lot of older people won't consider trying anything new. Well, don't look at me that way, Jeff. You've never been sensitive about age yourself, and I'm sure Alan already knows that he's older than a lot of people—chronologically, that is."

"Thank you," said Norlund, half-abstractedly. Then a moment later he had to make a conscious effort to recall just what he was thanking the young lady for.

Sitting on the edge of Holborn's desk, he had just seen something that distracted him from conversation. Being used as a paperweight on the desk was a small, nearly cylindrical object, made of what looked like dark ceramic, with slightly tapered ends and mounting flanges. It looked exactly like the devices that he and Jerry had worked for two days installing in Chicago.

TO A YEAR UNKNOWN

Jerry Rosen, on the morning that he agreed to work for Schiller, was given time for a shower, shave, and breakfast. Then he left Ginny Butler's apartment in company with Andy Burns and other people. They went down in the elevator to the underground garage, and crossed its parking area to a different corner, where a small, unmarked van awaited them. Jerry and Andy got into the almost windowless rear of the van, along with a nameless young man who saw to it that the two of them were blindfolded as soon as the doors were closed. There followed a ride of what Jerry privately estimated as one to two miles, all in city traffic. Then the van pulled inside another building and stopped. Jerry could hear the large garage doors opening for them, and closing again behind them after they'd pulled in.

Next he and Andy, still blindfolded, were helped to grope their way out of the van and into some other vehicle. Another van, or else some kind of a truck, Jerry couldn't tell for sure.

Their new transportation started up, and drove out when the doors opened again. Or maybe these were different doors. Because as soon as they were left behind, the sound and the *feel* of the unseen world around Jerry changed abruptly.

This time the ride lasted for no more than a city block. Whatever carrier they were riding in stopped, and he and Andy, both of them with eyes still covered, were helped out of it. Jerry could feel that he was now standing on a comfortably soft surface, but he didn't know if he was indoors or out. The silence around him was inappropriate for the middle of a big city. A hand rested lightly on his arm, and a voice murmured something commonplace by way of reassurance as he listened to the truck that had brought him drive away.

The hand fell free. "You can take off the blindfolds now," said the young man who was their guide, speaking in a normal voice. Jerry was startled to see that this was a new guide, with an oriental face.

The world as revealed by sight was now gray and timeless-looking. Underfoot, slightly yielding dark gray, like a smooth seamless carpet. An overcast sky above. Between ground and sky ran high gray walls like dark concrete, forming a smooth concave curve a hundred feet ahead of Jerry. The curve of those walls if carried on would have defined a circle perhaps half a mile in diameter. Directly ahead of Jerry as he faced the wall it was marked with a pattern of thin lines, like the sketch of a tall gate. He wondered if the van or truck had gone out that way.

"This way, gentlemen, please." Andy was still at his side, but their guide had moved behind them. Jerry turned to confront more curved gray walls. These were closer and convex, and given a more human scale by an almost ordinary door that now stood open at ground level. Jerry realized that the three of them were standing in a kind of courtyard, adjoining a large building. The shape of the building, perhaps two stories high, blurred almost indistinguishably into that of the higher wall surrounding; from where Jerry was standing, he could only guess at the full extent of either.

He looked up again, at the gray sky overhead. Or was it a natural sky at all?

"This way, please."

With Andy he walked forward, over the courtyard's gray carpet—or was it pavement?—toward the open door.

"Where are we?" Jerry asked the question urgently, but it wasn't answered.

Andy didn't appear to be all that much impressed by his surroundings. "Ah been here before, when they was givin' me mah new arm," he told Jerry. Then Andy looked around. "Or was it here? It was a lot like this."

The inside of the building, white-walled and plain—at least in the first few rooms they entered—seemed a much more normal environment. In part, Jerry realized, this was because when they entered, normal background noise re-established itself: the sounds of a large building with people in it.

Other people came to meet them, conduct them, talk about how they were going to be checked in. Everyone here except their oriental guide—who had now disappeared—wore some variation of gray garments, almost a uniform. Most people looked distinctly informal, nothing was tightly buttoned up. Along with the gray appeared brighter colors, but whether worn as insignia or simply decorations Jerry couldn't tell.

Getting the two newcomers checked in appeared to consist, for the time being at least, of issuing them their own uniforms of decorated gray, and leading them to the rooms in which they were going to live for some unspecified period of time.

Jerry, hauling an armload of new clothes that he had been assured would fit him perfectly along a commonplace corridor, tried again: "What is this place?"

A colored man with a dazzling smile and a wrestler's build reassured him. "This place is a school—among other things. I'm sure you were told that you'd get some training. You'll get the best that we can give you, until you're ready to do your job."

"My job? What's my job?"

"You've agreed to do one, I'm sure. Else you wouldn't be here. If they haven't told you what it is yet, you'll have to talk to someone else about it."

It was suggested that they change into some of their new clothes, and hang up the rest in their closets. Things like laundry were explained. Andy and Jerry had been assigned adjoining rooms on the long corridor that no longer looked quite commonplace. It was gently curved, making it impossible to see how long it really was.

The two of them were left more or less alone. Andy Burns, leaning in the doorway of his newly assigned room, had pulled his own shirt off already. Across his thinly muscled right shoulder and the upper part of his right arm ran a line defined by two slightly but definitely different skin tones. Andy was frowning at this area, pinching and rubbing at the skin just below the line, like someone worried about sunburn. And now something that he had said earlier fully registered with Jerry for the first time:—*when they was givin' me mah new arm*—

When he saw Jerry looking at him, Andy said: "Mah new arm. Lost mah own in the war. Don't know if Ah told you about that yet."

Jerry watched the fingers of the right arm flex. The whole arm looked good, natural. Yet when Jerry looked at it very closely he could see that there was a mismatch with the left arm. A slight one. He had to believe that Andy was perfectly serious, that the arm had been somehow grown or grafted on.

"You know," said Jerry with a sigh, "I think we ain't even in nineteen eighty-four any longer."

"Ah think you're right. Not that Ah know which year this is. Sometimes they just won't say."

"Jeez," said Jerry. He stood in the hallway, forgetting about putting his new clothes away. People going by looked at him in passing. Some of them smiled lightly, in a friendly way. All went on about their business. And here came, yes, it had to be, a robot, a metal shape rolling on swift wheels, threading its way among human traffic. No one gave it a second glance.

After a while Jerry asked, "I wonder if, by *now* maybe, someone has got to the Moon?"

Their first class, in what was called Weaponry, was scheduled not many hours after their arrival. Jerry was impressed with how well things were organized here. People evidently got to where they were supposed to be, and did what they were supposed to do, but nobody kept hounding you all the time. There was none of the continual nagging by authorities which was the thing he remembered best from the few schools he had attended. Maybe, he thought, this is the way a real college is always run. Jeez, me in college. You had to call it a college, didn't you, if adults were here as students?

The first class, at least, wasn't conducted in a schoolroom, but at an indoor firing range. The instructor turned out to be a woman, and at first it struck Jerry as odd and humorous that she was going to teach the three of them—Andy was there too, and a third student, also a woman—how to shoot guns. But Jerry was not dumb enough to comment on the instructor's sex, or to let his amusement show. From what he'd seen of what these people could do, he was willing to let them conduct classes in any way they wanted. Besides, here was Andy who had been in the army and had fired a good many guns, and he took this dame very seriously. Besides again, the weapons she had on display didn't look like any firearms either of the men would have seen before.

The first one up for consideration, what the teacher called a creaser, looked to Jerry more like a skeletal model of a flashlight, or the rings and spine left over from one of those snap-shut notebooks. There were variations of the creaser with pistol grips, and others that you just pointed, like magic wands or something. Again, having read some science fiction was a help in taking these things seriously.

The instructor told them that the operation of the real guns, out in the field, would be almost soundless. The models used here on the range for training were harmless and emitted little signal beeps when triggered.

"Point-blank range is always best, but this particular weapon can be used effectively up to one hundred meters—that's a little over a hundred yards."

"What does it do?"

"All you need to know, basically, is that the creaser here has an effect on the human mind, which usually results in a reversal of loyalties. It's not a long-term effect, and it's not very dependable either. But it could make you turn around and shoot your buddy, instead of the enemy."

"Who's the enemy, anyway?" This was Jerry.

The instructor faced him squarely. "Hitler. I think you've been told that much. You'll get the rest in History. Hitler, and the people who are fighting for him, whether they realize they're fighting for him or not. Imagine a world where Hitler is brought into the future, instead of being killed in nineteen forty-five or earlier. Brought forward in time, established in power, with everything that the people of the future know about maintaining power used to maintain him? Think about it." And with scarcely a change of tone she turned back to the weapon under discussion. "A second creaser jolt will often reverse the effects of the first one, so you can try that if your partner starts after you some day. But a second jolt may well take the recipient out of action completely, perhaps fatally. A third jolt within a matter of an hour will almost certainly finish anyone off."

There were a couple of other weapons to be discussed today, and there was range-firing with several. Tomorrow would be Armed and Unarmed Tactics, and History. Next the three students were to be allowed a break, and were then to report to another room for Discipline. Jerry didn't like the sound of that one especially. He wondered if they were going to be sent outdoors to march.

On their way out of what passed for a coffee shop, Andy and Jerry rejoined the young woman who was their fellow student for the day. Her name was Agnes Michel, and she spoke English with a more pronounced accent, and a different one, than most of the people here had. In today's Weapons class Agnes had impressed Jerry as being one tough gal, maybe almost as tough as the instructor herself.

Now, as Jerry wondered how to go about opening some kind of a conversation, Agnes took the initiative. "This is the Legion of the Lost, guys. Nobody who's sent to this place ever gets home again—did you know that?"

Andy took it calmly. "Ah knew it 'bout mahself," he said. But he looked across at Jerry with concern.

"I'm going home," said Jerry, walking toward Discipline.

"You think so," said Agnes, keeping pace in her gray slacks. Agnes was small. She looked mousy, when she wasn't looking tough, which was most of the time. Not bad-looking, with qualifications.

"They told me I am."

Agnes didn't seem to find that worth any direct comment. "This army is your home from now on. At least until you retire."

The option of eventual retirement somehow made the grim prediction more believable. Jerry felt a chill. He repeated: "I'm going home."

"And, when they do let you retire, if you should live so long, it'll be to some place that you've never been before anyway."

"How do you know?" asked Andy, curious at least about retirement. But he got no answer.

Jerry wasn't going to let her leave it at that. He kept after her. "Where are we now? Do you know where we are?"

She nodded, smiling, as if she had gotten him to admit that he agreed with her. "Those big gray doors you saw, outside, when you arrived? It's twenty thirty-three outside those doors."

Now it was Andy's turn. "How do you know?"

"They can't send you home, man, knowing about this place. At least they're not going to. They won't send any of us home, no matter what they've said."

1933–34

The phone rang in Norlund's bedroom in the middle of the night, and he struggled into wakefulness to answer it.

It was Jeff's voice that he heard from the receiver, and in the circumstances this was disorienting. Jeff ought to be in his own bedroom two doors down the hall, and how was he managing to phone from there? Then Norlund remembered. Holborn had been called away on one of his fairly frequent business trips, this time to Chicago. It was the fourth or fifth time he'd gone out of town during the ten weeks or so that Norlund had been staying with him.

"Yes, Jeff . . . what is it?"

"Can you talk freely?" asked the voice on the phone. "I take it you're alone?"

Norlund had a lamp switched on now, and squinted into its glare at his bedside clock. It was two in the morning; he felt vaguely complimented. "Yes, I'm alone.

What's going on in Chicago?"

"I'm here making sure for the Fair people that the mooring mast on the Skyride tower is ready. We don't know if the *Graf Zeppelin* is going to want to use it or not, and it hasn't really been tried as yet. Anyway, I'm sorry about the hour, but this is important. I'm calling on a private line, you see."

"A private line?"

"I'm saying that a special phone arrangement has been made, to connect me with you directly, privately. Understand? To conduct business of the kind that brought you to my house."

"Yes, all right. I'm awake now." They're about to send me somewhere else, thought Norlund. He didn't look forward to hearing where they wanted him to go now. I'm going to have to insist on seeing whoever it is that makes these decisions, he thought; I'm going to have to get my career settled.

"There's an important job you have to do, Alan. Tell Holly that I called, and that I want you to take a close look for me at the top of the mooring ring on top of the mast on the Empire State. It's a copper-plated structure, holding heavy pulleys and so on, about ten feet in diameter, almost at the very top of the mast. To do it from the air will be the most practical way; she'll have to fly you. You're going to have to use her plane, because the equipment for the real job's installed in it."

"What equipment is that?"

"I'm told you'll recognize it as soon as you see it, and that its use is already familiar to you. If you want to prove to Holly that you're interested in the mooring ring, you can find some drawings of it on my desk in my study there at home. Take the drawings along."

"All right, but what's the real job, that I'm to do with this special equipment?"

"I'm to tell you that you'll get your final instructions when you turn the equipment on, after you're airborne." Holborn paused. When he spoke again it was in a less constrained, more open tone. "Does that make sense to you?"

"I'll know for certain when I try it. But yes, I think it makes a kind of sense."

"Good. It didn't make much to me. And Norlund."

"Yes."

"Holly knows nothing of what's really going on here. She must know nothing. She thinks that all that special gear in her plane is for some kind of survey of the strength of radio broadcast signals."

"I understand," said Norlund.

"Good night, then. Or good morning. Tell Holly I'll be seeing her in a few days."

"Yes. Good night, then, Jeff."

It wasn't a regular click when the connection broke, but a smooth fade into dial tone.

As usual, Norlund once awakened had difficulty in getting back to sleep. He was awake when Holly came home, not long after the phone call. He could hear her quiet movements down the hall, and the closing of her bedroom door. As far as Norlund could tell, no one had entered the apartment with her. Doubtless she had been out with Dr. Niles, a young bachelor physician who was coming round more and more.

Norlund had learned early on in his stay that Holly was married but separated. Mrs. Rudel. Husband Willy, a native of Germany and a pilot too, had gone back to his homeland some months ago to assist in building the New Order, the Third Reich as it was sometimes called. Either by direct action or subterfuge he had succeeded in taking seven-year-old Willy Jr. along with him. Norlund had heard mention of divorce proceedings, though they weren't really started yet, he gathered. He would have highly recommended them in this case if he had dared. Doubtless Dr. Niles would have, too.

Norlund got snatches of sleep off and on through the wee hours. Then he got himself up early, afraid of missing Holly, who seldom slept very late even on the infrequent occasions when she came in that way. He went to have his breakfast in the room they called the library, overlooking the yellowing October leaves of Central Park. This room did have more bookshelves and books in it than any other in the apartment, but Norlund had yet to see either Holborn or his daughter sitting still anywhere long enough to read a book. Holborn himself had read some of the books during the last ten weeks, and had taken long walks, and seen some shows, and had spent some of his money. He thought that a middle-aged but not unattractive widow he'd met at one of Holborn's friends' parties a couple of weeks ago was probably interested in him. Norlund, though, wasn't interested in her.

Now he sat looking out the window at autumn leaves and sipping his coffee while he waited for Holly to appear, and listened to the radio. The radio was giving the news.

"—the British government today continued to preserve an attitude of calm toward the crisis precipitated by the German withdrawal from the arms conference, and from the League of Nations—

"—meanwhile, the *Graf Zeppelin*, after battling strong winds yesterday to reach Akron on the second leg of its goodwill tour of this country, was off again today, attempting to reach Chicago. Its appearance there in conjunction with the World's Fair is scheduled for tomorrow—

"In other news: near Springfield, Illinois this morning, some ten thousand striking coal miners are still confronting troops in labor unrest that continues to sweep the country—"

"They're all Communists, that's what Dad would say." Holly had arrived. She had materialized before the library mantel while Norlund's thoughts were elsewhere, puzzling over the mooring mast and Skyride tower. And in the second before he looked at her, she might have been looking at the photo on the mantel, of Willy and little Willy Jr. Norlund had once heard her say that it was the best picture of her son she had.

She had dropped her gaze into the dark empty fireplace now. "Almost cold enough for a fire these mornings," she said. And in almost the same tone added: "Yesterday I got a letter from Willy."

For a moment Norlund looked at her hands, expecting to see in one of them a letter ready to be crumpled up and consigned to flames. "Bad news, evidently," he said with sympathy.

"Oh, Alan, I've been hoping, expecting, that when he'd been in Germany a while he'd wake up and see what a . . . I've never been there myself, what do I know? But I can't believe this Hitler is really any good. He has done some good for Germany, I guess, got the people standing up on their feet again. . . ."

"Those who haven't been knocked down by Storm Troopers."

"What? Oh, I suppose." Holly, in the way she had, paused and seemed really to focus on Norlund for the first time. "Well, good morning, Alan. You're up early."

"I had a call from Jeff last night."

"Oh. Did he ask for me?"

"No, just business. And it was two in the morning."

"Funny I didn't hear the phone ring. Of course I was out late."

Norlund, avoiding any comment on that, gave the explanation that Jeff had prescribed of what they wanted to do. "And besides getting a look at the mooring ring . . . I take it that there's some special radio gear that's been installed in the cabin of your ship?"

"Oh, that. Yes. Dad asked me a couple of months ago if I would mind. I told him no; after all, it's still mostly his money that keeps me flying. Are they really broadcasting from that mast already?"

"So, it's possible for you to give me that ride as Jeff requested?"

She hesitated, lifting the cover of one of the breakfast dishes, sniffing the aroma with healthy appetite. "Today?"

"Jeff did sound in a hurry. I think he would like it to be taken care of today, yes."

"All right. I'll go phone the airport now." Holly went to the window and took a quick look at a partly cloudy sky. "Doesn't look bad. Then I'll grab some breakfast and change, and we'll be off."

"Thanks. I suppose you had something else planned," Norlund said when Holly came back from phoning. A silent maid had by now arranged her breakfast for her, across from Norlund's place at the library table. His dishes had already been collected. He marveled, in passing, at how quickly and easily he had gotten used to being waited on.

"It can wait," she said, sitting down. "Your project will take my mind off things."

"Dr. Niles last night?" Norlund asked, and then instantly regretted it. "It's none of my business."

"No, it isn't." But she didn't sound angry. "Maybe later I'll start talking about it all."

After breakfast Holly changed into garments that Norlund had seen her in before, and recognized as flying gear: what looked almost like army pants, and a man's shirt. "Let's go," she said.

The lobby of the apartment building was lifeless as usual. A uniform opened the front door for them. Griffith was already waiting with Holly's roadster in front of the building, at a curb kept clear of casual parkers. After holding the car door for Holly, the chauffeur saluted and walked away.

"You don't mind if I drive, do you Alan?"

"You're going to have to do all the driving when the time comes to switch vehicles. But if you want to drive this one too, suit yourself."

"I like to drive."

"I've noticed." They had been together on a number of outings of one kind and another, most recently to the Whitney Museum. Norlund wondered if his name and Holly's would someday appear, linked, in somebody's gossip column. Maybe they already had; he never read the damned things and thought that she didn't either. Jeff probably did. Or would, if he ever had the time, and perhaps would have seen his own name more than once. His wife, Holly's mother, had been dead now for a good number of years.

Holly, as usual driving a little too fast, said, "I wouldn't be surprised to find out that you could handle the airplane, too."

"You would be surprised, if you bailed out up there and left me to try it. I think you'd be out one . . . you've never told me what kind of a ship you have."

"Lockheed Vega." Smiling a little smugly, she glanced over at him. "I think you'll like it. No, it's not a seaplane." Her enthusiasm for the waterfront skyport in Manhattan had become a gentle standing joke between them.

She never does talk to me, thought Norlund, as if there were forty years of chronology between us. That was probably why certain fantasies on his part were becoming harder and harder to dismiss, and why he had disliked Dr. Niles from their first brief meeting.

"It's strange, in a way, that you and Jeff are working together."

If there were any logical consistency behind the way she sometimes called her father by his first name and sometimes did not, Norlund hadn't yet figured it out. Anyway he couldn't very well deny now that he and Jeff were partners in some enterprise. "How so?" he asked.

"Just that you're so different from each other." Holly paused with traffic, shifted expertly, and was off again. "In one way you're alike. Good at keeping secrets. There's a whole area of Dad's life that he never allows me to get into. I don't mean his girl friends; I can pretty well see what's going on there. I used to think it was something to do with the War, that maybe he'd been in Intelligence work, though he never would admit to that, and some of it was still going on somehow . . . but now I wonder." She looked over at Norlund. "Whether it was the War or not, I think it was something to do with you."

He tried to frame his answer carefully. "I can't talk about my work. Not much, anyway. Not even to you."

"I didn't expect you would. You probably wouldn't be much good at your work, whatever it is, if you did."

They rode in silence for a while, into and out of the Holland Tunnel. West of the river the land was largely flat and empty marsh, with screaming birds hovering above it. When Norlund turned his head to look back from the curving highway, he could see the Empire State hovering on the horizon, standing above the flatness to what appeared to be a mountain's height.

Holly spoke again. "Well, Dad never begrudges me my own life, my own secrets."

Norlund asked on impulse: "Have you heard very often from your kid since they've been gone?"

"When his father has him write. Or lets him. Or makes him. I don't know. They both talk about my going over there to join them."

"What will you do?"

"I've been unable to make myself do anything. I don't want it to wind up with lawyers and courts."

In the next fifty years the Newark Airport was going to change by an even more mind-boggling amount than the metropolis across the river. For one thing, thought Norlund, the airport was going to become vastly less convenient to use. As it was now, Holly knew the people who ran it, and they knew her, and the necessary things got done with a minimum of fuss and formality.

Cloud-shadow alternated with sunshine out on the ramp where the Vega stood waiting for them. It was a big high-wing monoplane, thick-shouldered, and the single air-cooled radial engine looked enormous. The craft was painted white with stripes of red and blue. Norlund looked for some kind of name on it, but there were only the official numbers.

Norlund felt reassured to see Holly doing a thorough walk-around check before they boarded. She even pulled the caps off the fuel tanks and checked the levels inside directly; the fuel guage must be unreliable, he thought, or non-existent.

They entered the plane by the cabin door, in the side of the fuselage toward the rear. Inside there was plenty of room for four passenger seats, but only one on each side had been installed. A lot of the remaining cabin space was taken up with what looked like radio gear; it was the back of the Radio Survey truck all over again. With a difference. Each side of the cabin had a row of small windows, and the center window in each row was furnished with a special small mount, bolted in place, and holding what looked like a telescopic camera on a swivel. The lenses stared out through the flat glass. The rest of the equipment was neatly safety-wired into racks, in the best military aviation style. There, on one cabinet accessible from a seat, was his row of dials that ought to be settable like the combination on a safe.

Holly had already gone on forward, through the tiny hatch leading to the cockpit. And now that big radial engine was coughing into life, shaking the furniture. Norlund had forgotten how loud big engines were.

A slim arm sleeved in a man's shirt reached back through the open hatch and beckoned to him. Norlund moved forward. He was halfway through the hatch before he realized that the tiny pilot's compartment ahead of him was meant to accommodate only one. Two smallish, thin people could probably squeeze in, but it was going to be a tight fit. And there would be only one safety belt.

Holly had squeezed herself over to one side. "Come on, Norlund, I won't be able to talk to you if you ride back there. I've got to know how close you have to go to the damned tower, and when you've seen enough of it. Then you can go back in the cabin and play with your radios."

He stuffed himself into the seat somehow, with Holly's thigh pressed tightly against his. Then he reached back to pull the cabin hatch closed behind him. The safety belt was going to go unused.

They taxied, with guidance by arm-waves from a man trotting beside them on the ground. In tail-down position the aircraft's nose was so high that it was almost impossible to see anything directly in front of it from the cockpit. Then Holly evidently got some kind of visual signal from the tower, for the next thing Norlund knew they were in a takeoff roll at deafening full power. He tried to find something other than a control handle to hang onto.

The engine had plenty of power. In seconds they were off the ground, gaining altitude fast.

Holly leveled off amid cloud-puffs, at about two thousand feet. She shouted toward Norlund's ear: "How come Jeff just thought of this?"

He tried to make plausible noises. "Maybe something he noticed about the mast in Chicago. You know the airship people are getting nervous, especially since the *Akron* went down." That had been only last February; Norlund had been catching up on his current events in newspapers and magazines. "Seventy-three men lost. They want to be really sure about everything before anyone tries mooring over downtown Manhattan." He had been privately racking his memory of his previous sojourn through this decade, and he couldn't recall anything about a dirigible ever actually mooring there. There was only the faintest suggestion that he might have heard of such a project once being planned.

Holly grumbled something that he couldn't hear very well, about damned Nazis and the *Graf*.

There was a momentary drop in rough air, and

Norlund felt a pang of motion sickness. Even through it he remained acutely conscious of the pressure of Holly's leg on his. An angry thought followed: Does she think I'm so old that I can't react, it doesn't matter?

They circled the Empire State at a distance of no more than a few hundred feet, with Norlund looking under the banked-down wing at the great copper mooring ring. Fortunately the regulations on flying were non-existent compared with what they'd be in fifty years. As far as Norlund could tell, the mooring ring looked just as the drawings suggested that it should.

Still he went through the farce of jotting down notes, as if he were paying attention to details. Then he yelled into Holly's ear that she should just circle over the city for a while at about two thousand feet. Then he pulled himself out of the seat and got back into the cabin.

There he strapped himself into the handiest chair, turned on the equipment, and set up his old combination on the dials. The screen immediately lit up with text:

> NORLUND: YOU WILL SURVEY THE RECORDING DEVICE NETWORK HERE AS YOU DID AT THE PREVIOUS INSTALLATION. IT IS IMPERATIVE THAT EACH RECORDING DEVICE BE IN WORKING ORDER. IF ANY ARE DEFECTIVE OR MISPLACED REPORT THROUGH HOLBORN. IF ALL DEVICES IN GOOD ORDER, REPORT SO.
>
> HARBIN

At last, some word from those people. Norlund began to operate the equipment, in the routine that he'd been taught. Again a pattern of "recording device" installations appeared, marching across countryside, suburbs, and city in a pair of miles-long lines. Again the lines pointed roughly east, converging on a point. And it was obvious that this time the convergence point was the Empire State.

Two pairs of lines—one in Illinois, one in New York. Two convergence points. Two towers, two mooring masts. What—

Norlund's screen went blank, about two seconds before the aircraft lurched. But his equipment was not dead, far from it. Thrown sideways in his seat by what felt like the sudden start of a spin, he saw that the telephoto cameras had come alive, twirling on their gimbals. One of them projected what looked like a concentrated spotlight or a laser beam out through the side window glass in front of it, swerving on its mounting, spinning the beam from right to left.

Holly pulled out of the spin, into a tight, steep-banked turn. In a shadowplay that raced across white cloud below, Norlund saw the aircraft that he was in, and something else. A roaring, crackling something that passed the Vega with the speed of a jet fighter or a bullet. Around the Vega's shadow was a haze of red. Or was it only the after-image of the beam that the swiveling lenses in the cabin projected outward?

Now the Vega was flying almost steadily. It climbed, on the verge of stalling, groping for flying speed. Taking a chance, Norlund unstrapped himself from his safety belt, grappled his way forward, and opened the communicating hatch. "Are you all right?"

Holly's face, whitened by fear and shock, turned to look at him over her thin shoulder. "What was *that*?"

"Stay out of clouds. Get down on the deck, in view of lots of people. Get back to Newark, fast, and land."

Norlund could scarcely speak. It wasn't fear or shock so much as anger at himself. Ten weeks of safety and luxury had made him fat, dumb, and happy, and now he had almost been a party to getting Holly killed.

She didn't argue or question. The plane was nosing down already, in a new banking turn, and Norlund had to fight his way uphill to get back to his seat in the cabin. The waist-gunner's position, he thought. There were the little telephoto devices on their swivels, but no place for human hands to grip them, even if human hands could have swung them fast enough.

His little screen had now turned itself on again.

ATTACK IMMINENT MAN DEFENSIVE POSITIONS

Which would be fine, if he just knew how.

He strapped himself into his seat again, and sat there trying not to hold his breath, until he saw a windsock out the window, with the ground not fifty feet below. In another few seconds they had landed. Smoothly. Holly was undoubtedly a good pilot. Cool under fire, once given a chance. She would have done well in combat.

His screen said: ALL CLEAR. AUTOMATIC DEFENSES OFF. Then it went dead.

Before they had finished taxiing, Norlund had stuck his head forward into the cockpit again. As soon as they had stopped, and Holly had cut the engine, she turned to him. "What was that?" she repeated.

He couldn't tell if she really thought he knew. His own hands were trembling now with delayed reaction; his gut felt as if he'd swallowed lumps of lead.

Holly said: "I'm reporting it to the Department of Commerce, whatever it was."

That, of course, would be this decade's equivalent

of the FAA. Norlund had had a little time already to think up an answer to that one. "It wasn't something that I'd want to describe." He put just a little emphasis on the personal pronoun. At the same time he did his best to look calm. There was an inference for Holly to draw: hysterical women, pilots or not, saw things like that, and a lot of people had known all along that all women were hysterical.

"Alan, you saw it too."

"I saw nothing that I could describe very well. Oh God, Holly, I'm sorry. For getting you into this. It's not going to do the least bit of good to try to report it." He was coming close to letting out secrets, and Ginny Butler, perhaps still with her hand on the valve of Sandy's life, was going to be angry. Well, to hell with her. Norlund was angry, too.

Driving the roadster back toward New York, Holly began to talk. "What makes you tick, Norlund? You can tell me that, even if you can't tell me what almost killed us both just now."

Still gripped by rage, at himself and at the world, he started, "Every time I —" and then he couldn't go on.

"What?"

He tried again, more slowly, getting a grip on himself. "I suppose I've loved five or six people in my life."

She glanced at him, waiting, listening in silence, evidently satisfied that in his own way he was trying to answer her question.

"There was a girl. When I was young." Ten years in the future from the year he spoke in now. "There was a war on. She lived in London, doing war work. There was — an aerial attack." In his mind he could still hear the buzz-bombs, as he had really heard them sometimes. When the engine sputtered and then cut

off, that was the time to duck. Before that, Norlund
had killed a German or two but had not hated them.
After that it had been different.

"Those zeppelin raids, yes. I remember hearing
about them. How sad."

"I was off — getting shot at, sometimes expecting to
be killed. But she was the one who was killed. Holly,
I'm trying to tell you what makes me tick. I really
wish I could."

She asked: "How did you meet Dad?" And when he
didn't answer, added: "Never mind." In a moment she
went on, in the same tone, with what at first seemed a
change of subject. "I've had one bad crash since
I've been flying. It was in upstate New York, the
Adirondacks. Really out in the sticks. Jeff happened to
be with me. The plane was really a total loss, and I
was knocked out for some time. When I came to, I had
a lump on my head and a ghastly headache, and my
nose was bleeding too. The front of my clothes looked
like rags out of a slaughterhouse. My father didn't
have a scratch on him, but he was practically in
hysterics when I came round at last. He'd really thought
that I was dead." Holly paused. "Sometimes I wonder
if he didn't get a knock on the head, too. Ever since
then . . ."

She didn't finish, and Norlund didn't ask.

On New Year's Eve Norlund was sitting in a chair in
Holborn's library. A good part of the time he looked
out into the darkness over the snowy park. Now and
then he faced back into the lighted rooms of the
apartment, and talked with people, while Holborn's
annual holiday party raged near him and around him.
Norlund had a scotch-on-the-rocks in hand, quite legally.
Prohibition had finally died, a matter of weeks ago. It

seemed that everyone who arrived at the party had some comment to make on that subject, most of them the same one.

"All legal now, hey? Takes some of the fun out of it."

"I suppose it also lessens the chance of being quickly poisoned." That was from Dr. Niles, who had just come in dashingly bareheaded, snow on his young black hair, his black bag in hand from making house-calls. Through the library door Norlund watched the maid taking his coat.

"I like that, quickly! Ha hahh!"

Jeff was off in yet another room, livening up with a few drinks in him. Norlund could hear his voice. The two of them hadn't exactly sought out each other's company since Jeff had gotten back from Chicago and Norlund had privately expressed his anger about Holly's being brought into this. *This* was about all they could call it, this secret and plainly deadly game that both of them were in, for presumably separate reasons which they had never revealed to each other. There wasn't a name for this project to which they were bending their lives—or if there was, Norlund at least had never heard it.

It had been borne in on him that neither of them knew what they were really about in what they did for Ginny Butler and her associates. Norlund didn't even know if Jeff had ever met or heard of Ginny Butler, or if his orders came through someone else. And how had Jeff been recruited? By the promise of someday being shown what streamlined design would really look like in fifty or a hundred years?

"Jeff, you kept telling me that Holly knows nothing, must know nothing, of what we're really doing."

"That was my intention. It still is."

"Did you or did you not know that our airplane was

likely to be attacked? Just answer me that."

"I will not tell you anything about that. I will say only that *this* is a matter of honor to me. Of . . . vital importance. And I am going on with it." Jeff was plainly under a great strain in this confrontation, which had already gone on for some time. But he was also obviously determined to stick to his position.

There was a pause, that seemed to Norlund himself long, before he answered. "All right. We'll go on with it. Wait for our next orders."

Holly, like Sandy, like all the rest of the world, was caught up in war and subject to its blows. Whether most of them knew about it or not.

Now at the party Holly was acting as hostess, wearing a dazzling red evening gown supported by one shoulder strap. Her bare feet were encased in high-heeled gold sandals that she wore as skillfully as if they were her everyday footgear instead of practical shoes or even flying boots. She moved in and out of the library now and then, as other people were doing. There were enough people in the room, coming, lingering, going, so no one could accuse Norlund of hiding from the party. An old man, let him sit still if he wanted to.

Holly stopped and spoke to him now and again, as others did, and once she rested her hand on his shoulder. That horror they had faced in the sky over the Hudson back in October had not recurred. Norlund had worried about it, and had insisted on going along with her next time she flew. With Holly, insisting hadn't done him any good, and she had gone up alone. And, fortunately, returned without incident. While she was in the air he had belatedly realized that she might be a lot safer without him along.

Dr. Niles, following Holly into the library, had smiled indulgently when she touched old Norlund on the shoulder. Norlund could have stabbed him at that point. With every passing week, with every passing drink tonight, the doctor's attitude of possessiveness toward Holly became more open. And her attitude toward the doctor? Neutral, at least whenever Norlund was around.

Christmas. Yes, Christmas. That night a week ago had been pretty grim around here, with the word from Germany short and almost formally cheerful. Longer messages were promised soon.

People in the other room, Holly among them, were arguing. Some of them wanted to go next week to see the newly opened play, *Tobacco Road,* on Broadway.

Some other woman, getting drunk, was bemoaning the fact that her children weren't around. Or else the fact that she'd never had any, Norlund couldn't tell for sure.

The Victrola was playing in one room, the radio in another, the piano in a third. Who were all these people, anyway? There seemed to be at least a score of Holborn's distant relatives, business associates, friends of one kind or another.

Holly came from nowhere to sit next to him again.

Norlund asked her, "What's the word from Germany?"

"Does it show?" Her beautiful face was slightly flushed. "I'm getting so I can't hide anything from you. What's your wife like, anyway?"

"No wife, not any more. She's dead."

"Killed in London, you said."

"That," said Norlund with a sigh, "was someone else."

"Didn't you once tell me you had a daughter, twelve years old?"

"Did I really? I suppose I did. I'm getting so I can't hide anything from you."

"I'm having trouble getting the chronology of your life all straightened out the way it should be."

He realized she was a little tight. Perhaps more than just a little. Change the subject. "There's something about the way you gesture with your hands. Always makes me think you ought to be holding a cigarette."

Holly made a face. "Have you seen all those damned cigarette ads, aimed at women? The ads without the smoke are enough to turn my stomach." She fluttered fingers in a maidenly gesture, and put on a voice. " 'She was all tired out from diving at the Olympics— and then she smoked a Camel. It gave her energy enough to—' Never mind."

A couple of more people were coming into the library. The door, recently almost closed, was now wide open, so that voices came in more clearly from the noise outside.

"Roosevelt is a radio crooner—his legs are the strongest part of him."

Laughter.

Someone else, angered, spouting liberal dogma with the fervor of a new convert, denounced the Nazis. Roosevelt didn't matter. They'd all see, in a few years, that a new world was being born in Russia. The future was visible there already, and it worked.

What was going to happen to the League of Nations now?

Steer clear of foreign entanglement, that's what Washington warned this country.

Norlund's old leg wound was paining him tonight, in an unusual way. Tingling. He wondered if the weather was going to change, a giant blizzard bearing down on the city. He wondered if Ginny Butler had forgotten where she'd left him. There was a comfort in that thought tonight, but he didn't really suppose that she had.

Someone—yes, Jeff's voice—spoke up now, in a hesitant, reasonable tone, for Hitler. "You must admit he's really straightened Germany out. Look at the terrible problems they were having. The aftermath of the War. Inflation. Reds and Jews. Now there's peace, people are working, they have some sense of pride in themselves again."

"Rearming, too," someone objected mildly.

"I think it's part of the sense of national pride."

"Is Roosevelt really going to invite him to this country, do you suppose?"

"There are a lot of German voters."

Holly was still beside Norlund. He took her hand, and pursued her quietly: "What's the word?"

She looked at Norlund more directly than before, and now he could see the redness in her eyes. "The word is that they're not coming home. Willy talks about sending me a ticket so I can join them there, as if lack of a ticket were all that held me back. He writes like he's issuing orders now. As if I were the deserter, but he's willing to overlook it. Oh, he isn't really like that. Not when you know him."

"I'm sure he's not." The bastard. A pilot, too. Maybe some day in Forty-three young Norlund would aim a machine gun at him. But no, in a decade Willy would certainly be thought too old for fighters. He'd be some strutting, high-rank friend of Goring, maybe.

People across the room were starting to turn and look at Holly, and she got up from the arm of Norlund's chair and went to the fireplace, where coals were dying down. She started to grab the poker, and burned her hand on it and dropped it with a little cry.

Norlund was at one side of her in a moment, with Dr. Niles at the other. Between them they led her to a chair, from which she immediately jumped up again.

"Stay here," said Dr. Niles to her firmly. "I'll get my bag." He moved off quickly.

Norlund examined the burned finger, which looked white along one side. Taking Holly by the arm, he led her unresisting into the kitchen. He put ice cubes into a clean glass, ran some water on top of them, took Holly's hand and immersed the finger.

"Ah." Her blue-green eyes trusted Norlund. "That does relieve the pain."

"It'll do more than that. It'll help the healing. Better than anything he can put on it."

It took Niles a couple of minutes to find them, having missed them in the library. An authority figure with black bag now in hand, he demonstrated outrage at Norlund's practice of medicine. "Who told you to do that? Do you want the worst blistering you can imagine? Holly, give me your hand."

When she wouldn't, he tried to pull her finger forcibly out of the healing cup. But Holly snatched her arm away. "Don't ever grab at me again."

It was said in a way that compelled the doctor to retreat, black bag and all.

It was hours later, well past midnight and into the New Year, but Norlund didn't really feel tired. The party had sagged a little and had then swung on. Jeff had actually been somewhat relieved to see Niles go away mad. Scandal, you know; Holly was after all a married woman. Not that Jeff had actually said anything. A few other people had departed, but other celebrants had arrived from another party elsewhere.

Now what promised to be a die-hard group was singing around the piano in the other room.

Holly and Norlund had both gravitated back to the library. She had brought along her cup of icewater, into which she still plunged her finger at intervals. A maid came around now and then, replacing melted cubes.

At the moment Holly was studying her finger curiously. "That was a bad burn, but it hardly hurts at all now. There's a mark. But nothing much."

"I'm glad."

"That's not what they tell you to do for burns. I burned my arm on an engine manifold once, and there was no end of salves and dressings and bandages. And pain and blisters, too."

"Depends on who you listen to," said Norlund, unable to resist.

Jeff came and went in the background, his expression hard to read.

Norlund poured himself a little more scotch, after helping himself to one of Holly's ice cubes. At the moment she didn't want any more to drink.

She turned to Norlund. "Tell me about you. I've been aware for some time that that's really a forbidden topic. But tell me anyway."

"And violate my oath?" He tried to make it sound like a joke.

And at that moment the pain hit him. It struck up under the breastbone like the thrust of a jagged dagger. It twisted, and then a piece of the blade broke off and flew down through the veins of his left arm.

He wasn't fainting, not yet anyway, but he had his eyes clamped shut and he knew that his drink had spilled. It was his heart. It was a heart attack, and this was it, he was dying and at the moment none of the rest of it, none of anything else, mattered in the least. People were bending over him, but he couldn't really hear what they were saying.

Now he was stretched out on his back on the sofa, and with every breath the world was slipping a little farther away. The jagged knife had stopped thrusting and twisting, but it was still heavily embedded in the wound.

Holly was bending over him. He could smell her, and he opened his eyes. "Alan, just lie still. We're going to get you help." As she ought to be, she was cool when the crisis came. Norlund watched her, while she undid his tie and collar.

"I'll call for an ambulance; I'll do the calling." That was Jeff, over in the corner by the phone, taking the phone away from someone else. And Jeff was dialing now. It was as if he had the number already memorized.

IN A YEAR UNKNOWN

Norlund rode the train across Manchuria again. He felt confident of being able to defend the train, because he knew he'd ridden it before. His fifty-caliber Brownings were ready, one swivel-mounted at the waist position on each side of the Pullman car, and he stood keeping watch out of one of the side windows, looking for the hordes of mounted Japanese that ought to appear at any moment. But the attacking cavalry didn't come. There was only the gray steppe, slow gentle waves of land going on forever like the sea, out to the gray horizon.

At last Norlund began to grow tired of standing at the window, and, when he remembered that he was now a heart patient, a little worried. But his heart continued to beat. He realized now that it was keeping time to the pulsation of the rails that carried the train forward so endlessly . . . so endlessly . . . he had just decided that he was never going to wake up, when deep night cut off everything.

When darkness lifted again, he saw enough to know that he was not dead, but in a hospital room, real and brightly lighted. He could tell also that it was a modern hospital, not some Thirties horror. Ginny Butler was at his side—yes, really there; she took his hand and told him that he was going to be all right. Thus reassured, he slept.

But dreams were not through with him yet, though from now on they were mixed in with reality. There was a large woman, a nurse or perhaps a doctor, anyway a large woman who had a Chinese face and dressed in a flowing gray gown of interesting pattern. She came to Norlund's bedside frequently, and fed him things and gave him drinks and talked to him. But right now he had to get back into his Radio Survey truck, and play his equipment, which was really nothing but a giant video game. President Roosevelt spoke to Norlund out of the truck's receiver, delivering a fireside chat. Another familiar voice came on with play-by-play action, and said that the Cubs were threatening to score. Lines marching across his little screen, converging on the Empire State, showed where the recording devices were. And now Adolf Hitler, his face part of a newsreel, gray and grainy, looked up at Norlund from the screen. Hitler spoke to him only in German, but still Norlund could recognize the word *zeppelin* when he heard it.

And now Norlund awoke, more fully than before, gasping and trying to wave his arms about. He was in his modern hospital bed, in some gray time that felt like the middle of the night.

And he thought that he understood at last what job he had been doing for Ginny Butler.

Ginny came to visit him briefly fairly often, at various times of day and evening, but Norlund didn't try to talk to her about what he thought he had inferred. Later would be time enough for that. He lay continually in his bed, stark naked and very weak, between sheets that seemed never to be changed but still remained unalterably crisp and cool and clean and comforting. The bed kept putting forth padded extensions of its elegant machinery, and these stroked at Norlund, nuzzled at him, blessed him with tingling anaesthesia whenever pain threatened to arise, which was fairly often. His chest was kept tingling almost all the time. The tingle was in its own way a nice sensation, but whenever it gave promise of becoming outright pleasure something happened to moderate it back again toward nullity, the absence of sensation.

From time to time he was quite sure that he was helplessly wetting or soiling his bed. But if there was any stain or mess, it was gone again within moments from the impossibly white sheets, and from his body. Norlund dreamed again, this time that he was visiting Sandy in her own hospital room . . .

And woke up, thinking that he'd just seen Sandy, and that she and her mother were visiting him. But the more fully awake he became, the better he understood that no such visit would be possible. Not here, in this hospital. This was not Chicago, at least not in nineteen eighty-four.

Ginny Butler had no trouble getting to see him, though. She came in again, in a dress of decorated gray, to stand real and solid beside his bed.

Again she took his hand. "How are you, Alan?"

"Pretty good." Feebly he pressed her fingers, glad to see her, glad to see anyone. "I've been dreaming a lot. Outside of that, you tell me."

Three more people were following Ginny into the private room.

"I am Dr. Cucusus." This was a black woman, almost as large as the oriental nurse. From the way this woman introduced herself, there was no doubt that she was in charge, medically at least; her tone suggested that Norlund had been wondering all his life who Dr. Cucusus really was.

Norlund nodded.

Ginny gestured. "This is Mr. Tak, and Mr. Schiller."

Tak was thin and brown, his features suggesting Southeast Asia to Norlund's not very expert eye, and he sat apparently half-crippled in a small conveyance vastly different from any wheelchair that Norlund had ever seen before. From the way Mr. Tak nodded, and the way the others looked at him, Norlund assumed that he was in charge of the world, medical affairs being only one department thereof. Schiller was colorless, and not very large. He nodded to Norlund too.

Ginny continued. "Alan, there's a decision you're going to have to make. No one else can do it. We've waked you up completely for that purpose."

And indeed his mind felt perfectly clear. It was only that he was weak. He said: "I've had a heart attack."

"Yes, a very severe one," agreed Dr. Cucusus. "And now you have a new heart."

"Ah," said Norlund, and pulled in his chin to look down at his naked chest. The hair on his chest had all been shaved away. A huge capital I of a scar, its lines very narrow and delicately pink, marked him as if he were a letterman from Illinois. Or as if he had been pretty well eviscerated while he slept, his innards somehow reprocessed and then packed back in.

"The scar will be all gone when we're through," Dr. Cucusus soothed him.

"A new heart," said Norlund. At the moment it seemed no more than his due. "So what's the decision that I have to make?"

"Medically speaking," the large black woman informed him, "there are two ways that we can go from here. And we can't, or we shouldn't, put off deciding between them any longer. The first way would involve leaving you basically as you are. With your new heart, we project that you may have twelve or fifteen more years of life—perhaps more than that, perhaps less."

"Twelve years," said Norlund.

"Your arterial system," explained Dr. Cucusus. "It is not an immediate threat to your life, but it is not all that good, either." She stopped there, and looked at Mr. Tak.

"Another important thing about the first way," said Mr. Tak, speaking in a dry penetrating voice, "is that when you are up and about afterwards, you may still be able to go home, should you choose to do so. I emphasize *may*. I should estimate the odds as approximately even. But on the other hand, if the second course of medical treatment is adopted, your return home becomes definitely impossible."

Mr. Schiller spoke up for the first time. "The second course of treatment will not be available to you unless you volunteer for a certain combat mission to be performed when it's completed. A mission for which you seem to be uniquely qualified, but not physically fit for presently."

Dr. Cucusus: "The second medical path we can take is rather difficult, and very expensive in terms of resources. In most cases it would be prohibitively expensive. It is really a rather general rejuvenation treatment. Blood vessels. Endocrine system. Muscles. All systems must be integrated into the treatment as much as possible, if it is to be successful. Roughly speaking, the effect will be to make you thirty years younger."

"Of course," put in Ginny, "there's no guarantee that you are going to survive the combat mission afterward. But you will have a fighting chance."

"There are no guarantees of anything," said Norlund. "I know that much." He tried to think about what rejuvenation might be like, but he was too weak to imagine it very well. He thought things over while they all waited. Then he asked: "What if you try to send me home, and it doesn't work?"

"We'll have a job for you," said Mr. Tak. "Somewhere. Behind the equivalent of a desk. Good routine medical care. I suspect you might live longer than twelve years." Norlund couldn't tell if he was smiling or not.

"Well," said Norlund. "Suppose I take the second course. And the combat mission. And I do survive it. What do I do if I can't go home?"

"The war will go on," said Mr. Tak. "There will be other missions for you, other jobs—some with desks and some without. You'll have some choice. Eventually retirement, somewhere you find pleasant."

Ginny, standing closer than the others, was nodding. "It's not a bad life," she said calmly. "I've been at it for a few years now, in Recruiting."

Norlund looked at her, then back at Tak. "So what is this big combat mission that you need me for?"

Tak's face creased with the wisp of a smile. "An old soldier like you should know better than to ask. You volunteer first, then find out."

"Okay. Then where is it? Where and when? Can you tell me that much?"

A brief whispered conference took place among the

three non-medical visitors. "Somewhere in the United States," said Tak at last. "In New York, most probably. In nineteen thirty-four."

Norlund lay back and closed his eyes. "If you can make me young again," he said, "let's do it."

Undergoing the second course of treatment proved to be more uncomfortable than the mere aftermath of heart-replacement surgery. Not that the machinery permitted anything like real agony. Norlund was for the most part unconscious during actual treatments, and was told little about them. There were long stretches of dull discomfort. Gradually impatience came to dominate.

Some time passed before they let him see a mirror. When they did, a strange face peered back at him— half-recognizable, like the face of some unknown relative—peeling as with sunburn, but with the old skin pale over the stubble of a new brown beard. The face was certainly not sixty, not old any longer. Whether it was young was quite another question.

1934

Holly, in the gray dawn of the New Year, was arguing with her father. She was still wearing her one-strap red gown, but the gold sandals had been kicked off somewhere, making it easier to stalk around, which she liked to do while arguing. She had plenty of latitude, social as well as physical, in which to move around and yell; the servants, dismissed the night before somewhere around midparty, were not yet back from their own celebrations or their rest to commence the cleanup job. The apartment was a terrific mess, but Holly and her father had the freedom of being alone in it.

So far Jeff's attitude had remained one of patient soothing, though Holly was really flaring at him.

"There's something very funny about it, Jeff. You had hardly hung up the phone before those men with the stretcher were coming in the door."

Her father was sitting wearily on the sofa in the

library. Sometimes he looked toward the window, as if he wished he could be out there somewhere. "Holly, if I just tell you that he's getting the best care possible, isn't that enough? Can't you just accept that for now?"

She paused in her angry movement, to look at Jeff. "Oh? And how do you know that he's getting the best of care?"

Jeff sighed and shook his head, looking old and tired. Obviously he hadn't expected this much of an argument.

Holly could feel sorry for him, but she wasn't going to let up. "Why don't you tell me what hospital they took him to?"

They had been over this ground several times before; still Jeff remained, in Holly's view, surprisingly patient. He said: "I don't know where the hospital is."

"And I suppose you don't know what it's called, either."

"Actually, I . . . no."

"Who runs it?" Holly asked sweetly.

He shrugged.

"Oh Jeff! For God's sake! You don't know where or how or who, but you do know he's getting the best of care. Do you expect me, anybody, to believe that?"

Her father had turned his face to the window again. He stared out of it, into space, at nothing, as if he were just waiting for her to get tired of this.

She was very tired, but not going to give up. "Why were they just waiting in the wings to rush him off? Did they know that he was going to get sick? How did they know?"

Jeff's eyes came slowly back to her face. "No, they didn't know that. Not until I called them."

"I suppose they just happened to be driving by. With a radio in their ambulance, I suppose."

"They do have a radio, I'm sure. As you say, how else could they have been so quick?." Jeff paused, then, as if unable to help himself, asked, "What did the ambulance look like?" The tone of the question was almost wistful.

Holly stared at her father. She knew that look; it was his usual expression when he wanted to see something very new, an invention or a design, that he thought was going to be important.

Against Jeff's urging she had gone down in the elevator with Norlund and the attendants who had come for him, and she had tried to follow when they put him into the ambulance. In this case her usual forceful ways hadn't done her the least bit of good. The attendants had calmly but forcefully put her aside, and slammed the doors, and sped away. There had been no cabs in sight, or she would have tried to follow.

"It looked quite ordinary," she said now. "On the outside, at least. There were . . . respirators, I guess, and things inside. I didn't get a very good look. Why, are you wondering if it was streamlined properly, according to your rules?" If she had to fight, she might as well be nasty about it.

Her father didn't appear to notice. He had forgotten, at least for the moment, about the ambulance, because a sudden overriding suspicion had seized him. "Holly." His voice dropped. "There wasn't anything *between* the two of you, was there? You and Norlund?"

She could feel the unaccustomed tears start in her eyes. "And what if there was?"

Jeff was, predictably, aghast. "He's more than old enough to be your father. And Willy. What if Willy should find out?" Jeff had always been certain that there would be a reconciliation.

Rage came back, to dry tears like the heat of flames. "Dad, I'm not just going to drop this. You know me. I'm warning you that I'll go to the police, the newspapers, wherever else I have to go, to find out what's happened to him."

"Alan Norlund," Jeff said, as if to himself. Still he stared at his daughter in disbelief. Then another urgent question started to grow behind his eyes.

Holly forestalled it. "No, Alan and I haven't slept together. But that's not the point right now. The point is that I'm going to find out where he is, and how he is."

Jeff was pulling himself together. "Holly. Look. Sweetheart. It won't be good for Norlund, or for me either, if you make too much of this. In time we'll find out how he's doing."

"How will we find out?"

"It won't be good for *you*."

"You're going to have to explain to me why. Convince me. Or I'm going for the police, right now. You're talking as if you and Alan are involved with gangsters, and I won't believe that of either of you." And she started for the door, not bluffing.

Jeff, who knew her, gave up. "All right!" he called after her. When she stopped and turned, he held out his arm to her. It was a slow, old man's motion. "All right," he repeated. "I'll tell you what I can. But you must sit down and listen. Hear me out, and don't jump up and do anything until I've finished. Okay?"

"Okay," Holly said softly. She took her father's hand and held it, and sat down close to him.

"The reason I haven't told you any of this before," he began slowly, "is that I'm afraid, as I just said, that I could be putting your life in danger if I do. Still want me to go on?"

Memory flashed in her mind: the strange attack

during her flight with Norlund. But she only said: "Go on."

"Of course. It was a silly question. All right." He sighed deeply. "It all goes back to that day we crashed."

For some reason Holly felt no surprise. She had long realized that day marked some kind of a watershed. "All right. When you thought that I was dead."

Her father was looking at her very strangely now. He let go of her hand, and got to his feet as if with some definite purpose in mind. But then he only paced a lap around the room and came back to stand in front of her.

When he spoke, his voice was so low that Holly could barely distinguish the words. "I still believe that you were dead."

"What?"

"Listen to me, my dear. You were just lying there, all covered with blood. I couldn't find any pulse. And as far as I could tell, you were not breathing."

"But I was only knocked out. I woke up."

Her father was shaking his head. "Listen to me, I say. While you were—lying there—two people arrived."

"What two people?"

"A man and a woman. I thought at first that they were only hikers; there were no roads, and they arrived from somewhere, I couldn't quite see how. And they offered to help me. But only under certain conditions."

"Dad, you must have been hurt yourself."

"No. I know it sounds that way. I was in a tremendous state of shock, certainly. Beside myself with grief, because I was sure that you were dead. At first I wasn't quite sure that the people talking to me were real. But, as it turned out, they are very real indeed. Just as real as those ambulance attendants that you just saw. As all that special gear, installed in the cabin of your plane." Jeff's voice dropped again. "As real, God help me, as whatever it was that attacked you when you were on that flight with Norlund. I never expected that, I swear."

He had never raised the subject with her before. "I didn't know you knew about that. Do you know what it was?"

Her father shook his head helplessly. "Let me finish telling you what little I do know." He drew a breath, and went on. "The two people who arrived at the crash. I've said I couldn't quite see how they got there. But there was a sort of . . . rushing sound, I thought, in the sky. A moment of oddly colored light. And then there they were."

"A rushing," Holly murmured. And an odd light? If she had been trying to describe the strange phenomenon in the sky during her flight with Norlund, she might well have chosen the same terms.

Jeff misinterpreted what must have been the odd way that she was looking at him. "I tell you, those people were real enough. I've seen one of them since then, and I've talked with her many times."

"A woman."

"A young woman, of fairly ordinary appearance. Her name is Ginny Butler, or so she says. I never learned the man's name. The pair of them bent over you, looking at you closely. The man took one instrument after another out of a backpack that he was wearing, and he kept probing at you with them. I remember asking if he was a doctor, but he didn't answer. Instead he conferred for a moment with Ginny Butler, and then she led me a little distance away and talked with me. She told me you were beyond ordinary medical help."

"Oh, Jeff."

"But, she told me, there was still one chance. If I helped them, worked for them afterwards, she swore that they would do everything they could for you. She assured me that there would be nothing wrong or illegal in any task they would ever assign me. Of course I raged at them for making conditions. But then I swore I would do anything.

"With that, the man went to work on you at once. The woman kept me from watching very closely. She kept telling me what a great cause it was, that I was now going to work for, how it would one day make the whole world a better place. Well—one's heard all that before, of course. Still, I did swear a solemn oath to help them, and to keep their secrets." Jeff paused, sagging. He moved again to the sofa and sat down. His voice had fallen to a whisper. "Now I'm breaking my oath, and I don't know what the result is going to be. Are they perhaps going to—withdraw their investment?"

"I don't understand."

Jeff looked sadly at his daughter. "When I was first pleading with them for help, they put it to me this way: they couldn't afford to help all the accident victims in the world. Therefore they—invested their help carefully. It was given only in cases where they could expect a return, in the form of help for their own great cause."

"Which is—?"

Her father's smile was ghostly. "I've never found that out, exactly."

Despite herself, Holly was growing afraid. It was not that she did not believe her father. It was that she did. "And you've been helping them?"

"Yes. Doing things that seem harmless in them-

selves, if sometimes strange. Allowing that equipment
to be put in your plane, for one thing. They of course
sent men to do it—what it's supposed to do, I really
have no idea. Norlund does. He's one of them. Or else
he's simply working for them, recruited by them as I
was, perhaps. It was their phone number that I dialed
last night, when he collapsed—a number that Ginny
Butler had given me to memorize. And it was their
ambulance that you saw, taking him away."

Holly sat down beside her father. "This woman,
Ginny Butler. You say you've seen her many times,
since the crash?"

"Seen her a few times. Talked to her often, mostly
on the phone. They like to do business by phone." Jeff
pushed himself to his feet once more and went to an
abandoned bar-cart, where he managed to put together a glass of ice and mineral water. "An ambulance came for you too, you see. It wasn't an ordinary
vehicle—there was no road, remember? And it wasn't
an autogyro. I never really saw how they did it, but
I know they took you away, somehow, to somewhere
else, while the woman kept on talking to me, distracting
me. Then almost before I could be sure that you were
gone, they were bringing you back. You were still all
bloody, and unconscious. But now you were obviously
alive."

The whole thing sounded very unreal to Holly. And
at the same time she could not seriously doubt it.
"They aren't bringing Alan back that fast."

Jeff examined his icewater as if it might possibly be
of some rare vintage. "No, they're not. It occurs to me
that there were other people here last night, who saw
him taken away with what certainly looked like a heart
attack. If he were brought back very quickly, in good
health, it would look strange." He drank quickly, and

paused. "I'm sure we'll get news of him quite soon. Almost sure," he added in a low voice. He looked at his daughter. "I'm rather surprised that you're not telling me I'm crazy."

There was the equipment in her plane, like nothing else she had ever seen before. There was the sense of strangeness about Norlund, and his work with her father. And one thing more, the clincher. "When I was flying with Alan," she told her father, "that thing that came after us in the sky . . . I can't imagine any reasonable, natural explanation for what it looked like. And I've tried."

Jeff seemed suddenly on the verge of being crushed by remorse. "The people who recruited me are fighting against some other force, some other group, with the same kind of powers. It's a kind of war I've gotten you into, I see that now. God, Holly, at least I can tell you now how sorry I am about that. But it was either that or—or—"

On impulse, Holly flew to his side, and gave him an enormous hug. The impulse was genuine, but in a moment she pulled back. "What else can you tell me?"

"I think not much. I think nothing at all. We'll just have to see where we go from here." Jeff sucked at his icewater, and she thought that he was still concealing something. He went on. "We'll wait. We'll hear, in time, about Alan." Then he demanded suddenly: "Why can't you make things up with Willy? He's your husband."

Holly was not going to be distracted right now. "That phone number you have, the one you dialed for the ambulance."

Jeff shook his head vigorously. He looked horrified. "You wouldn't get any questions answered with that.

I'm afraid you'd just create serious trouble for both of us by trying to use it. It's for dire emergencies."

"The phone company . . . "

"You might just as well go to the harness and buggy-whip company for help." Then the bitterness in Jeff's voice was abruptly transmuted into enthusiasm; it was as if he could not help himself. "Holly, the things that Ginny Butler and her people can do. They're—" He checked himself, as if on the verge of some improvident guess, or revelation. "Knowing what can be done, I'd give my right arm to see what the future is going to be like. Generations from now. The science, the healing, the discoveries . . . "

Holly's fingers, nervously clasping, had rediscovered her small burn. Already it felt more like a healed scar than a recent injury.

Jeff, in spite of everything, could still be distracted, almost enraptured, by thoughts of the future. "Would the people of five hundred years ago have believed someone who claimed to come from the future? They'd have cried witchcraft. But today we ought to know better. Today we ought to believe in the future that science can create." And with that he shut up suddenly, like a man who knew that now he'd said too much.

Suddenly Holly had to get away. "Dad, I'm going out. No, it's all right, I'm not going to repeat to anyone what you've been telling me. But I have to get out, walk, get some air, think. I'll be all right."

She hurried out of the library, to grab boots and a fur coat from a closet and put them on. There was a last hurried exchange of waves between her and her father, assuring each other that they were all right. Then she was gone.

At this early hour on a holiday morning she had expected to have the elevator to herself, but it stopped at the floor immediately below hers and a man got on. He was youthful in appearance, and well-dressed in homburg hat and topcoat, as if he might be going to work today, holiday or not. Not your ordinary overstayed party-goer heading home at dawn, but quite sober and wide awake and freshly shaven. He was a little taller than average, blond and lean, but not exactly German-looking. Not exactly handsome, either, to Holly's taste. She couldn't recall seeing him around the building before.

He gave his homburg a little tip. "Mrs. Rudel, good morning." His voice had authority in it, and a trace of indefinable accent—again, she thought, not German.

"Good morning," Holly answered automatically, mildly startled. She studied the man again. "I'm sorry, but ought I to know you?"

"I am very glad to meet you at last, Mrs. Rudel. My name is Hajo Brandi, and I represent the law."

IN YEARS UNKNOWN

Jerry Rosen was seated inside what looked to him, by God, like an almost recognizable phone booth—one big difference was that this was too comfortable. He was physically alone, though he knew that Ginny Butler or one of her people would be listening in when his call went through.

He was at last, after being here in this still-unnamed school or whatever it was for several weeks, getting his chance to phone home.

Just above Jerry's eye level, as he sat comfortably in the booth, were certain numbers and indicators on its wall. What their current readings meant, as he had been taught to interpret them, was that the call he was trying to place, if it could be completed on schedule, would be received at the Monahan residence in Chicago at some early hour in the evening of Christmas Eve, nineteen thirty-three.

There was no need in this booth for him to hold a

receiver to his ear. Just sitting there, hands nervously clasping and unclasping on his knees, Jerry waited, listening. The quiet in the booth was almost absolute, except that now he could hear the ringing of that distant phone. Jerry kept hoping that the call was going through early, as the indicators said, before Judy and her Ma set out for midnight mass. They would probably leave the baby at home, for the half-grown girls to watch, but they might take old Mike along if they judged him sober enough—Christmas Eve was a special occasion—and if he felt like going. They might—

Someone picked up the distant phone. And in another moment Jerry could hear his wife's voice, as if she were right there in the booth with him, saying: "Hello?"

"Judy? It's me."

He had been warned to expect a certain delay in response time, probably enough to be noticeable. One component of the delay was deliberately built in, so he could be cut off if he tried to say something he wasn't supposed to say. Another component was apparently inherent in the way this cross-time communication worked. Still, the pause that followed after Jerry had identified himself was a little more than he had been expecting.

Then his wife was able to talk. "Jerry. Oh my God. Where are you? What's happened?"

"Listen, I'm all right. I may not be able to get home for a while yet, but I'll get there. Did you report me missing?"

"Jerry, it's been five months. Yes, we reported you. Where are you? Are you coming home?"

"I can't come home right now. I'm gonna, later, I swear it. Are you and the kid all right?"

There was a burst of something like radio static, which immediately cleared up again.

"—yeah," Judy was saying. "The other kids had measles, we just got the quarantine sign down off the door." Her voice shifted off-phone. "Ma, Ma, it's Jerry." Back again. "Yes, we're all right. Jerry, my God, my God, I made novenas . . ." A new change in Judy's voice. "There was a telegram came, about your father. Did you get that news?"

"My old man? What about him?"

This time the delay stretched on and on, to conclude not with Judy's voice but in a vast explosion. Not at the Monahans', either; a hell of a lot closer than that. Jerry could feel the floor, the whole booth, quiver with it. All the lights in the booth, including the digital readouts, momentarily went dead, leaving him in pitch blackness. A moment later the emergency lights from outside the booth came stabbing through the dark, penetrating transparent panels.

Jerry found that the door was slightly stuck now, but he forced it open and got out. The people who had been in the larger room that contained the booth were gone, and in the distance an alarm was hooting. Just like the practice alerts they had been holding during the past few days, thought Jerry, with an effort recalling himself from thoughts of his father and his wife to face his present situation. But this time, with the lights gone out, and starting with a bang like that, he doubted that it was practice.

Something outside the high gray walls was battering at them like a gigantic tank, and they were going down.

Norlund observed this from a distance, over a remote monitor, while he was pausing to regain some breath after a considerable run. He took one look at the image of those crumbling walls and then ran again, on legs newly taut with youth, their firm muscles fueled by fear. Corridors flowed past him, holding a scattering of other people, some of them running too. By now Norlund had been up and about long enough to know his way around here pretty well. Just as in a normal alert drill, he was heading for the weapons rack where his sidearm was ordinarily kept.

He reached the rack, and amid other scrambling hands and arms snatched his assigned weapon out. He automatically checked the charge, even while jostling his way past other people, away from the arms rack and on toward his next destination.

Which was not far. Norlund hurried among other scrambling bodies through the wide entrance to the huge Operations Room, then across the hangar-like spaces of Operations to the particular launch rack where his assigned vehicle waited. This was an armored personnel carrier with time-travel capability, much different from anything that Norlund had ever ridden in or ever seen. The elephant-sized body of the APC was all slanted planes of dull gray, with the protrusion here and there of a weapon nozzle or some kind of sensor. The two large front wheels were gray, also, and almost spherical. The rear of the body rode on extended, shapeless globs of something that took the place of the endless armored treads of an old-style military halftrack.

The uppermost hatch of the APC was open, and Norlund quickly clambered atop the vehicle and slid down inside. Ginny Butler was already occupying her assigned place, the observer's position toward the front of the cabin, while Andy Burns was in one of the seats toward the rear. The two other assigned mem-

bers of the combat team, Jerry and Agnes, had not yet
arrived. Norlund had just time to get himself secured
in his own seat when Jerry came bursting in through
the hatch above, swearing energetically at things in
general.

A moment later, Ginny turned round in her chair to
hand Norlund a moderately large white envelope. He
thought that the expression on her face as she looked
at him was odd.

He accepted the envelope, with some surprise.
"What's this?"

"This is obviously more than an alert, right?"

"Right."

"So I've opened our sealed combat orders." Ginny
nodded toward the envelope now in Norlund's hands.
"The first one appoints you to take over this group as
RM."

"What?" Norlund felt dazed. "You're the ranking
member."

"As long as we're in training. But no longer. At this
point I just wish you good luck, and stand by for
orders myself." She nodded at the envelope again.
"There are the rest of the orders, still sealed. They're
for you to open now."

Norlund looked down at the envelope he was holding.
Then he pulled out the first sheet of paper that it held;
the paper unfolded and uncreased itself to comfortable flatness as its corners cleared the enclosure. The
message printed on it was short. In terse language it
made official what Ginny had just been telling him:
as soon as combat started, at the base or elsewhere,
Norlund was to take over as commander of their small
group, and was charged with immediately moving to
carry out their assigned mission.

Under that first sheet of paper, an inner envelope,

still sealed, was thick with detailed orders—or something. Norlund pulled out the inner envelope only far enough to read the warning that it bore: FOR COMBAT RM ONLY. OPEN ONLY AFTER FIRST COMBAT LAUNCHING AND RE-EMERGENCE.

Ginny, Andy Burns, and Jerry Rosen were all looking at Norlund when he raised his eyes. He thought he saw in their faces less surprise than he felt himself. Well, maybe it was logical. He did have real combat on his record, even if it had been in a different army and . . . a different war? No, perhaps not even that. And he was older than the others, and they knew it, even though he no longer looked as much older as he was. The mirror these days showed him the face of a man of thirty, a hard-bitten face that he supposed could easily look authoritative enough.

And, he supposed also, he knew the job.

More explosions sounded. Somewhere outside of Operations, but still uncomfortably close. Voices were yelling, some of them in panic.

The panels at the driver's and observer's positions indicated that the vehicle was ready, fueled and targeted for an emergency launching into time. To get it away safely, ready to fight somewhere, sometime, had to be the first objective of its crew and their commander.

But all the crew was not here yet; Agnes was still missing. Swearing, Norlund got himself out of his seat and stuck his head up through the hatch. Operations was chaos, in which no trace of Agnes could be seen. He dropped down again, pulling the hatch closed above him. Jerry Rosen, in the driver's seat, was looking up at him expectantly.

"Drive us out, Jerry," Norlund ordered.

Jerry didn't move at first, except to look over at Ginny as if requesting confirmation.

"I'm RM now," said Norlund. "Do it. Get us the hell out of here, somewhere fast."

Three seconds later the APC launched. There had been nothing surprising about Jerry's assignment as first driver, given his high scores on the simulator tests in training. And from the start of training Jerry had insisted that these APC's weren't as hard to control as their reputation had it. "They just tell us they're tough to keep us from trying to use 'em to get home."

The launching at Jerry's hands now was barely in time, for a last explosion, very near, almost overtook the vehicle. Norlund, watching the observer's screens, could see how the reaching tendrils of that blast came after them, spreading like cracks in a fine vase across the last milliseconds of their existence within the Operations chamber. Then those computer-drawn lines were gone, along with all other information from the world of normal timeflow. The vehicle with them in it had survived the blast, but it was obvious to everyone that it was going to be thrown off course.

What wasn't obvious at first, at least to Norlund, was how far off they were going to be. Their passage through the brightly-colored world between the years continued through hours of subjective inside-the-vehicle time, a much longer period than any normal launching would have entailed.

From time to time during these hours, Jerry would lay hands on the controls, and make some minor adjustment to them, and reluctantly take his hands away again. Given the magnitude of the initial deflection caused by that explosion, there was probably little that any driver could have done in the way of correcting course. It would be necessary to wait until some destination was reached, and try again. Meanwhile indications were that the computers were laboring to do their best.

Norlund glanced several times at the envelope containing his sealed orders. But the warning on it was plain—he was to wait until first emergence before opening it.

Some of the hours of passage time were occupied by getting into combat clothing and gear, something of a struggle in the cramped space available. When everyone had done that there was really nothing more to do but wait, and be ready for emergence when it came. The vehicle felt as steady as an airliner in smooth flight, and was almost quiet; muffled chaotic noises came and went outside the hull at intervals, and now and then there was a perceptible movement, a shift as if gravity had altered slightly. The waiting conditions were endurable, so far, if not comfortable. An APC was built for survival, not comfort, and with four people and their gear aboard the interior was dense with equipment and supplies and bodies.

Norlund, trying to relax in his chair—trying above all to look confident—could close his eyes and hear to right and left the engines of the old Fortress. But the engines he heard were far too quiet, and he was too warm and relatively too comfortable, for the illusion to be in the least convincing.

At last the colored lights that made up their surrounding universe began to change, their images in the viewscreens signalling imminent emergence. Presently Ginny in the observer's position announced that the early sensors were beginning to recover, another sign that they were fast approaching normal timeflow.

Moments after Ginny's report the vehicle lurched more strongly than before, and those inside briefly knew the sensation of free fall. This lasted for only a fraction of a second before the APC found solid footing, wheels and tracks bouncing and then coming to rest with brushing, crackling noises, in what sounded like tall grass.

Now the screens showing the outside were filled with a different color, what Norlund took to be gray daylight. "Battle stations," he ordered, and realized even as he spoke that he ought to have given the command sooner.

Stillness reigned, inside and outside the vehicle. The crew looked over their surroundings as well as they could, with instruments that were still recovering from passage through time. It was impossible as yet to tell where and when they had emerged.

"Clear from stations," Norlund said at last. He looked again at the envelope of sealed orders. It would be legitimate to open them now, but he felt that finding out where they were took precedence even over that.

"I'm going out to take a look around."

When he opened the top hatch the air that came in was chill. The sun was hidden in a thick overcast, and Norlund was struck immediately by a couple of drops of rain, feeling cold as snow. When he stuck his head out of the hatch he saw that the vehicle was surrounded on three sides by miles of tall, brown grass. Near the horizon the grass made islands out of groves of trees, looking brown and leafless. On the fourth side—there was no telling which compass direction it might be— the grass was cut off at about a hundred yards' distance, by a rank of tall sand dunes.

Climbing free of the vehicle, Norlund dropped into the tall grass, which crunched under his combat boots. Just behind the APC were the three or four yards of tracks it had left between materializing in the air and rolling to a stop. Norlund's crew followed him out, some of them with sidearms at the ready. He thought that the dismal peace around them mocked weaponry.

Jerry, after a moment, holstered his gun. "I bet this ain't nineteen thirty-four," he said.

"Toto," said Norlund, "I don't think this is Kansas." Seeing how blankly the others looked at him, he sighed. "Or maybe it could be. All right, I'm going to climb to the top of one of those dunes and take a look around from there."

"We could drive up it," Andy suggested.

Norlund shook his head. "I'd rather keep the APC in time-mode, save a few seconds on a quick getaway if it's necessary. If we move it spatially we lose that, right? Jerry, you come with me. Andy, Ginny, you stay here."

In silence he trudged with Jerry through crackling grass, over to the nearest dune and up its flank. Their feet slid frustratingly on the slope of sand.

Increasing elevation revealed nothing but more of the same landscape—until they reached the top. Then a plain of water came into sight, stretching from just past the line of dunes out to a calm gray horizon.

"The lake," said Jerry, true Chicagoan.

"Maybe." Norlund was scanning the expanse for sails, for smoke, for any sign of human presence, but finding none. "I don't know what our geographic displacement was on that launch. For all I know, we could be in Asia now."

Jerry, as if his natural navigator's or hot-shot pilot's instinct were affronted by this idea, shook his head and muttered something vulgar. He was plainly not impressed by Norlund's recently acquired rank.

Gesturing for Jerry to follow, Norlund went sliding and scrambling down the side of the dune toward the water. Meanwhile he scanned the narrow beach for footprints. Only bird-tracks were visible in the strip of damp sand until he and Jerry crossed it. At the very shoreline Norlund squatted to scoop up in his palm a small sample of a cold, gentle wave. He tasted it and found it fresh.

"Maybe this is Lake Michigan," he said, standing up again. "Anyway, I'm not sure that really matters to us now." He surveyed the world, which from this viewpoint contained only the dull sky, the lake, the wind-carved dunes—all speaking of slow time. Small waves lap-lapped on sand. The breeze lofted birds that looked like gulls, and stirred the sparse, tough grass that half-clothed some of the dunes. It urged the small waves in from the horizon to the shoreline that smelled vaguely of dead fish.

And suddenly Norlund knew fear; this time not combat-terror of the enemy, but a more subtle and inescapable dread of time itself. He felt sure that they had been deflected further into the past than any of them realized. Further, perhaps, than anyone ought to go. He understood vaguely from his brief training that there were limits that ought not to be transgressed. He was afraid of what Ginny might tell him when he got back to the vehicle, afraid of hearing what the numbers really were.

"What now, chief?" Jerry, untroubled by metaphysics, was waiting to be given orders and be informed about what happened next.

Norlund shrugged, concealing his feelings. "Let's get back to the APC."

As they approached the carrier, they found Andy standing sentry in the open top hatch. Inside, Ginny was back in the observer's seat, busy at the panel. As Norlund entered she looked up. "I'm not going to be able to determine where we are without a number of additional readings, and then some lengthy calculations. Anyway, the computer indicates that it might not be worth the trouble of trying to find out."

"No?" Norlund felt obscure relief.

"No. Our best move in this situation may simply be to take a good guess as to where we are—or a bad guess, even, if it works out that way—and then start moving. We ought to be able to zero in on our target year by a series of successive approximations. We can tell if we're moving toward it, even if we don't know what time we're starting from—where we are now." And Norlund thought that Ginny shivered slightly as she spoke. He wondered if she were frightened, too, of time. The thought was not reassuring.

He nodded briskly. "All right, let's do it that way."

He got into his chair again, and there was the envelope of sealed orders, still waiting to be opened. As casually as possible he added: "While you guys are getting set up for another launch, I better take a look at this."

He settled himself back into his seat and took up the envelope and ripped it open. He skimmed through the contents, saving details for later study. Several times in the course of scanning the papers he looked up from them, and each time found at least one member of his crew observing him.

Whatever they might be able to read in his face, thought Norlund, it was probably not surprise.

Once more he read through the key sentences in the orders. He looked up to find that his crew were all ready for launching, watching him and waiting.

Norlund told them.

"We're going to kill Hitler."

1934

As Norlund had feared, it took a long struggle, a good many subjective, inside-the-vehicle hours, to get back to their proper target year. Almost a full day passed, the crew grumbling and stiffening in their cramped positions, as the APC hunted from one approximation to another, before the change of exterior light and the revival of early instruments signalled once more that a full emergence was at hand. But in a sense the hours passed more quickly than those of that first deflected trip. Driver and observer had more to do, working out a course and staying with it. And Norlund used the opportunity to brief and drill everyone on the details of the plans and alternate plans that the sealed orders had presented.

"Roosevelt invited Hitler t'visit the US?" Andy Burns, for all the classes they'd all had discussing timelines, was having trouble with the idea.

Norlund sighed. "Yeah. The idea was that between

them they could maybe work out some way of keeping world peace. Getting out of economic troubles."

"But it wouldn't work."

"No, it wouldn't. But it gives us our chance at him."

Andy nodded, probably not understanding much —a waist-gunner following orders, being briefed for the next mission.

An hour came when signs of emergence began to develop, and then a minute came when the signs were very strong.

"This is it, guys."

"This is it . . . yeah, no doubt about it this time. Here we are, nineteen thirty-four."

"The New York site? Chicago?"

"We'll see." That one wasn't possible to answer so confidently.

As before, abrupt momentary free-fall was followed by a crunching landing. This time arrival was on what sounded like packed cinders.

The first glimpses of the outside obtainable through viewscreens were ambiguous. Again Norlund got the definite impression that he had probably not reached Kansas. More to the point, the APC did not seem to be in either of the landing slots, in New York and Illinois, that its crew had been attempting to reach.

"This is one of the emergency alternate sites, I'll bet. The autopilot must have found it for us."

"Or else the navigational grid diverted us again. . . . "

Suddenly there were more possibilities than had been readily foreseeable. There was no absolute certainty. Anyway, sensors showed that this time the APC had come to rest in comparatively warm near-darkness, on a cindered or graveled flat of land. In the distance, Norlund thought he caught just a quick glimpse of something pyrotechnic—a skyrocket? A volcanic flare?

A cliff-like surface reared up close on the right side of the vehicle, cutting off the view in that direction and shadowing it from what was probably faint moonlight. In the opposite direction trees were silhouetted against sky, and Norlund recognized a palm. Near the palm was another shape: lower, peculiar. . . . It wasn't until Norlund had led the way out of the APC to reconnoiter, and had taken a couple of steps in that direction, that he recognized the horned head of a triceratops.

Norlund was still almost frozen, his weapon on the way to being leveled at the dinosaur, when brisk human footsteps off to one side distracted him. The single approach was quiet, though not really stealthy.

Norlund shifted his aim. "Who is it?" he called sharply.

"Mercury," a low voice replied, as some yards away the footsteps stopped. It took Norlund a moment to recognize in the answer one of the code words that he had been taught to expect—in this case it was one of the less likely ones, the code name of a local agent at one of the alternate emergence sites in Thirty-four.

"Okay, come ahead." Puffing out his breath, Norlund relaxed his aim. A quick glance back at the triceratops assured him that it had not moved.

The footsteps again came nearer, slowly, as quietly as could be expected for a man walking on cinders. Mercury on arrival was quite ordinary-looking: a youngish man dressed in overalls, an appropriate outfit for some Thirties caretaker or janitor. Now Norlund could see that the cliff-like surface right beside the vehicle was really the stuccoed and almost windowless wall of some huge building.

Mercury gave the vehicle a looking-over, and also

the people emerging from it. He did not appear to be enormously impressed. "How many of you, four? You'll need clothes, I suppose. Not weapons, I see. If you need money, I'm a little short but I'll see what I can do. You can just leave the vehicle right where it is if you want to; it'll be all right for an hour or so. Then I can get rid of it."

"Where are we?" Norlund demanded, almost hopelessly.

Mercury blinked at him, surprised that Norlund did not know. "This is the fourth of July. Uh, nineteen thirty-four."

"But *where*?"

"Why, Hollywood. This is the Paramount back lot."

At Mercury's suggestion the travelers stayed with their vehicle, while he went to a nearby building. He emerged again in a few minutes, clothing bundled in his arms. They had told him what sizes they required.

"Little short of money right now," he repeated as he rejoined them, dumping his bundle down. "Even if I put in some of my personal funds, things are kinda tough, you know? But here's six bucks each." And he counted out fives and ones, pausing before he gave Ginny her share, as if he thought that for some reason a woman might not really require it. Meanwhile Norlund was silently cursing the decision, made higher up, for them to refit and resupply locally this time.

"And there's the clothes," Mercury went on. "I got extras' stuff out of Wardrobe. Hope that dress fits you, lady."

Ginny ducked inside the APC to change. The men meanwhile shuffled garments on and off while standing on the cindered lot. Norlund, fortunately for him, had got both legs into his new pants before the futuristic gunfire struck at them from the general direction of the palm tree and triceratops—he was able to hit the dirt without breaking a leg in the process.

The defensive shields of the APC had already reached out to embrace the exposed members of its crew, saving Norlund's life and Jerry's. For Mercury and Andy Burns, standing a trifle closer to the foe, the protection came fractionally too late, and they both were hit.

Norlund, sprawled on his belly in cinders, pumped silent and almost invisible death rays from his sidearm out into the darkness, toward the enemy's concealed position somewhere near the dinosaur, while Jerry lying beside him did the same. Then, just above their heads, the heavier weapons of the APC lashed out, in the same spooky silence. Plaster triceratops and real palms were pretty much unaffected, but the enemy fire stopped.

Norlund turned his head. Mercury's body and Andy's were shriveled husks inside scorched clothing; it was obvious that they had been somehow fried to death. Only Andy's artificial right arm was still moving, as if there might be a trace of life left in it. . . .

"Clear now, chief." Ginny's voice, quavering but functional, came through a small external speaker in the APC's armored flank. "My scan shows they're all dead over there. Are you getting back aboard?"

"Thanks, Gin," Norlund said. There was a smell of cooked meat in the air, and Jerry was being sick. Temporarily, Norlund hoped. He himself had been inoculated by the events of twenty combat missions. "Some of us are getting on. Just stay alert in there, and give us a minute to do some things out here."

Jerry recovered quickly. Between him and Norlund they loaded the two casualties of the crew into the vehicle. There was no place to put the bodies but in seats; Ginny was going to have a grim trip back. Norlund rifled Andy's and Mercury's pockets for the local money that they had just been issued, but the bills were burned into unusability.

Ginny looked on, pale-faced in the concentrated interior lighting.

Norlund draped blankets over the bodies. Then he thumped his hand on the inner surface of the hull. "We can't use this vehicle here in Thirty-four, and we can't just leave it. I don't know what Mercury's method of hiding it or returning it would have been. So I want you to take it back to home base, Ginny. If the base isn't there any more, or you can't reach it, do what you can."

"What about the mission?"

"Jerry and I are going on. You're the utility person in the lineup, and this is where we need you."

She nodded, more relieved than anything, Norlund thought. Then she remembered to give him back the few local dollars that Mercury had just given her. He split the money with Jerry; now the two of them had nine dollars each.

Norlund asked her to delay departure briefly while he went with Jerry to look over the enemy dead. There were four scattered bodies in Thirties clothing. Again, no money was salvageable; their dropped weapons were unfamiliar to Norlund, and what he thought was probably a communicator of some kind was dead.

He went back to the APC with Jerry and called for different weaponry. In moments all trace of the enemy dead was gone. There was only a faint scorching noticeable on what had been cindered ground anyway. Let Hajo Brandi wonder what had happened to his people—unless one of those bodies by some good luck had been his.

Moments after that the APC, with Norlund's final wave to Ginny, was out of sight as well.

In the moon-shadow of the huge studio building, Norlund stood facing Jerry. "We split up here," said Norlund. "Get to Chicago and—hell, you know what you have to do."

"Yeah."

They shook hands. Norlund waited until Jerry's footsteps had died away before he moved himself.

Norlund during his more or less sheltered Depression youth had often heard about but never actually seen hobos riding freight trains across the country. According to the usual expression they "rode the rods", which meant that in some perilous way that Norlund had never quite understood they traveled slung beneath the cars, taking their ease within inches of the rails and ties and roadbed roaring past beneath them.

In his own first five days of traveling by freight, Norlund had yet to see the trick performed by anyone in quite that way. Most non-paying riders, he had observed, followed the method he had chosen for himself--clinging to the top of a boxcar or else riding lower and more sheltered in a gondola. Some few were successful in getting inside, like the men Norlund had glimpsed during his own recent period of prosperity, when he'd been riding the *Twentieth Century* first class.

One idea his last five days' experience had refuted—a cynical suspicion born during the time when he'd been paying for his passage. He was now quite sure that freights took just as long as passenger trains to cross the country. At least the ones he had been riding did. Five days, five times he'd watched the sun go down on dusty plains or desert, and he was still no farther east than Texas—crossing which, of course, promised to be an epic struggle in itself. Five days . . . or was it six?

With only nine dollars in his pocket at the start, there hadn't been very many means of transportation open to him. And he knew that Jerry would prefer hitchhiking, and he was determined to travel separately from Jerry, determined that one of them at least was going to get through. Either of them, of course, could call for help, from Jeff or other local agents, but after being ambushed in the presence of one such agent Norlund didn't want to do that just yet. There were a few days to spare. The *Graf* should not yet have departed from Germany, and to cross the Atlantic would take it a couple of days at the very least, even assuming favorable winds. Norlund meant to work his way east, closer to New York, and call for help when he was nearly there.

At least that had been his original plan on leaving Hollywood. Now he wasn't so sure. In one sense his plan was working; at least Brandi's people, Hitler's people, hadn't caught up with him yet. But on the other hand he wasn't all that much closer to New York, where on the twentieth of July the *Graf Zeppelin* was due to tie up to Jeff Holborn's ingenious mast atop the Empire State, and where the great dirigible would then discharge her illustrious passenger and his entourage to begin his state visit. . . .

And Norlund was having other problems. He had eaten only twice in the last three days, and not too often in the three days before that, even if you could call swallowing the kind of stuff he had ingested eating. Three days ago he'd been granted a share from an iron stewpot hanging over a fire in a tramp encampment lodged between railroad tracks and a highway bridge in Arizona. And the day after that he'd been fed at some religious charity's soup kitchen in a New Mexico town of modest size whose name Norlund had never learned, any more than he had learned with any certainty the name of the religious group who ran the charity.

He was traveling alone, which had its good points and its bad. One point about it, good or bad, was that he had to decide for himself when he had passed the point of being merely hungry and had started actually starving, in the sense of growing dangerously weak. Clinging now to a boxcar's top in the fifth or possibly sixth dusty sunset of his trip, he knew from the way the train's swaying motion made him feel that he now qualified as starving. Next town he came to, he'd have to take some serious steps about getting food. He still had his nine dollars.

As soon as a scattering of lights appeared ahead, and the train began to slow, Norlund made his way to the iron ladder at the end of the car, climbed down most of the way, and watched and waited for his chance. You had to be careful of more than being run over by the train, old hands at this game had warned him. You couldn't just stroll on and off, in and out of railroad yards. In some yards, some towns, the local cops or the railroad bulls lay in wait for unpaying passengers and beat them, sometimes just for the fun of it, or hauled them off to stand before a magistrate and then fill the ranks of work gangs on the county roads for thirty days. Personal and esthetic considerations aside, Norlund couldn't afford that kind of a delay.

The train rattled swaying around a curve, as the lights ahead grew closer. When Norlund had judged that the train had slowed enough, he jumped, tumbling on the uneven footing in the dark, but luckily not spraining or breaking anything.

He lay still until the train he had been riding on was past, then dodged across the tracks toward the lights. A fence presented no very serious problem. All was quiet.

Five minutes later, Norlund was walking up the dusty main street of another southwestern town whose name he did not know. He had brushed off his clothes as well as possible as he walked into town, wondering how close he could still come to an appearance of respectability. Not very, he had been forced to admit. His suit had been new-looking when he'd put it on in Hollywood, but after almost a week of continuous wear in hobo jungles and atop freight cars it was in bad shape. And Norlund himself was unwashed and unshaven. He had a necktie in his pocket if he wanted to put it on, but under the circumstances it was not going to help.

Any decent-looking eatery had to be considered off limits. Fortunately the sign of the soup kitchen was visible for a block away, with a dim light shining on it like some fading hope for salvation. The Mission for Unfortunates, or some such name. Norlund drew no attention as he entered and took his place amid a handful of other clients, most of them looking worse off than he did. He spent a dime for a bowl of soup and a chunk of bread, and in a couple of minutes was back to spend another dime for seconds.

Sitting down to savor this second helping, Norlund found himself alone at a converted picnic table lit by a bare bulb that hung overhead on its own wire. A sign on the wall across from him assured him that JESUS SAVES.

To keep himself from reading this over and over infinitely, he looked about for something else. There was old newspaper, spread on the other end of the table, where some messy project had evidently been carried out. Norlund grabbed what looked like a front page and pulled it nearer. It ought to be part of his job to keep up with the news, ready to cope with unscheduled and unforeseen events.

The first item, on the bottom half of the page, was reassuring.

> HITLER TRIP ON SCHEDULE
> Frankfurt, Ger., July 1 — Final preparations were in progress today for the state visit of Chancellor Adolf Hitler to the United States. Crews of men labored day and night to ready the *Graf Zeppelin* for the trans-Atlantic voyage, the most important of its success-ful career . . .
>
> This demonstration of German progress and aerial superiority, viewed by some in the United States as threatening, and by others as an encouraging sign of friend-ship . . .

Norlund sighed faintly, wishing for a more recent newspaper as a source of information about possible changes of plan during the past few days.

He flipped over the folded page, bringing its top half into view on the stained table. Here the headlines, also expected by Norlund, were bigger.

HITLER CRUSHES REVOLT BY NAZI RADICALS
STORM TROOP CHIEFS DIE

Killed Or Take Own Lives
    As Chancellor and Goering Strike
REACTIONARIES ALSO HIT
Wife Shot With Schleicher
    as He Resists Police
Head of Catholic Action Slain
LOYAL FORCES HOLD BERLIN
    IN AN IRON GRIP

The famous purge of Ernst Roehm and his trouble-
some Brownshirts. According to the plan, it should
not result in Hitler's visit to America being called off.

Looking for more information, looking for he knew
not what, Norlund flipped the paper over to page two.

DILLINGER RAIDS BANK IN SOUTH BEND
Officer Slain, Loot $28,000

Even the nation's most wanted criminal had been
pushed to page two by Hitler's news. Even . . .

FLYER RUDEL DEAD IN CRASH
Berlin, July 2 — Willy Rudel, 37, well-known
aviator known also as the son-in-law of the
famous designer Geoffrey Holborn, died Saturday in the crash of his small plane in the
Bavarian Alps, it was announced today.
Rudel's son, Wilhelm Jr., 9, also perished
in the crash. The aviator's estranged wife,
Holly, was reported in New York . . .

There was a very little more.

The phone available in the mission was the kind
you had to feed with coins for a long-distance call.
The people behind the soup-kitchen counter had plenty

of small coins with which to make change, when Norlund thrust dollar bills at them. If his manner was somewhat wild when he approached them, they had doubtless seen wilder, and made no comment.

Now, Norlund told himself, it was necessary for him to contact Jeff at once instead of waiting until he got closer to New York. Jeff was to be his prime contact on this mission, and anything likely to affect Jeff's capacity to function was something that he, Norlund, had to check up on as soon as possible. And a disaster like this striking at Jeff's daughter was certainly going to take a toll on Jeff.

To hell with all this justification, Norlund told himself. His fingers were busy clipping a small dull jewel—his bug-detector, part of his small store of secret equipment—on the receiver cord where it clung like a dark bug itself. The truth was he didn't know if it would be a mistake to make this call or not, but he was going to call her anyway.

He told the operator what number he wanted to reach, and fed in coins. Eventually there were two rings at the far end. And then Norlund recognized the voice of the butler answering.

"Rupert, this is Alan Norlund. Is Holly available? It's very important that I speak with her."

There was a pause. "Mr. Norlund, sir?"

"Yes, it's me." At least he had not been totally forgotten.

"Very glad to hear your voice, sir. We were all worried . . . I'll fetch Miss Holly to the phone immediately."

Long seconds passed. Norlund watched his bug-detector. So far the line appeared to be safe. He rearranged his little piles of coins on the little shelf before the phone, ready to feed in more money when the operator should break in to ask for it. He thought that he could feel the proprietors of the mission staring at his back.

Again someone picked up the receiver at the other end. "Hello?" said Holly's voice. The unbearable grief that Norlund had been bracing himself to hear in her voice was not evident. What he heard sounded to him more like simple suspense.

"Holly, it's Alan Norlund. I've just now heard. God, I'm so sorry for you."

"They killed them, Alan." Maybe the feeling that tightened her voice was not suspense either, but rage compressed and waiting. She'd had days now to get it under control, but still it seemed to leave no room for surprise at hearing from him so suddenly. "Those bastards killed them. It wasn't any crash, at least not accidental. The big purge was on, gangsters settling scores among themselves. And I know Willy had enemies, Goering and others. I've had word from people who got out." At last her voice did soften. "Alan, where are you, how are you?"

"At the moment, in Texas. And I'm in good shape." And still the bug-detector remained inert; Norlund supposed that Brandi's people were having their problems too, trying to defend in a dozen or a hundred places against the attack that they must know was coming, trying to avoid the crushing paradoxes that could make some regions inaccessible to time travel. "Could you find out anything through the State Department? If Jeff—"

"None of Jeff's friends were able to do anything. If the German government says it was an accident, then officially that's what it was. Even if we all know better. With that son of a bitch coming on his airship, nobody wants to stir things up."

"How's Jeff doing?"

"About as usual. He's out working, even if it is almost midnight. But you. Was that a heart attack? Jeff tells me that you . . . that you got the best medical care available anywhere."

It sounded like maybe Jeff had told her more. Norlund sighed. "Better than you'd believe. You won't know me when you see me again. That's going to be soon, I hope."

"Are you coming here?"

"Holly, I want you to tell Jeff something for me. Something very important." The detector still indicated that no one was listening in, but there was no telling how long it would stay that way. "Tell him rendezvous Jupiter, a couple of days from now. Will you do that?"

"Of course. Jupiter, in a couple of days. Is that all? What does it mean?"

"No, goddamn it, that's not all. That's very far from all. I want to see you, I've got to see you, but I can't see you just yet." And the device on the line sparked suddenly, emitting a sharp gem-flash of light directed at Norlund's eyes. He tried to change his voice. "I'll be talking to you, Mrs. Rudel. Good-bye."

The abrupt closing of that phone conversation was probably not the strangest thing about it, Holly thought, nor was it perhaps even the most alarming.

She knew where to look for her father. It was very doubtful that she would be able to reach him there by phone, and anyway in this case she preferred a face-to-face confrontation.

Griffith drove her to the Empire State, and waited at the curb. With a judicious combination of brass and cash, Holly got herself first into the building lobby and then into an elevator.

In a narrow service passage on the level of the

observation deck she encountered Jeff, who was just coming down from a climb on stairs and ladders to even greater heights. He was coming through a door, with the sprawl of the city's midnight lights behind him.

Holly stepped forward. "Jeff, I . . ." The rest of the sentence was never said. Descending immediately behind Jeff was the man she had encountered in the elevator on New Year's morning. Like Jeff, he was now wearing engineer's coveralls over his suit.

Holly's father, though startled for a moment, did not appear enormously surprised to see her there. Instead he became—not exactly embarrassed, Holly thought, he never really did that, but he got the look he usually wore when dealing with some social difficulty. "Holly, what's up?" he asked.

She grinned. "Just an impulse." She knew that from her such an explanation was likely to be accepted readily. "I timed it well, I see."

As the man behind him stepped forward smiling lightly at Holly, Jeff turned to him. "Ah, Mr. Brandi, this is my daughter."

For a moment Holly had the idea that Brandi might click his heels, Prussian-style, and bow. But he only grinned and put out his hand in an open, quite American way. "We've met once," he said.

Jeff was surprised. "Oh? Where was that?"

Holly told him briefly, not mentioning what had been said that time in the elevator. "I just didn't want to bother you with it, Dad; I didn't think it would turn out to have any importance. But what . . . ?"

Brandi cleared his throat. "A mutual friend introduced me to your father. I have been helping him on some matters connected with the mooring mast. We are making sure that it is safe."

Holly got the impression that when Brandi said those last words he was watching her closely for a reaction. "Good idea," she acknowledged, while wondering all the more what was going on.

Brandi had turned to Jeff. "At our earlier meeting, I told your daughter that I represented the law—but then I had no formal credentials to present. So she sent me off about my business, for which I can scarcely blame her."

Jeff nodded, as if he already understood why Brandi would have introduced himself in such a way. Meanwhile Holly, looking at the pale man, decided in her own mind that he was really not German at all, though that had been her first impression. Brandi didn't sound like a German name—at least she didn't think it did— and his faint accent seemed to be from somewhere else, she was not sure where.

"Then you do represent the law?" she asked him now. "Or don't you?"

"Holly." Her father's voice, to her surprise, was actually reproachful. "There are times when real life is not that simple. Washington and Jefferson had to take existing law into their own hands, in order to create this country. There were days when Lincoln himself had to suspend civil rights."

"And now you and Mr. Brandi—?"

"Don't worry about it, dear." Then Jeff caught himself, hearing in what he had just said the overtones of don't-bother-your-pretty-head-about-it. As he knew very well, that was about the worst imaginable way to go about enlisting his daughter's co-operation in anything.

He tried again. "There are times, yes, when good citizens have to act, even without formal credentials. Times when their country is in peril. Right now the Jews and the Reds between them have such a grip on

Washington . . . " Jeff's eyes were moist, and he almost choked on the last words. For a moment Holly was able to see the depth of his emotion.

"On George, that is?" Holly asked lightly. "Or on the city?" She turned to Brandi then, fluttering her eyelashes sarcastically. "I really don't understand a thing about politics. But I hope that at least the mooring mast is safe. Is there political significance to that?"

And only then, only in the moment after that last line had been delivered in perfect innocence, did she connect the day's largest headlines about the *Graf's* imminent departure from Europe and who would be on it and when and where it was scheduled to land, with what was going on before her eyes.

"There is now," said her father brusquely, bumping past her in the narrow passage, perhaps in an effort to conceal from her his own emotion. In the process he incidentally blocked Brandi's view of her face at what might have been her crucial moment of realization.

Then the moment was over. Brandi was saying: "Allow me to offer my sympathy, Mrs. Rudel, for your recent bereavement."

Holly had herself well in control now. "Thank you. I suppose no one could have prevented the crash. It's just one of the things that aviators live with." She paused. "Sorry if I was nasty just now. I'm afraid I'm still rather wrapped up in my own affairs."

"Of course." Brandi looked and sounded quite naturally decent and sympathetic. "I'm no pilot myself, but I am interested. Maybe some day when you feel like it, we could talk about flying."

"Yes, certainly." Holly hesitated, a new idea coming to mind. "Actually I'm going to take Dad to Chicago in a few days. There's a similar mooring mast there, as you must know if you're concerned with this one. You could come along with us."

"Right," said Jeff, visibly relieved at his daughter's change in attitude.

"That would be great," said Brandi, smiling. "If you're sure there's room."

"In my Vega? Plenty. Of course there's some extra equipment in the cabin . . . " Holly turned to her father doubtfully.

"I want to have Mr. Brandi look at that equipment too," said Jeff somewhat grimly. "Before we fly."

Holly hesitated momentarily, then brightened. "I'm going out tomorrow morning and have a look at the kite. Mr. Brandi can come along then if he wants to. And you too, Dad, of course."

"Sounds like a fine idea," Brandi agreed at once.

"Right." Jeff was pleased that things were now going so smoothly, though he shot Holly one almost-suspicious glance. "Shall we get together around nine?"

In a mood of general agreement, chatting about weather and the difference it made in flying, the small group of them moved along the passage, down one short interior stair, and thence to an elevator.

In the lobby Brandi excused himself to make what he said was a rather important phone call in one of a row of midnight-empty booths. Jeff accepted this without apparent surprise, and took the opportunity to turn Holly aside and speak to her with some urgency.

"Holly, you remember Alan Norlund, of course."

"Of course."

"You haven't heard anything from him lately, have you? Or heard of him?"

"No, why?" She had always, she thought, been an accomplished liar.

"Or of—anyone who might be connected with him?"

"Jeff, for Pete's sake! How should I know who

might be connected with him? I don't even have any idea whether or not he's still alive." Among the other concerns running furiously and simultaneously through Holly's mind was the thought that sooner or later Rupert was bound to say something about Mr. Norlund having called tonight and spoken to her. In fact, Rupert had almost certainly mentioned it already to some of the other servants. There was no use Holly's wishing now that she had pledged the butler to silence before she left home.

Jeff was again relieved, this time enough to smile. And suddenly his daughter could perceive him as vulnerable. "You'll tell me, won't you dear, if you should hear from Norlund? Or anything about him?"

"Of course, if you like. But what's the big deal? Is this Brandi tied up in the same business?"

That turned Jeff sad again. He gave Holly an odd look, and shook his head. "Holly, I wish I'd never got you into this at all . . . but that was forced on us, and it can't be helped now. Brandi has promised that we'll get all the support we need, even if those others should be able to withdraw theirs." He glanced toward the row of phone booths, where one door was still closed. "One more thing, quick. That phone number you once talked me into giving you—something else I shouldn't have done. Tell me, have you ever used it?"

Jeff's warnings on that point had been so convincing that she hadn't quite been able to make herself give it a try. "No, you warned me not to, unless some tremendous emergency came up. Why? Anyway, I'm not sure I even remember it any more."

"Thank God." He patted her arm. "Don't remember it. And don't *ever* use it now, as you value your own welfare and mine. Just put it out of your mind. Will you do that for me?"

Put it out of your pretty little head, thought Holly. Her very exasperation with her father—how could he be such a fool about some things?—seemed to provoke a corresponding surge of love. She wished that she could help him now, but she saw no way. "Sure," she said soothingly. "Dad, are you sure of what you're doing?" There was the sound of a phone-booth door opening, and she raised her voice slightly. "Ready to come home with me?"

"Not yet," said Jeff. "You run along." He glanced toward Brandi, footsteps hollowly approaching on the marble, and she could see in Jeff's face his shining certainty of the future. "Mr. Brandi and I have more work to do tonight."

Jeff had taken a couple of steps away from her, then spun back to show her something that he held in his clenched fist—one of the small ceramic things he had once told her were special recording devices. He had one of them, she remembered, in use as a paperweight in his office. He called back now: "I was taken in, Holly. Badly taken in. I'm trying now to make amends."

"Taken in by who, Jeff?"

"Don't worry about it. It's all going to be all right." Those were his parting words. Brandi waved to her, and the two men still in their engineers' coveralls went out through the lobby doors to the street.

Holly followed, in time to see them pull away in a car that had to be Brandi's. She walked quickly to her own car.

Griffith stood beside it, waiting. "Home, Miss?"

"Yes, but find me a telephone on the way. There's an urgent call I have to make."

Encased in the booth in the all-night drug store, she dialed the number her father had just warned her not to use, and listened to the peculiar ringing produced somewhere at the other end of the line. Someone picked up the phone there before she could decide just what was so peculiar about the ring.

"Hello?" It was a man's voice, sounding as if he might be right with her in the booth.

"Hello," she said firmly. "My name is Holly Holborn, and it's very important that I talk with someone there."

There was only the slightest pause. "My name is Harbin," the man's voice responded eagerly. "And you can talk with me."

Less than an hour later, at approximately one o'clock in the morning, Holly was speeding through the warm night on her way out to the Newark airport. Griffith was still at the wheel in the big car. He was not overly big himself, but quite tough, Holly thought, and certainly loyal. So she had made a point of bringing him along, and had also made sure he understood that there might be some kind of trouble.

"Sure, Miss. What kind?"

"Physical trouble. Where I might need a friend who's bigger and stronger than I am. I'm not certain. But be ready, would you?"

"Sure." Griffith had sounded pleased.

Then they had made a flying trip to the home apartment, where Holly had gathered from closet and bureau drawers and hidden safe some money and other things that she expected she might need. Then, to the airport.

In the back of the car, hunkered down, she changed into flying clothing as they drove.

When they reached the airfield, there was a light on inside the operations shack. Holly had no idea whether or not that was usual at this time of night. The light went out as they drove up, as if someone inside had wanted to look out through darkened windows at the arriving car. Then the light came on again, and a couple of outside lights as well. As Holly and Griffith disembarked from the auto, two men stepped out of the small building to meet them.

One of the men she knew, a regular employee at the field. The other she had not seen before, but he impressed her at once as looking somehow like Hajo Brandi's cousin, only larger and more muscular.

The regular worker was plainly surprised to see her there at such an hour. "What can we do for you, Miss Holborn?"

She moved forward cooly, swinging her pilot's gloves in one hand. "Is my plane ready?"

"Why . . . " The regular man was really puzzled.

"Get it ready," she ordered. From the corner of her eye she saw Griffith easing forward a little, near her side.

The stranger spoke now: "Field's closed right now, Miss." The words were courteous enough, the voice inflexible.

She turned to Griffith and gave him a slight nod.

"We're opening it up," the chauffeur said, and strolled a step ahead of Holly. He was casually tapping some metallic automobile tool into the gloved palm of his left hand, like a policeman with a billy club.

The regular employee blanched.

The stranger smiled. Smoothly he pulled something out of his pocket and shot Griffith with it. It was some kind of small and silent gun that made very little noise as it sent the chauffeur staggering back and dropped him to one knee.

From Holly's hand, where she'd concealed it with her pair of gloves, her own little revolver barked right back, and barked again. Not silent, but effective. Brandi's cousin crumpled, looking immensely surprised, before he could do anything else. She'd bought the weapon a couple of years ago, to take along on a flight over Yucatan jungles, and had never fired it till now except on the practice range.

She turned to the petrified attendant. "This is life and death, Alfred. Get my plane ready right now, and I'll look after these people. And don't even think about trying to use that phone."

Griffith was flat on his back now, not hurt as far as Holly could see, breathing steadily, but quite unconscious. She tried to shake him awake but failed. It couldn't be helped, she'd have to leave him here. Brandi's cousin looked dead, if her experience with accident victims was any guide. She picked up his exotic weapon, hesitated, then threw it far away into the night. Then she ran into the shack and tore the telephone loose from its wires before she followed the stumbling Alfred out toward the hangars.

The runway was very dark for a takeoff, but Holly thought she knew both its direction and its length by heart. Once airborne she turned into the northeast, as the patient, pedantic voice of Harbin had advised. Following his advice on another matter also, she had turned on certain switches controlling the equipment in the cabin. Now she would fly northeast to meet the early dawn, and land somewhere in daylight. That was the first step.

Six days, Norlund was thinking, to get to Texas, and now he'd lost track of how many more days he'd spent in getting up to Iowa. On one freight train after another he'd zigzagged up from the South to the Midwest, through the midst of one of the worst heat waves on record in this or any other decade. The old newspapers he had managed to look at here and there were full of stories about people dying in this unprecedented heat that blanketed the middle of the nation. And of Dillinger and his exploits: robbing banks, shooting lawmen, kidnapping doctors to tend his wounds. And of the *Graf*, that had encountered certain technical delays, but would any day now slip its Frankfurt moorings and head west.... Norlund hadn't yet seen a paper or heard a radio broadcast that told him he was too late. It was possible for him to hear the radio sometimes, when changing trains or begging food.

Nighttime, Norlund was thinking now, was perhaps after all the best time for hopping off a freight if they were likely to be waiting to club you when you landed. He had belatedly discovered that the small town in Iowa that his leaders had code-named Jupiter was known in different circles as having some of the toughest, meanest railroad bulls in the entire country. And now in the darkness, as the cars beneath him groaned and clashed and shuddered their way toward a total stop, Norlund could see flashlights up ahead at trackside, their beams of light bobbing with the running motions of the men who carried them. The hunt was on. And now there was a shrill, carrying outcry of pain, as of someone being beaten.

With a final grinding of its steel wheels the train lurched to a stop. Now the train was silent, save for the puffing of the distant engine, and Norlund could hear the pairs of running feet along the roadbed, and more voices shouting—some in fear and some in triumph. And now a shot was fired.

Norlund pulled from his coat pocket what looked like an old cigar case, made of cheap metal, scratched and dented. It had ridden with him all the way from base. Appearing to be not worth a robber's stealing or a lawman's confiscation, it held not cigars but pseudo-memorabilia: fake family photos and worn, faked letters. Under finger pressure at the proper points, the case changed. Metal silently and swiftly unfolded and reshaped itself. The photos and letters vanished back into it, inside a clip. And now the device was dark and hard as ebony, fitting the hand like a well-made target pistol.

Ready as he could be, Norlund dropped from the stopped train. At once flashlights shone in his direction, and heavily-built shapes came toward him in a lumbering run. As soon as the first flashlight caught him in its beam, he sent his own beam invisibly back. One of the railroad bulls cried out. His brain ecstatic with the contrary currents of creaser energy, he turned to swing a club at his companion.

And Norlund turned the other way and ran.

It was midmorning when he hiked over the last hill of the dusty gravel road outside of town and came in sight of the primitive airfield. There was no sign of Holly's Vega; Norlund couldn't tell from here whether or not it might be in one of the small hangars. And he could discover no other clue that anyone, friend or otherwise, might be waiting for him here.

Limping past the buildings on tired feet, peering into the open hangar doorways, he drew the attention of a man in coveralls, who looked back suspiciously at Norlund from a distance. Norlund kept on going, as if he had never had any intention of doing otherwise. He kept going to the edge of an enormous cornfield that bordered the airfield on the east, and moved in a short distance among the rows and sat down with a sigh.

From here he ought to be able to keep watch on anyone coming or going by road or by air.

The heat had remained fierce during the last few days, and was now mounting again as the sun approached its zenith. Knowing what the weather was going to be was one of the things that a time traveler into the past could feel most certain of, but knowing it gave little help in enduring it. Presently Norlund got to his feet again, and walked farther east, through corn tall enough to hide him if he crouched, following a descending slope of land toward a line of trees where experience told him there was a chance of finding water. There was a small creek there, surviving the summer though running slow and shallow. Norlund drank, of water that tasted less muddy than it looked. Then, sheltered by corn and hedgerow, he stripped for a quick bath in a tiny pool. Afterward he felt fresher if not actually much more clean.

Dried and dressed again, he sat for a while in shade, then crouched his way back to the western edge of the cornfield to resume his surveillance of the airstrip. He sat there wondering to himself just why he'd picked this particular site for rendezvous. But he knew why, if he wanted to admit it. It was an airfield, and that increased the chance that a certain pilot would be at the meeting. . . .

He was still there, in what he had thought was an almost concealed and certainly inconspicuous position, when the man in coveralls came bouncing toward him across the field in a small truck.

The man pulled up nearby and stuck his head out the truck window. "You still here?" he yelled at Norlund. "No bums! Get moving, or I call the sheriff."

Norlund was on his feet, and about to start insisting in one way or another on his rights, when he heard the engine. It was a sturdy airborne blatt of sound that he'd heard before, now steadily growing closer. Raising his eyes, Norlund was sure from the very first glimpse of dark outline against cloud that he could recognize the Vega's shape.

Norlund ran, leaving a shouting voice behind him. The truck followed and then overtook him, but the proprietor of the airfield was not about to run down someone in the middle of a runway, at least not on his own field when his first customer in some time was perhaps about to land.

The Vega landed into the wind, on the cross runway. Norlund ran on to meet it as it taxied in along the grass strip, toward the hangars and what passed here for an operations shack. He could recognize the color scheme of Holly's aircraft now.

She was climbing out of the aircraft, her head and shoulders in flying clothing already through the hatch that opened directly over the cockpit, when she saw Norlund running toward her. She paused for a moment, then looked away and went on with what she was doing. Then, completely out of the hatch and sitting on the wing, she looked back and her movements came to a halt. Norlund thought that her body was even thinner than before.

Very near the aircraft now, he slowed to a walk, then stopped. Holly, her face a study in wonder, dropped to the grass to confront him.

"Hello, Holly."

She said it quietly. "Oh my God. It is your voice."

Still, some minutes passed before she could totally accept him as the elderly Alan Norlund she had known. As they walked off down the field together away from the man in coveralls, seeking privacy for conversation,

Holly suddenly came up with the theory that he was really the son of the man who'd been hauled off on New Year's morning at the point of death.

"No, it's me. You say Jeff has told you something about the people we're working with, some of the things that they can do. Well, they can do a lot. It's me all right. And God, I've missed you." He reached out and took her arm as they kept walking.

"I believe it is you. I believe it is. Oh, Alan."

It was difficult not to keep his eyes on her, but at the same time he had to keep looking warily around at the almost empty field, and up into the empty sky. "And now I've got to get to New York in a hurry, so you're going to have to give me another ride. But I can't promise we won't be shot at again—"

"I'm ready. The plane's ready."

"—so this time I can't ride up in the cockpit, much as I'd like to. I'll have to be in the cabin, and be ready to use the gear back there." Norlund stopped suddenly. "Where's Jeff? Who told you this was the Jupiter site?"

"A man named Harbin told me, on the phone. Alan, there are some things I've got to tell you about Jeff."

Norlund drew a deep breath. "I've really got you into a bloody mess, haven't I?"

She gave him a twisted smile. "Not you. Let me tell you about what's been happening in New York."

He was suddenly alarmed. "What day is it today? Where's the *Graf*?"

"It just left Germany this morning. Take it easy. We've got time."

Just after takeoff Norlund was busy in the Vega's cabin, monitoring local radio traffic, trying to get some news. One voice after another was coming out of the speakers, when one of them abruptly struck him as familiar. He didn't really think it belonged in the Thirties, but at first he couldn't place it. It was only some Des Moines radio announcer, sportscasting a baseball game involving the Chicago Cubs.

With the voice coming, as it were, out of left field at him, Norlund needed a full minute to identify the owner. Ronald Reagan.

It was nearly sunset on the same long summer day when Holly set the Vega down on what looked like an abandoned airstrip, or possibly just an accidental stretch of flat, packed sand. They were on the eastern shore of Lake Michigan now. An hour ago, as they started across the lake, they had passed within sight of Chicago, well to their south and below broken clouds. As far as Norlund could tell by using the equipment in the cabin, the enemy did not have them under observation. One of the things the equipment could do was make the Vega hard for a sophisticated searcher to detect.

The region where they were landing was sparsely inhabited, mostly dunes and cottages and occasional small towns. The landing strip was surrounded by dunes and a second growth of forest, and a couple of abandoned-looking shacks stood near it. As Holly tax-ied toward one of these, a man came hurrying out of it with what looked like a huge bundle of dull-colored cloth in his arms.

That cloth had not been fabricated in the twentieth century, Norlund soon decided. When the three of them spread the almost weightless folds of it over the parked aircraft, and tied it down, the Vega virtually disappeared from sight. At a few yards' distance it appeared to be a small sand dune of irregular shape.

The code name of the man who ran this small site on his own was Hannibal, and he was small and rather plump, with gray curly hair that made him look at first glance older than he was. He welcomed Holly and Norlund in and asked them what they needed; headquarters had called to say he should give them every possible assistance.

"If there's nothing more urgent to be done at the moment," said Holly, "I'd like to start by cleaning up a little." And her face indeed looked filmed with grime.

"*You've* got to clean up?" Norlund's voice sounded hoarsely tragic, as if he were pleading for his life. He looked at Holly, and she at him, and suddenly the two of them began to laugh.

The shacks were better equipped inside than their exteriors suggested. Norlund soon got a real bath, and an offer of a shave—but he decided he'd let his youthful brown beard grow for a while, if it turned out that Holly didn't mind. And there were some clean clothes that fit tolerably well.

She was fiddling with Hannibal's local radio when Norlund rejoined her in the main room of the shack. The agent had gone to town on a trip for more supplies.

"They say now that the weather in New York doesn't look good for Sunday," Holly greeted Norlund as he entered. "They're saying now that maybe the *Graf* won't try to tie up there at all. Possibly it'll go to Lakehurst instead, or more likely right on to Akron or Chicago." Akron had a well-equipped airship facility.

"That's good." Norlund nodded; he hadn't been relishing the possibility of having to conduct an aerial battle above Manhattan's crowded streets. He had vague hopes that Chicago, with its dirigible mooring mast right at the edge of uninhabited water, would be different if the fight should take place there.

"Hello," he said to Holly now, as if this were really the first moment of their reunion. She got to her feet. And then he was kissing her.

A little later, with a kerosene lamp lighted in the shack against the night outside, they started talking business. Holly was saying: "I was always surprised that Roosevelt ever invited him to come here."

"I expect our people, Ginny Butler's people, in Washington and Berlin had some hand in that. Apparently it's extremely damned difficult to ever get at Hitler in Berlin, in any timeline."

Holly digested this, or tried to. "I should imagine. If we—when we get him, how big a change is it going to make?"

"Enormous, so I'm told. More than the assassination of almost any other leader in world history. National Socialism just collapses in timelines where he's removed from the center of it."

"I should think there'd be no shortage of other bastards, ready to take over."

"Oh, there are, and they try. But—" Norlund gestured futility. "It all splinters. Adolf has a power of influencing people that's fortunately very rare. It comes along once a century or so. Napoleon. . . . Oh, there are still good chances of some kind of major war in Europe, up to the point where nuclear weapons are introduced—"

"*What* kind of weapons?"

"Oops. Said something I shouldn't have. I ought to bite my tongue." But he was two-thirds joking. Here was Holly, with him, and for the moment Norlund could feel no real worry about anything.

In a little while, after an informal and hearty meal, Norlund and Holly were out in the summer night, strolling along the beach. Norlund was speaking.

"You see, the plan all along has been to use your plane. That's why our people installed all that special stuff in the cabin. But the idea was to use our own trained pilot—she didn't make it." His sealed orders had informed him that that was to have been Agnes' job. He still didn't know what had happened to her, back at the base. "And with two trained weapons specialists aboard: myself and a kid called Andy Burns. Andy didn't make it either."

"And now there are the two of us. We'll make it."

And still later, lying in the sand, they were inescapably talking business again. They began with how tomorrow they would install an intercom in the plane so that it would be possible to talk freely between cockpit and cabin. Gradually the conversation became distracted.

Holly began, "I wish . . ."

"What?"

She raised herself on one elbow in the sand, staring out at the moonlit lake. "What are we going to do afterwards? Is there a getaway plan?"

Norlund could hear the waves lap-lapping. "Anywhere we might go in this decade," he said at last, "we'd be wanted terrorists at best."

"I suppose." Holly sounded thoughtful. Doubtless she was having difficulty trying to apply that label to herself.

"On the other hand, I'm sure that Ginny Butler will be glad to see us." He had by now told Holly just about everything that he himself knew about Ginny Butler. "If we can pull off a thing this big we'll probably be offered honorable retirement right away. Or desk jobs somewhere, after a vacation. Anyway, a career of fighting Hitler doesn't strike me personally as all that bad."

"But if we kill him now—"

"Other timelines. Other times, other people who are just as bad if not so famous. It's not all assassinations, understand. I couldn't follow any plan, any career, that consisted of just that. There are a lot of ways of fighting."

Holly was silent for a time. Then: "Sounds like you're telling me there's no end to it."

"No War to End All Wars. There really isn't, as far as I can see. Let me tell you sometime how the Forties were, the first time I lived through them. That's why I'm here now."

And they began on practical tactics. Norlund cautioned, "I want to make sure you understand, we're not going to be shooting at just a gasbag. The *Graf* will have an escort when it gets here."

"You don't mean just the Army planes. . . . "

"I mean something a whole lot worse than that, from our point of view. I mean Hitler's angels. You know in all timelines he's a bastard to try to kill. Brandi's people, from the future, protect him with the best that they can send."

"I see."

"And even if we do get the *Graf*, Hitler's still likely to get away. You've probably heard something about it on the radio, or read about it: they're carrying a little Junkers seaplane slung under the keep. A two-seater; just room for Hitler, and his favorite pilot, Hans Baur . . ."

Holly stopped him, putting out her hand and turning Norlund's face up to the moonlight. She studied him for a time, then asked, "What are you trying to tell me, Alan? That you want to drop this and head for South America?"

"No. Although I wish we could."

"How far away is South America?"

He thought over the meaning of her question. "Not far enough," he had to admit.

"Then let's forget about it and get on with the job."

Hannibal brought in an up-to-date newspaper next morning.

HITLER TO SKIP NEW YORK
. . . President Roosevelt kept in Washington 'temporarily' by the press of business . . . Vice-President Garner has boarded a special train to Chicago . . .
. . . the city's Jewish population demonstrates . . .

HOLLY STILL MISSING
No trace has yet been found of the Lockheed Vega monoplane in which the young aviatrix disappeared. Within days after the deaths of her estranged husband and her son in Germany in a crash that was claimed as accidental . . .

TWENTY YEARS AGO NEXT WEEK THE WORLD WAR BEGAN

NAZIS TORTURED POET TO DEATH, SAYS WIFE

... details of the killing of the poet Erich
Muehsom ...

FLAPPER REIGN OVER,
PSYCHOLOGIST SAYS
... nation going conservative ...

PORTLAND BREAKS
 WATERFRONT SEIGE
... trucks, guarded by police, moved gas-
oline through the ranks of the strikers ...

50 PERSONS SHOT
IN TWIN CITY RIOT

HUGE WAVE FELLS SCORES
AT CONEY ISLAND

REDS HUNTED DOWN
IN CALIFORNIA CENTERS
... by police and vigilante wrecking crews
... in the agricultural sections it was per-
sistently reported that ranchers and citizens would "take care" of Reds in their own
way where legal technicalities interfered ...

Inside the cabin of the Vega, under the concealing
camouflage wrap, Holly helped Norlund finish testing
the intercom. Then she looked over his shoulder as his
equipment brought to the little screen an image of the
Graf, now locatable over Lake Erie and heading east.
According to the latest reports from regular radio
news, the zeppelin was now intending to bypass the
naval airship facility at Akron, and come more or less

straight on to Chicago. The weather at Chicago was reported good, and the World's Fair presented a prime target for the German propaganda effort.

Norlund also showed Holly the other images now crossing his screen, faint poisonous-looking blurs that came and went like distant heat lightning. "There. And there."

"What are they?"

"Hitler's angels. I told you about them. The things that are going to try to kill us when we go up after him."

She stared at the screen. "You'll be able to cope with them, though?"

"I hope to hell I can. With all this stuff. I've spent some time in learning how to use it."

The images seemed to fascinate Holly more than they frightened her. "Whyever should anyone in the future be that keen on defending him?"

Norlund shrugged. "I've not been told any definite reason for that. One idea we kick around is that eventually they mean to bring him to their time, to establish him there somehow. In the time of our grandchildren. Nice to think about, hey?"

Holly had no words with which to answer that. But it was the first time Norlund had seen her looking really ill.

Their talk necessarily soon moved on to tactics, and Norlund reiterated the obstacles before them. "Remember, just trying to ram the gasbag isn't likely to work. There'll be something to stop us. Even if we were ready to kill ourselves to get him."

And Holly replied, "I remembered to bring parachutes."

In his private car aboard the special train that was hurrying him west to Chicago, "Cactus Jack" Garner,

Vice President of the United States, was holding forth, surrounded by cigar smoke and a small crowd of his favorite reporters.

The laughter from a joke had just died down, when one of the reporters toward the rear of the huddle ventured a question: "Sir, do you think that the President is now making an attempt to avoid or delay meeting with the Chancellor?" The phrasing of the question suggested the reporter's hope—it could not have been a very large hope—that the question would be answered with some degree of seriousness.

Garner, small blue eyes twinkling from under white brows in his preserved-red-apple face, looked at the reporter sharply. "There's a regular meeting scheduled for next week in Washington. Don't you boys read your own papers?"

"Yes sir, but don't you think that perhaps the President now wishes that he hadn't invited the Chancellor over here at all?"

"I don't wish to speculate on the President's thoughts in this matter, son, not even off the record." Garner paused for thought. "Off the record, I will say that after all, Mr. Roosevelt is confined to a wheelchair. And he is very busy, and he can't go runnin' off all over the country after a dirigible when we don't know for sure when or where the damned thing is going to come down. Anyway, I think this planned welcome in Chicago will certainly be diplomatically adequate, and you can quote me on that. Yours truly will be there, for whatever that may be worth. And some State Department people, and I understand Governor Horner of Illinois."

"Unless he finds a way to get out of it," someone mumbled. "Maybe send the Lieutenant Governor."

That comment, if heard by the Vice President,

was ignored. "And Mayor Kelly of Chicago . . . "

A reporter muttered: "*He* probably just hopes no one opens fire." There was cynical laughter; Kelly's predecessor as mayor had died in a burst of gunfire from a crazed assassin, while standing close to Roosevelt.

Garner made a brisk gesture, declining a passing hip flask. "Boys, we can hope that the wind keeps blowin', and carries the son of a bitch on across the country and out to sea again. And I'll thank you for not quoting me on that!" His Texas laugh went up, leading the chorus.

In the small galley located well forward in the passenger gondola of the *Graf Zeppelin*, a young steward named Fritz was filling insulated metal jugs, one with coffee and one with hot chocolate, for a last serving to the crew before the announced landing in Chicago. The platform of the airborne *Graf* was as steady as the deck of an ocean liner in a calm sea, and the liquids poured without a splash.

Jugs filled, Fritz had to collect some mugs and put them as well on the compartmented tray. Not for the crew the fine Bavarian porcelain bearing the LZ initials of the *Luftschiffbau Zeppelin*, from which the passengers ate and drank. These were more serviceable mugs of enameled metal, stackable so ten or a dozen could be readily carried on the tray.

Fritz in his white jacket and steward's bow tie was only seventeen, chosen for this voyage as an exemplary specimen of Hitler Youth. Still, his hands were shaking just a little as they moved the tray. The last three or four days had been overwhelming. Not only to have crossed the ocean, but to have done so as a member of the crew of the *Graf Zeppelin*, and above all in the personal service of the Fuhrer himself . . . even now there were moments in which Fritz wondered if he was dreaming.

When the compartmented tray was ready, Fritz carried it out of the galley into a short and narrow corridor. To his left was only one door, closed now and leading outside. Through it the passengers ordinarily boarded and left the airship at the beginning and end of a voyage. Facing the steward and slightly to his right was the closed door of the passengers' lounge-dining room, from behind which now came the murmur of voices and a burst of laughter. Shortly Fritz would be needed again in there, but right now he passed that door, turned right, and entered the radio room.

One of the two operators on watch asked for coffee, one for chocolate. The one who had his earphones on said in German: "Hey, Fritz, what do you think? I've got a Chicago news broadcast. Dillinger has just been shot, by the American government agents." Everyone on board the *Graf* knew who Dillinger was, after two days of listening to American news.

Fritz paused, holding the tray. "In Chicago?"

"Yes."

"You're joking."

"No, not a bit. They shot him on the street, just as he was coming out of a movie house with his lady friend. He's dead." The man was smiling, but Fritz no longer thought that he was making the story up.

"And we're going to that city," the other operator murmured, leaning back in his chair with his headphones down around his neck. He smacked his lips a little, and the others knew that he was yearning for a cigarette. Not that there was any question of having one. Even if there hadn't been millions of cubic feet of gaseous fuel and lifting hydrogen aboard, with the omnipresent danger of insidious leaks, the Fuhrer's personal aversion to tobacco smoke of any kind was well known to be comparably explosive.

Out in the little corridor again, Fritz paused to listen. This far forward of the engines, the *Graf* was fairly quiet. Taking note of the muted, endless waterfall-roar of the huge twelve-cylinder Maybachs, he decided on the basis of several days' experience that one engine was probably down for maintenance again. Still, even with only four propellors turning, the *Graf* might be able to make fifty or sixty miles an hour, given a minimum of luck with regard to wind. Fritz fully intended to be an engineer one day, and in the last few days he had chosen an engineering job on a dirigible as his ultimate goal.

The door to the chart room was only a step farther forward, and Fritz bore his tray in there. The men bent over the wide tables growled, and muttered that they were too busy to be interested in coffee. And don't spill any of that stuff in here!

In the middle of the forward bulkhead of the chart room, another door led forward to the control car. This, on the *Graf*, was not a separate car at all. It was simply the front compartment of the single ninety-foot-long gondola that clung to the lower front curve of the enormous hull, and housed the ship's key control functions as well as the entire passenger quarters.

The man at the wheel wanted coffee. His companion, manning the engine telegraphs, asked for chocolate. Beyond the glass panels that made up the whole curving front of the control car, the sky was sunset, with broken and scattered clouds at the level of the dirigible and higher, in several layers. They were flying at about five thousand feet, and Fritz could see yet another of the Great Lakes—this one Lake Michigan, he knew—ahead. He didn't know whether to pass on the news about Dillinger or not, or whether these men might already have heard it. Finally he decided it would be unseemly for a Hitler Youth to appear overly excited about these foreign gangster matters, and said nothing.

Now the crew members farther aft who were not too busy had to be served as well. Fritz stopped in the galley to restock his tray, then headed aft. The commonly used way lay straight through the passengers' dining room. He entered the dining room and would have traversed it as unobtrusively as possible, but someone called to him: "The Fuhrer would like a refill."

Even after days of approaching Hitler closely, it was still a pulse-quickening experience. The Fuhrer was sitting now at one of the small tables in front of the portside red-curtained windows of the dining room, empty cup in front of him and sunset sky behind. Hitler wore his Bavarian sports coat of light blue linen and a yellow tie. His unique gold Party pin was prominent on his jacket.

As usual, Hitler himself was dominating table conversation. "Civilian informality is definitely best on an occasion like this," he was saying to his companions as Fritz approached. "The Doctor' '—Fritz knew that this meant Herr Doktor Goebbels—"agrees with me. Especially as we are arriving at a fair. And especially in America—ah, chocolate is here."

As Hitler's cup was being filled, he smiled lightly and raised his blue eyes to the steward's face. "Thank you," the Fuhrer said in English. He was obviously practicing a phrase for use during his visit.

Fritz spoke some English, and understood more —it was one of the things that had been taken into consideration in the selection process for the crew. He replied now in that language, as best he could: "You are velcome, my—my Leader."

Paul Schmidt, the English-language interpreter, who was seated now at Hitler's table, corrected the vee sound, pursing his lips and going *www*. Everyone at the two occupied tables had a small chuckle, except perhaps for Sepp Dietrich, the head of Hitler's body-guard, who was looking nervous as the time for landing drew near. Sitting near Dietrich were a couple of SS adjutants who on this trip were doubling as his assistants. They looked uncomfortable in the civilian clothes that they had put on within the last hour or so. Heinrich Hoffman, the photographer, was holding his camera before him on the table, ready for a chance at an informal shot. Albert Speer, the young architect and favorite confidant of Hitler, was in conversation with Baur, the airplane pilot.

As Fritz moved away, going on about his tasks, he heard the talk behind him start up again. In German, but about America.

Passing through the remaining width of the dining room—it was only sixteen feet square in all—Fritz stepped aside for a fellow steward hurrying through the other way. Then Fritz left the room by the aft door, leading to the central passage that ran aft through the rest of the gondola's length. This hallway too was narrow, conserving space, and lined on both sides with narrow doors. There were five small passenger cabins on each side, the Fuhrer's being first in line on the starboard. The forward cabins were minutely larger. Toward the rear of the gondola were the washroom doors.

From inside the crew washroom at the very end of the corridor, Fritz climbed into another passage that ran back through the keel for virtually the entire length of the ship. Here the enclosure of the walkway was no more than skeletal, a spidery work of duralumin structural members. Here and there an electric light shone on cloth curtains, and on the very walls of the great cell bags of fabric and goldbeater's skin that contained the lifting hydrogen and the gaseous engine fuel. The full length of this passage was more than seven hundred feet. But this time Fritz was going only two hundred feet or so, to the crew mess, where he set down his tray on a plain, lightweight table.

He was on his way back carrying another tray, this one loaded with dirty dishes and miscellaneous garbage, when he stopped for a small personal detour. A cramped side passage, used by men who had to go out in flight to work on a particular engine, led to a glass-windowed small door. Inside this door Fritz crouched, pressing his face against the cool glass, looking out at the curve of hull and the engine pod outlined against a darkening sky. The pod, reached by a spidery catwalk, was mounted on long struts that held it some yards from the hull, giving the long propeller—idle now—plenty of room to spin. He couldn't see the man working inside the pod, but the small hatch on the side of it was open. Fritz looked forward to being allowed out there some day.

Below was all water now, the ocean-like expanse of Lake Michigan sinking into the shades of night. Above, the great round of the dirigible's hull cut off the higher sky. Along the curve of silvery-gray fabric Fritz could see only a fringe of the uppermost layer of broken clouds on which the sun still shone.

What wonderful things, he thought, I am going to be able to write in my next letter home. And when I get home again, what things I will have to tell. . . . He thought for a long moment about a certain girl, and about the long time that he was going to arrange, one way or another, to spend with her when he got home.

How marvelous, Fritz thought, is the world. Especially, above all, now in the New Age to which the Fuhrer leads us. . . .

Not far ahead now, though still invisible, lay Chicago. He hoped for some time off in which to see the Fair, and the great and mysterious and dangerous city. In large part it must be a mixture of inferior races. And of course a city of gangsters, but they were never to say that to anyone, of course, while they were there. Even if Dillinger . . .

Someone was calling after him from the direction of the main passage. Had all the coffee been put away?

Yet the steward lingered at the window for a moment longer, hoping to see the beacon that was called the Lindbergh Light.

He thought that he could see strange shapes of light flicker past him through the darkening clouds.

As soon as the Vega took off from the concealed strip, the enemy was able to locate it again. As it climbed into the sunset sky it was the target of quick and intense attack. Norlund was strapped into his cabin seat, wearing a metallic headband that wirelessly connected his brain's alpha waves with the ship's weapons—the projectors that looked out of the cabin windows on either side. Norlund's hands, like any human hands too slow by far to man these guns, lay clenched or folded in his lap, or gripped the seat's armrests. As he watched the screen, his very thought was melded with computer output to establish a priority of targets and select the type of beam to be projected.

The first attacks came in quick succession, one on

either side, and were beaten off. Without, as far as Norlund could tell, any substantial damage sustained on either side.

Now Holly's voice came to him, over the newly-installed intercom: "Got it in sight ahead, at about four thousand feet." She was talking of course about the *Graf*, and they had timed their interception effort well. She might well be still unaware of the skirmish already fought, so swift and silent and nearly invisible had that clash been.

They were still some miles east of Chicago, over the great plain of water. On his screens Norlund could watch the *Graf* descending gradually toward the distant lakefront Fairgrounds that its crew could probably not see yet. He could see that one engine of the *Graf* was for some reason idle. That would slow her down somewhat, all to the good. But the four remaining engines propelled it easily on into the mild breeze, into what looked like perfect weather conditions for a landing.

At a relative speed of about a hundred miles an hour, the Vega overtook the dirigible swiftly. Within a very few minutes after takeoff, at a range of about half a mile, as had been planned, Norlund beamed off his first broadside at the airship. It was a heterodyned mixture of rays and particles, calculated to be difficult for Brandi's people to block.

But block it they did, successfully, somehow, though they probably had no gear mounted on the dirigible itself. The *Graf* flew on, unharmed and unaware of an attack.

Norlund ordered Holly to turn back for another pass, this one from closer range. But this one, too, was ineffective, though the projected ray was changed. Demonstrating an aptitude for fighter tactics, Holly broke off the pass into a twisting dive that carried them right beneath the *Graf.* In the light of the airship's own running lights, and the now-visible reflected beacons of the still-distant Fair, the gray hull looked faintly shiny, the hanging seaplane dark and small. The shape passed above Norlund at a hundred miles an hour, like some elongated planet. There was the gondola where Hitler rode, and Norlund had been unable to so much as scratch its paint.

And that last pass, Norlund thought, was probably our last free one. Hitler's angels were back on his screen now, materializing and closing fast.

"Once more, and closer!" he ordered on the intercom, not knowing if they would have the time.

Halfway up the eastern tower of the Skyride, exposed to the mild night on a half-open service platform, Geoffrey Holborn was listening to Hajo Brandi swear. Jeff could tell from the tone of voice that the man was swearing, though the language was as strange to Jeff as Hindustani. Brandi was speaking over a small communicating device he had pulled out of his pocket, apparently an unbelievably tiny two-way radio of some kind. Jeff, privileged to see this artifact of the future, stared at it in fascination.

Brandi had chosen this platform as his temporary command post. For the past several hours he and Jeff, along with a crew of men that Brandi had called up from somewhere, had been secretly searching the Fairgrounds and particularly the towers for evidence of sabotage—specifically, for ceramic devices of the kind that Jeff himself had once been induced to put in place around the Empire State Building. Every time Jeff recalled how the Red aliens had duped and forced him into that, his rage flared up anew—

But now time, even for rage, was running short. The *Graf* was coming on. By now it must be only minutes away, out in the darkness over the lake.

Nearby, elevator cables whirred. Perhaps more engineers, local security people, airship experts, all going up to the top of the tower three hundred feet above, where the actual mooring was to be accomplished. The Navy's *Macon* had been here twice in the past month for practice moorings, and it had been proven that the new Holborn system worked.

Brandi continued to look out over the fairyland of electric light that sprawled below, while he swore monotonously and incomprehensibly into his communicator. At intervals he paused, listening to unsatisfactory answers that Holborn could not hear. Brandi until tonight had kept the communicator hidden from Jeff; that Jeff was now allowed to see it reassured him that he was finally completely trusted.

But time was passing mercilessly; the *Graf* was coming in. . . .

"Hank!" Jeff called sharply now, trying to get the other man's attention. For some days now, Brandi had been asking Jeff to go on a first-name basis and call him Hank. It was part of what seemed to be a calculated but somewhat clumsy effort on Brandi's part to appear as just one of the fellows in American society of the Thirties. Jeff—rarely just one of the fellows himself—had mixed feelings about the effort, feeling sympathetic and at the same time in some way repelled by it.

Hank or not, Brandi now continued to pay him no attention.

Jeff was beginning to feel truly desperate. There were between fifty and a hundred men on that dirigible, and if there was real danger of sabotage the docking *must* be stopped. He looked round him almost frantically, as if some forgotten source of help might be available. From this high vantage point he could pick out the horizontal cables of the Skyride itself, running a hundred feet below him and still twenty stories or so above the paved Fairgrounds and the lagoon those cables crossed. Of course the cable cars were not running now; their activity, like that of most of the Fair, had been interrupted for tonight's great event. A truly vast crowd of spectators had showed up to see that, and now filled most of the open space within the grounds, except for the roped-off acres around the east tower, above which the docking maneuvers would take place.

Down there, on the cleared picnic grounds, some four hundred men were waiting, most of them Navy people with experience in landing a dirigible. Jeff had serious doubts about how useful they were going to be, even in an emergency, when actual docking was going to take place six hundred feet above their heads. But there they were, organized into squads, ready to catch dropped mooring lines and do what they could.

And now a vast, oceanic murmur was rising from the extended crowd. Out over the lake, the *Graf*, approaching head-on, had become visible. There were its running lights. And there, a flash of gray, caught for a moment in the edge of the Lindbergh beacon's revolving gleam.

Something *had* to be done now.

Jeff caught Brandi by the arm, forcing the wiry man to turn round. "Hank! If there are any sabotage-units here on the tower, we haven't been able to find them. It's time to call in the authorities and get them to call the landing off."

For a moment Brandi only glared at him, not even

appearing to understand what Jeff was talking about. Then, bringing his attention to Jeff with an effort, he shook his head decisively. "No! I keep telling you, Jeff, we must handle this in our own way. What evidence have we that the authorities here are going to accept?"

"They'll listen to *me*, if I tell them that something is seriously wrong."

"And afterwards, when you still can produce no proof?"

Jeff shook his head violently. He was having trouble believing this argument. He waved his arms in desperation. "My God, man, at least we'll have saved lives!"

"Jeff." Brandi had his bland mask fully in place now, and he was trying to be soothing. "Hitler can get off the *Graf* safely, with his seaplane and his pilot; in fact I've sent word to our man on the dirigible to get him to do just that."

"Hitler?" Jeff was aghast. "Who gives a . . . what about the others? The crew, the . . . "

"There is a great deal more at stake here, Jeff, than the lives of a few individuals. It is the Lawgiver's wish." He nodded at Jeff solemnly. "I know you cannot understand that now. But trust me."

"Trust you." Jeff's echoing voice was low. Once he had trusted those others, too, who had brought healing with them and then turned out to be assassins. "This is madness," he said loudly. "I'm going to stop it."

"Jeff, don't do it!" Brandi ordered. But the local was already out of his reach, moving swiftly along the other side of a kind of metal fence or railing that divided the platform, and heading for stairs and elevator.

Brandi shot him silently in the back. Jeff crumpled to the platform.

The Lindbergh Light swept round again, showing the gray face of the *Graf* a minute closer than before, out over the plain of water. Now its engines could be heard, their waterfall-roar mingling with the renewed noise of the crowd.

Brandi glanced round. It was highly unlikely that anyone anywhere could have noticed the shooting. He pocketed his weapon and made his way around the railing, approaching the fallen man with professional caution. Looking down, he was sure that Jeff was still conscious, though he had hit his head in falling and his forehead was bleeding slightly. The eyes were open, and able to move, and Jeff was breathing.

The small secret communicator in Brandi's pocket was signalling for his attention, and he whipped it out and spoke into it, again using the language that Jeff had not been able to understand.

"Hail the Lawgiver, Brandi here. I still cannot report success . . ." There was a pause, during which the blond man listened intently while his eyes widened. "I understand, sir, the Lawgiver's personal wish that Hitler land here . . . yes sir, if you *wish* to explain, of course. Because . . ."

Again a pause. Then Brandi swiveled on taut muscles to the south railing of the platform. His eyes, suddenly awed, bored down into the night, where scattered pieces of the crowd stood near the seaplane landing at the edge of the South Lagoon. His voice became a whisper of exultation. "The Lawgiver himself? *Here?* Yes, we will of course give up our lives if need be to provide security, but . . . here. He is, of course, incognito . . . yes, sir."

Hardly had he closed the communicator when it throbbed again for his attention. "Hail the Lawgiver, Brandi here . . ." Now his tone became savage, the

words altering to the familiar, contemptuous form
provided in his language for addressing a subordinate.
"If you've found one unit, then remove it, fool! It will
at least weaken the effect, and we won't have to report
complete failure. The House of Tomorrow?" Again his
gaze swiveled, raking the ground and the structures
within the broad roped-off area below. "Well, fool, if
there are two men defending it, kill them!" he snarled.
"I'm on my way!"

Brandi took a long stride toward the stairs and
elevator. Then he turned and, almost as an after-
thought, lifted the paralyzed body of Geoffrey Holborn
in his strong arms and put it quickly over the safety
railing at the platform's edge. No one was at all likely
to see anything that happened on this shadowed por-
tion of the tower; all eyes were on the approaching
silvery shape, now steadily visible above the lake.
Skyrockets were going up, at a carefully emphasized
safe distance from the landing area and the *Graf*, and
boat whistles were sounding.

The still-living body struck one of the horizontal
Skyride cables a hundred feet down, and went caroming
off. Brandi did not delay to witness the final impact.

The House of Tomorrow was within the area that
had supposedly been cleared of people for the dirigible's
arrival, but Jerry Rosen had still managed to get
inside the building and find a hiding place. There
was a stunned Fair policeman sleeping things off
in a closet, who could expect to wake up tomorrow
sometime, with stiff muscles and a headache, wondering what had happened to him.

Jerry would have been tempted to switch places
with that cop right now, if he'd been made the offer.
He was hiding in another closet with the door cracked,

able to watch from where he hid the single doorway to the room in which he'd hidden the last ceramic pulser, back in those dear innocent days when he'd just been working for a man named Norlund. . . . Now somebody was coming through the house, trying to be quiet.

Jerry tensed, a weapon in each hand. These future guns were really neat, but one of the first things he'd done on getting back to Chicago was to visit an old bootlegging friend and arrange to borrow something a little heavier and simpler. He'd come to like the feel . . .

It was two of Brandi's people who were coming, detectors in their hands, and Jerry eased open the closet door and let them know that he was there. Lethal sizzle from his left hand, bang from his right.

And fire came back from one of Brandi's men and struck him down.

When Fritz saw the men hurrying grim-faced toward him through the narrowness of the keel passage, he pressed himself and his dishes back against the fabric wall and girders in surprise, making as much room as possible for them to pass him. Dietrich came first, moving in long strides. Next, one of the SS adjutants, looking just as somber; and after him, the Führer, eyes fixed straight ahead, now wearing a long coat over his blue linen jacket. Hitler was carrying a small dispatch case in one hand. The second SS man followed Hitler.

"Baur has the engine running," someone muttered, as the small cavalcade pushed past the flattened Fritz. And the engine noise from outside now did seem to be varying strangely. As if, thought Fritz, some airplane could be buzzing us. Dangerous; they shouldn't do that, especially now.

Looking after Hitler and the others, he saw them descending a small ladder; the Führer was, then, about to get into the seaplane and depart. Fritz set down his tray and darted aside to where he could get a good look outside through another window — by now he knew where all the good places for observation were.

The partly cloudy sky had become an entrancing show of lights. The moon, the distant beacons, the welcoming searchlights on ship and shore. The glow reflected from the approaching Fairgrounds, which made a glorious sprawl now close at hand. There were even fireworks at some distance. And, reflecting on one small cloud, Fritz thought that he saw lightning.

One of Hitler's angels had locked onto the Vega, and through Norlund's small video-game screen he willed death and destruction back at it. From the corner of his eye he saw within the cabin the vivid backflash of his lasers, first right then left as the enemy hurtled past. His beams struck home, and on his screen he saw the enemy escort fighter crumpling, not going down in flames but sliding sideways off the stage of nineteen-thirty-four reality, disappearing with a whisper into thin twentieth century air.

Holly's shaken voice came to him over the intercom. "The seaplane's just launched!"

"Go after it."

This, Norlund thought, would be the last shot of the game — win, lose, or draw. He concentrated on his screen, then saw it go blank as he felt the Vega lurch and shudder with some terrific impact.

They were still in the air, but even the intercom was dead, and they were going down. Not in a spin, anyway; not quite in a hopeless dive. Maybe Holly could somehow pull it up enough to make it a ditching and not a hard crash into water. . . .

There were more of Brandi's men inside the House of Tomorrow now, trying to get at Jerry. Though hit, he had not lost consciousness, and he kept rolling half-paralyzed from one side to the other of his chosen room, trading fire with them. He thought that his two weapons confused them, so that they thought there were two of him, and this slowed them down. And he thought, too, that he had hit them more than once.

Now he heard them calling to each other, urgently, in some language that sounded funnier than Polish. Now it sounded like they were going away. Some kind of trick, Jerry thought. . . .

And then for a time he could think nothing.

Jerry came to himself, if that was the right description of the process, feeling very strange indeed. Now he was able to sit up again, in this strange, darkened, unfamiliar house, and now he could even begin to think. There had been a fight. Yes, he had been fighting for his life . . . but over what?

Stumblingly Jerry got himself erect. The house, whatever house this was, was quiet now. But somewhere in the distance there was a sea-like murmuring, as of a vast crowd gathered, expecting something, waiting for it.

He could walk a little, too, though it took sustained conscious effort to force the large muscles of his limbs to work, and periodically stabbing pains transfixed his body. There had been shooting, he could remember that much now, and somehow he must have gotten himself shot.

At least he wasn't bleeding, at least not anywhere that he could see. Maybe inside, judging from the way he felt. He wondered which beam weapon had hit him. It must have been a beam reflected, like a ricochet, or he'd be dead. He realized that much in a flash of clarity. When he touched the skin on his back on one side it hurt like fire.

The world around him grew strange and muddled again, while he stood swaying. If he was hurt, the thing to do was get home. . . . Where was he, anyway? Oh yeah, the Fair. But he was very tired now, from . . . so much sight-seeing, maybe.

On his way out of the glass-walled, curtained house Jerry stumbled over something and looked down. Hajo Brandi's dead face looked up at him, a neat hole as from a thirty-eight right in the forehead. Jerry found this discovery vaguely alarming. The urge to get home suddenly became desperate, and he hurried on.

He was just emerging from the House of Tomorrow when a vast orange glow lit up the entire sky.

Baur had just landed the seaplane, with great skill and almost inconspicuously, right at the edge of the South Lagoon. This was an area of water well outlined by floating and shore-mounted lights, and the water was quite calm.

At the moment when the Junkers' floats touched down, the *Graf* was just easing through the final feet and inches toward contact with the mooring mast. And at the very moment of that contact, a ball of fire appeared amidships on the dirigible, the striking of some titanic spark. Almost before the first cries of alarm went up, the whole airship appeared to be in flames.

Inferno. A thousand voices screamed. The mooring failed; the airship was released from trailing ropes that had been already gripped by hundreds of hands below. The sailors below let go, and ran to get themselves out from underneath the flames. The dirigible drifted gently back to the east, so it was again entirely over water. The *Graf's* engines, or some of them, could be heard still running, even while the gasbag burned. Only half a minute had passed since the first ignition. Flaming, falling scraps of fabric drifted over the crowd on shore, starting new surging panic. Half melted sticks and spars of duralumin splashed hissing into the lake.

It took long seconds for the enormous shape, still half-supported by the rising air of its own firedraft, to fall six hundred feet, going down stern first. On shore the panic grew, as quickly as the fire above. By the thousands people screamed, milling, running at cross purposes. From the shore they could see men, some with their clothing already on fire, dropping from the burning zeppelin into the lake.

It was at this moment that the Junkers seaplane with Hitler in it came taxiing up to the small dock. The cabin door, opening, was surrounded at once by a huddle of men. When Hitler emerged from the huddle he was safe.

In a moment he had stepped up onto a nearby picnic bench, the better to see the fire's last moments, the climax of the disaster that he had just escaped.

"My fate holds good! My fate holds good!" He murmured the words over and over, as he stared with wondering, almost triumphant eyes at the vast, slow, quenching plunge that put the fire out, darkening the sky again.

The Lawgiver, with his own agents recalled from other efforts and scattered thickly through the small crowd here, got discreet help in moving up close beside the Führer. Most of the official welcoming committee, dozens of important men, were trapped in the surging confusion up there by the Skyride.

"Führer," someone muttered urgently in German, "this is Herr Zeitgeist of—of Milwaukee. He would like very much to meet you."

The Lawgiver reached up his right hand. It was an awkward pose for him, this, with himself physically below the other, but that could hardly have been foreseen and in any case it did not really matter.

He seized and pressed Hitler's hand. In his own recently acquired German he pronounced: "In our own New World, Führer, we are waiting eagerly for you to accomplish what you can in yours. We intend to build upon the fruits of your labors. Despite what all our enemies can do, we intend to support you in maintaining your rightful place."

"Thank you," said Hitler. It was a brief, abstracted reply, but under the circumstances nothing more could have been expected, and the Lawgiver was satisfied.

He stepped back, giving an inconspicuous signal. His own men now aided the locals' effort to get the Chancellor bundled away somewhere to safety.

The Lawgiver looked on contentedly; once again his power to mold events had been satisfactorily demonstrated. He had wanted this meeting, and now he had it, his enemies and Hitler's notwithstanding.

An aide, one of the modified Brandi-clones, was at his side. The man indicated by a certain breathless, doglike attitude in his silence that he wanted to be told what had to be done next.

"Now," said the Lawgiver, "I have seen Hitler, and shaken his hand."

"Yes, Lawgiver."

"I wonder if one day it may not be possible for us to talk at some greater length. . . ."

"Does the Lawgiver wish a plan developed for bringing Hitler to our own time?"

There had been a kindred spirit there behind those startling blue eyes, someone he could really talk to . . . but, perhaps, on second thought, too close a kinship.

"No," the Lawgiver said aloud. "That will not be necessary." He looked around. "Get me home," he ordered, "before they realize that they can strike at *me*."

There was a streetcar terminus very close to the Eighteenth Street exit from the Fair, and Jerry, moving automatically, boarded a waiting car. He was almost alone on it; few people were leaving the Fairgrounds just now.

Streetcars were never delayed for any humanly understandable reason like burning dirigibles and assassination plots, and this one started west promptly on schedule. Delirium began to set in almost at once as Jerry rode. And long shivering spasms came, threatening to stop his breathing—it took him a conscious effort at breathing to get through them. Don't pass out, he warned himself.

When he got to the Monahans', he would be able to see Judy, and the kid. That thought kept him awake.

He swayed along on the streetcar's deafening, jolting ride, under an occasional shower of blue sparks from the overhead trolley. It was the same old city, the same old streetcars—it was great to be back. He looked out the window. Now and then, through broken clouds and city glare, it was possible to see the pale and distant moon. I wonder, thought Jerry, if people are ever going to . . . but someone, somewhere, sometime, had already told him that they had.

Instinct saw him through the necessary transfer point, where he clung like a drunk to a streetlamp's pole until the proper northbound car approached. Jerry presented his transfer, and then stood on the rear platform of the car, afraid that if he sat down again he wasn't going to be able to get up.

Then the familiar stop drew near. He stood on the step, hanging on to the pole there, and when the car stopped to let him do so he dropped off.

His legs felt like they belonged to someone else, but still they served to get him home. Up the front steps at last. He didn't have a house key any longer, he remembered after fumbling for it in his pocket. It was Ma Monahan who answered the door, took one look at her returned son-in-law, and recoiled yelling.

Mike came from somewhere, and between the two of them they got Jerry into the living room and stretched out on the sofa, shedding his tattered suit jacket somewhere along the way. The radio in the living room was turned on, but Jerry noticed in a dazed way that it didn't sound like any normal program. Dillinger was dead, some announcer was saying. Hitler was alive and safe. The loss of life from the *Graf Zeppelin* was being counted up.

When they laid Jerry down on the sofa, the borrowed thirty-eight slid out of the waistband of his pants to land on the carpet with a revealing thud. The old lady pointed at it and yelled again, this time something about Dillinger.

"Shuddup for Christ's sake!" Mike roared back. Half-grown kids who had started to come into the room fell back in fright. "What's going on?" he demanded of Jerry in anguish.

"I been shot." Things were slowly starting to refocus. Why, why, Ma demanded, had he given up bootlegging, only to take up with Dillinger? Now Federal agents were going to be coming with machine guns to her house.

"No, Ma." Something worse than Federal agents might be coming, he realized dimly. He shouldn't have come here . . . but now there was nothing he could do about it. Judy came hurrying into the room, driving all other thoughts out of Jerry's mind.

The women peeled off his shirt as he lay raving. There were some burned-looking places on Jerry's ribs, but nothing that Mike would accept as real evidence of shooting. Mike had already hidden the thirty-eight somewhere. Judy was kneeling at her long-lost husband's side, crying over him and jumping up now and then to keep her mother from doing something daft.

Under these conditions Judy and her parents debated whether a doctor should be called. They had about agreed that it was unavoidable, when there came a knocking at the back door, and a man's voice called in: "Ambulance!"

Peering out through the glass panels with the porch light turned on outside, they made out the face of a tough-looking young man. He impressed them all in one way or another as vaguely familiar.

"We're friends of Jerry's," this man called in. "My name's Norlund—my father was here once, visiting; maybe you remember him. No, no cops! Far from it, lady. We got an ambulance waiting for Jerry out here in the alley. We'll take him to a hospital." And indeed, between garages the lights of a standing vehicle, its motor running, could be seen.

The people inside were reassured enough to open the door and talk. And then the young medical attendants who came in with their stretcher were more reassuring still. No hoodlums, these people, and apparently no cops either.

Young Norlund talked to the Monahans. "Jerry's done a great service for his country—no, m'am, we're not the Dillinger gang. Nothing to do with them."

And as Jerry was being carried out, Norlund took Judy by the arm and pulled her urgently aside. He spoke to her with quiet emphasis. "I want you to come along. And bring the baby. Nothing else. Don't stop for anything else."

Judy hesitated, looking Norlund over carefully. Then she obeyed. A slim young woman with auburn hair and blue-green eyes came in to help her hold the child.

Within another minute the ambulance, all passengers safely on it, roared away.

Mike, hurrying after it to the mouth of the alley, saw the vehicle disappear in a transient colored haze before it reached the corner of the next street. But Mike went to his grave without telling anyone he had seen that.

2034

The trim, good-looking sexagenarian lady and the three small children with her were inside one of the middle-aged buildings of the great Smithsonian Museum complex in Washington DC, supping themselves full with wonders, when the lady came to a halt in front of a large mural. It covered most of a fair-sized wall, and she thought that it probably dated back to the Seventies, being as old or nearly as old as the building itself.

The children soon noticed her concentration on the painting, and joined her in looking at it.

" 'Fortresses Under Fire,' " one of them read from a plaque. "What war was that?"

His grandmother did not answer him at once. For the moment, her mind was far away.

. . . *looking at the Fortresses, the great planes that seemed to be coming out of the wall at her, quaint shapes now but in their day the best swords it had been possible to build. She thought that she could almost hear their engines. They would be raiding Germany, or maybe occupied France. Trying to hit the military targets, but in the process ruining the cities below.*

"Grandma?"

... but if you were riding in one, she supposed, beset by flak and fighters, the best thing you could do was keep on fighting. Given the need, the cause ...

"Grandma?"

... but at the moment her duties were different and gentler. "What is it, dear?"

"Grandma, what war was that?"

"That," answered Sandy, "was the war my grandfather fought in. World War Two, they called it. As if they thought they'd better get ready for a whole series."

"Why were they fighting, Grandma?"

And another child interrupted: "Did I ever see him?"

"My grandfather? No, dear. He—disappeared. Went on a business trip and never came back, long before you were born. When I was only a little girl myself."

And at the far end of the railing defending the mural a man strolled into Sandy's view; an erect, distinguished-looking gentleman who might have been ten years older than herself. He smiled at Sandy briefly, then turned his gaze up to the painting, as if he were in no hurry to interrupt her conversation with the children.

"Disappeared?"

"Yes, dear. I was upset at the time. But later on I understood. When I began to go on business trips myself." Somewhat impatiently she called toward the man: "Dr. Harbin, how nice to see you. You chose an interesting place this time. I hope you don't mind that I brought the children. What news?"

Harbin strolled a little closer. "Good news. We've no

assignment for you at the moment. Alan sends his love; he's doing well at his desk job. In fact I can tell you he's had a rather large success; there's one more timeline without Hitler."

Two of the children, tuning out adult talk as usual, were moving on to the next exhibit. But there was one who, as usual, would not stop asking questions.

"What's a Hitler?"

THE END